CW00539484

Teaching a Horse to Sing

TEACHING A HORSE TO SING

Tales of Uncommon Sense from India and Elsewhere

Retold by

DELSHAD KARANJIA

ALEPH

ALEPH BOOK COMPANY
An independent publishing firm
promoted by Rupa Publications India

First published in India in 2021
by Aleph Book Company
7/16 Ansari Road, Daryaganj
New Delhi 110 002

This is a work of fiction. Names, characters, places, and incidents are either the product of the author's imagination or are used fictitiously and any resemblance to any actual persons, living or dead, events or locales is entirely coincidental.

ISBN: 978-93-90652-57-0

1 3 5 7 9 10 8 6 4 2

Printed and bound in India by Parksons Graphics Pvt. Ltd.

For
My Father,
Still my strength and inspiration

Contents

PART II

AN EMPEROR AND HIS WISE WAZIR

PART III

THE LORE OF COMMON SENSE

Introduction

Until recently, my passion for stories had been strictly one-sided, obsessed with reading rather than writing them. It was only after I was approached by Aleph Book Company with a proposal to retell stories of wit and wisdom of my choosing that I grabbed this opportunity to spin a few yarns of my own.

Coming from a family of bookworms—my parents were journalists closely connected with Indian cinema—I grew up surrounded by literature. Our spacious flat in Bombay's Chowpatty had several crammed bookcases in various rooms, and books and magazines were piled high on all available tables, desks, and shelves. The entire family—my grandmother, parents, siblings, and I—had a favourite chair or sofa in our large drawing room, where each of us could be found reading a book or magazine in pin-drop silence whenever we were at home. My mother had accounts with two or three major bookshops in the city, and several fresh-smelling books and glossy foreign magazines were delivered to the house every month.

There was never a shortage of reading material, and it was here that my fascination with stories began. Words on a page conjured up magical images, and enchanting stories whisked me off on thrilling adventures in faraway lands. It was here that I read and reread fairy tales, fables, and novels in vividly illustrated books. Being a sickly child, these exotic and exciting stories in beautifully bound hardbacks provided comfort, distraction, and some relief during various childhood illnesses. I began to realize that although truth may be stranger than fiction, fiction was invariably more fascinating than truth.

With human beings always needing to share anecdotes and experiences, storytelling has been a powerful force in every culture known to man. Long before writing was invented, it was through telling stories that people were able to quickly pass on information to others. To quote author Hugh MacLeod: 'Stories are not simply nice things to have; they are essential survival tools.'

As an almost natural consequence of this innate need to share information with future generations, stories of knowledge and insight flourished in cultures across the world. Wisdom, it is said, is a treasury that grows as you give it away, which explains why googling 'wit and wisdom' yielded more than fourteen million results: a profusion of fables, anecdotes, mythology, homespun philosophy, speeches, witticisms, deft definitions, and quotable quotes from across the globe and spanning the centuries. But the brief from my publisher was specific—to retell popular tales of wit and wisdom, so this feast of riches has perforce been pared down to three courses, beginning with the wise follies of Mullah Nasruddin, moving on to the enduring legends surrounding Emperor Akbar and his adviser Birbal, and rounding off with fables and folklore from around the world.

It came as no surprise to find a common thread linking these human experiences and behaviour, regardless of the origin of the tale. Storytellers of old, recognizing a good yarn when they came across one, would merely substitute the central character with a home-grown hero in their retellings. Hence, we have Mullah Nasruddin or Birbal, or some other smart aleck, facing identical dilemmas in variations of the same folk tale, the only difference being that the setting shifts to some other part of the world.

Sifting through this glut of information, the challenge was tantamount to filtering, remixing, and rebottling vintage wine while retaining its flavour and piquancy. Storytellers through the ages often used foolishness as a stepping stone to sound sense, as demonstrated in hundreds of anecdotes centred on the antics of wise fools and foolish knaves. In addition, love, jealousy, pride, miserliness, competitiveness, misunderstandings, and differences of opinion continue to be the leitmotifs of compelling stories about the human condition, regardless of their origin or age.

The forerunner of many a wise fool, Mullah Nasruddin's daft-yet-crafty escapades, dating back to the thirteenth century, illustrate that there can be traces of canniness in the most foolish of us and much silliness in the cleverest of us. In the mullah, we have a protagonist capable of being either a critical thinker or a buffoon when it suits him, using his gift of the gab to put a positive slant on the mishaps that befall him. Like many a present-day politician, the attention-seeking mullah permitted everyone to ask him questions, but didn't allow anyone to question his answers. Behind the wry humour and apparent foolishness, there are down-to-earth life lessons to be learned from the mullah's folksy insights and sharp tongue.

Although historical records make no mention of the legendary interactions between Emperor Akbar and his trusted aide Birbal, the stories have flourished, possibly because there is a touch of schadenfreude in discovering that crowned heads are not necessarily clever, and that a humble adviser, blessed with native intelligence and wit, can get the better of a mighty monarch.

History does, however, record that though not a lettered man himself, Emperor Akbar was a committed supporter of the arts and culture. To encourage intellectual discourse in his court, he sponsored talented people who excelled in their chosen fields. Together these individuals came to be known as the Navratnas (nine gems), Birbal being one of them.

All the stories involve Birbal using his quick thinking, sharp intelligence, and sense of humour to outsmart envious rivals and the emperor himself. It was these qualities—along with his unwavering loyalty to the monarch—that made Birbal a trusted member of Akbar's inner circle, who gradually outranked the other courtiers and became widely known as the brightest jewel among the nine gems.

The third section of this compilation offers pickings from folklore, myths, and modern-day tales from around the world, retold with the benefit of hindsight. As far back as the sixth century BCE, a Greek slave named Aesop ably transposed human foibles onto animals to drive home fundamental truths in a simple and straightforward manner. But what if the hare and the tortoise collaborate with rather than compete against each other? And having taught the carefree grasshopper a lesson, will the illustrious ant's hard work pay off in the end?

Fast-forwarding to our cynical modern age, could it be possible that an oak tree in a forest in northern Germany actually has magical matchmaking powers? And what if an aspiring immigrant realizes that the grass is not necessarily greener on the other side? ...overall, the stories have a lot in common, providing candid insights into human nature and, at their heart, demonstrating the basic differences between right and wrong, good and bad.

~

Stories have always been the common wealth of humanity and there was indeed an abundance of riches to choose from for this volume. What all this worldly wisdom revealed is that simple solutions can often be found to universal dilemmas, disputes, and predicaments if there is the will to seek answers and resolve issues. Forced to pick and choose from this bounty, I have opted for stories that struck a chord with me and will hopefully resonate with the reader. Time-tested tales of wit and wisdom can still comfort, guide, amuse, and inspire us, revealing as they do that people can be wise or otherwise and may even believe it possible to teach a horse to sing.

Delshad Karanjia
1 January 2021
Pune

PART I

THE MISADVENTURES OF MULLAH NASRUDDIN

Was Mullah Nasruddin Hodja a witty fool, a foolish wit, or merely an overconfident braggart who left people wondering if he said what he meant and meant what he said? No one knows for sure, but of one fact we can be certain: Mullah Nasruddin's legendary ability to put a positive spin on his folly and capriciousness have charmed, entertained, and edified readers from the thirteenth century to the present day.

So great is the mullah's popularity that several nations have claimed him as their native son. Having lived in numerous cities across Turkey, Persia, and Mesopotamia, he has been embraced by various cultures from Turkey to Arabia, Persia to Afghanistan, and Russia to China. In numerous retellings around the world and over the centuries, the artless but shrewd, naïve but worldly wise, and always entertaining misadventures of the contrary Mullah Nasruddin have resonated with a variety of cultures, dealing as they do with timeless tribulations such as tedious schooldays, domestic strife, the struggle to earn a living, and the daily challenge of trying to outsmart others.

For this retelling, the mullah's escapades are based in the small town of Akşehir, or white city, in the central Anatolia region of Turkey. A bridge between East and West since ancient times, Anatolia was a popular pit stop on the famed Silk Road, where the townsfolk were mainly involved in trade.

As the stories reveal, Akşehir's most famous son was a man of average intellect blessed with a sharp tongue, an inflated ego, the ability to think on his feet, and a proclivity for putting a positive spin on misfortune to snatch victory from the jaws of defeat.

1

The Birth of a Legend

He had the kind of face only a mother could love. On the day Nasruddin was born, his overjoyed mother Leyla proudly proclaimed: 'God has answered my prayers and blessed me with the most beautiful baby boy in the world.'

Yousef, the baby's father, gazed at the tiny form of his son—ordinary looking, red-skinned, with a wrinkled forehead and large, hairless head—and thought: Beautiful baby boy? No way! Leyla is probably delirious from the pain of childbirth. Could she be mistaking someone else's baby for our son?

From this muddled beginning, Nasruddin Hodja grew into a precocious little boy who was doted on by his mother and three older sisters. Small for his age but sturdy, with bulging eyes, a broad flat nose, and a head that seemed disproportionately large for his body, Nasruddin was never considered conventionally endearing or winsome (except by his mother) so he learned early on that the only way to get attention from those around him was by relying on his wits and cheeky ripostes, rather than his looks.

By the age of four, he was exasperating his family with endless questions. 'Why is the moon broken, Mother,' he would ask, 'and how does it become whole again?' or 'If I tied myself to a big bird, would I be able to fly?', and the inevitable 'Why do I have to go to school?'

Leyla was convinced that her son was extraordinarily gifted and extremely intelligent and told anyone who would listen: 'Mark my words, my Nasruddin is destined to become a great man. He will bring fame and fortune to our family.'

At least there Leyla was partly right: for although fortune may have given Nasruddin a miss, people are still talking and reading about her son's famed exploits more than eight centuries later.

2

Height of Innocence

Nasruddin's family moved to Akşehir when he was four years old, the town offering better business prospects for Yousef than the small village where his children were born.

Little Nasruddin was fascinated by his new surroundings, where everything looked bigger and better and brighter. Although the majority of the dwellings were one-level wooden structures, strengthened with wattle and daub, the more prosperous townsfolk of Akşehir lived in two-storey houses of brick and timber, with whitewashed walls. In his new home, Nasruddin delighted in running up and down the wooden steps leading to the loft, which housed the family's bedrooms.

Venturing out on his own one day to explore his new surroundings, Nasruddin was fascinated by the town's imposing mosque with its tall minaret, which seemed to be reaching for the sky. Just as Nasruddin was craning his neck to see the top of it, the muezzin's call to prayer rang out loud and clear. Not having heard the azan in such close proximity before, and not knowing a word of Arabic, Nasruddin mistook the muezzin's loud, urgent-sounding voice for a distress call.

Staring upwards at the muezzin open-mouthed, not knowing what to do to help him, Nasruddin was reassured when he saw several men hastening into the mosque. 'Don't worry,' he shouted out to the muezzin, 'lots of people are coming to rescue you.'

3

Dressing Down

Like all boys his age, Nasruddin attended a school attached to a local mosque in Akşehir, which was walking distance from his home.

One day, Nasruddin ran into the classroom panting and out of breath, wearing a jubah but no trousers. A few of his classmates tittered at this embarrassing sight and his friend Hussain asked: 'What's the matter, Nasruddin? Why aren't you dressed properly?'

'I overslept,' Nasruddin explained, 'and was so worried that I'd be late for the spelling test that I ran out of the house stark naked, carrying my jubah and a pair of trousers, thinking I could get dressed on my way here. I somehow managed to put on my jubah whilst running, but found it difficult to put on my trousers while I was hurrying to get here on time, so I gave up, tossed them into a bush by the side of the road, and ran here as fast as I could.'

'But what's going to happen when our teacher sees you without trousers?' one of his classmates asked.

'Oh, I'll just tell him that I'm starting a new fashion.'

4

Class Warfare

Nasruddin was far from being an ideal student and by the end of his first week at the village school, his antics had driven Halil, the schoolmaster, to despair.

For more than two thankless decades, the hapless Halil had been tasked with introducing his rowdy and apathetic charges to the rudiments of reading, writing, and arithmetic. The classroom was nothing more than a shed, where students sat cross-legged on mats on the floor, fidgeting, daydreaming, and staring at their teacher blankly for a couple of hours every morning. Fostering young minds was not Halil's forte, as generation after generation of boys had discovered. An embittered, short-tempered man with a downturned mouth, shifty eyes, and an unfortunate squint (which always left his pupils—the two-legged kind—in suspense as to whether or not he had his eye on them), Halil had daily confrontations with Nasruddin, his most defiant and troublesome ward.

One morning, called out of the classroom to attend to an urgent matter, Halil assigned a few simple arithmetic problems to keep the students busy and instructed one of the more obedient boys to maintain order in his absence. Before Halil even reached the school gate, Nasruddin had darted to the front of the classroom, leapt onto the wooden table that doubled as the teacher's desk, crossed his eyes, and proceeded to mimic the schoolmaster, which soon had his classmates rolling on the floor with laughter. Arithmetic problems were completely forgotten as spontaneous bouts of mock wrestling and a competition to knock fezzes off each other's heads ensued.

When he returned to the classroom, Halil's jaw dropped as he witnessed the mayhem. He immediately swooped on the suspected instigator, grabbing him by the collar. 'What is going on here? Did you start this chaos, Nasruddin?' he asked angrily.

'No, it was actually started by you leaving us in class unsupervised,' came the impertinent reply.

'I've had enough of your impudence, Nasruddin!' Halil yelled, his hands trembling with rage. 'You should be ashamed of yourself. In my twenty years of teaching, I haven't come across a more disobedient and disrespectful child than you.'

The schoolmaster's outburst had no effect on Nasruddin, who was grinning sheepishly, which angered Halil even more. 'Mark my words, Nasruddin Hodja, your insolence will be your undoing. You are not the first fool who thinks he is too smart. People like you are never as clever as they imagine themselves to be and invariably end up being objects of ridicule. Throughout your life, people will never laugh with you...they will only laugh at you. That will be your fate.'

5

In a Class of His Own

For Nasruddin and his classmates, school was an unnecessary evil, given that none of them wanted to be scholars, with most of them likely to become farmers or take up the family trade. With schoolmaster Halil completely failing to inspire a passion for learning in his students, they were always looking for opportunities to play truant.

One day, Halil entered the classroom carrying three glass jars containing fruit sweets and plonked them on his desk. 'Boys,' he announced, 'all the sweets in these jars will be yours if you can answer a simple arithmetic question. There are forty sweets distributed amongst these three jars. The first jar contains seven more sweets than the second jar. The third jar has three less sweets than the second jar. Can you calculate how many sweets there are in the first jar?'

Getting nothing but vacant stares and stifled yawns from his unresponsive students, Halil slowly repeated the question, but no one wanted to calculate how many sweets the first jar contained. 'Wouldn't it be quicker to empty the first jar and count the number of sweets?' muttered Nasruddin, eliciting audible approval from his uninterested classmates.

Clutching his head in despair, Halil declared: 'Shameless and impertinent boys! You are all completely incapable of acquiring knowledge or bettering yourselves. I don't know why your parents are wasting my time by sending you donkeys to school. You would be better off grazing in the fields outside with your four-legged brethren.'

This was just the excuse Nasruddin needed: 'You are right, sir! We would indeed be better off in the fields,' and turning to his classmates he said: 'Come on, let's go and join our four-legged relatives as our esteemed teacher advises.' With shouts of delight, following Nasruddin's lead, the boys raced out of the classroom, holding on to their fezzes as they ran whooping and braying across the fields to their homes.

Surprised to see Nasruddin back from school so early, Leyla asked what had happened. Her son narrated an edited version of the morning's events, omitting all mention of the unsolved arithmetic problem that had triggered the schoolmaster's tirade and his own role in leading the raucous exodus from the class.

'Your teacher was wrong to call a clever boy like you a donkey!' said Leyla, giving her son a hug. 'He needs to learn that even donkeys respond better if they're tempted with carrots instead of threatened with sticks.'

At school the next morning, the boys were somewhat subdued, expecting some form of punishment for leaving the classroom so unashamedly the day before, but were surprised that their teacher made no mention of the incident. Instead, Halil continued his mission to engage his unruly class in learning simple arithmetic. 'Boys, if you bought one onion, one cabbage, three tomatoes, two potatoes, and three carrots, how many vegetables would you have?' he intoned slowly and carefully, holding up the corresponding number of fingers for each vegetable to make things easier for his dull students.

Surprised to see his most difficult student raise a hand, Halil beamed: 'Nasruddin, please tell the class how many vegetables you have bought.'

'Enough to make a tasty soup,' came the reply.

6

Scoring a Hundred

Convinced that her son was a budding but unrecognized genius, Leyla was in the habit of praising even the most rudimentary of Nasruddin's achievements, invariably rewarding him with a treat for the smallest success.

Coming home from school and finding the aroma of cooking filling the house, Nasruddin sat down at the table for his snack and announced: 'I got a hundred in school today, Mother.'

'That's excellent,' his mother replied, piling an extra date pancake onto his plate on hearing this good news. 'In what subject?'

'Forty in reading, thirty in writing, twenty in spelling, and ten in arithmetic.'

7

Free Choice

A new bakery opened up on the main street in Akşehir, the same road that Nasruddin and his classmates took on their way to and from school. The aroma of freshly baked bread, pastries, and other delicacies enticed the boys although none of them had any money to buy the tempting goodies.

To attract new customers, the bakery put up a large sign: TRY OUR HOMEMADE BAKLAVA. THE BEST IN TOWN. FRESHLY PREPARED EVERY THURSDAY. FREE SAMPLES AVAILABLE.

Nasruddin and four of his friends went into the shop and asked to try the free samples. The kind baker placed a tray of baklava on the counter but before he could say 'help yourselves', five grubby hands had grabbed fistfuls of the sweetmeat and emptied the tray.

'Thank you,' they called out in muffled, chuckling voices as they scampered out of the shop with their mouths crammed full.

The next Thursday, the boys headed for the bakery but found that the sign had been modified. It now read: TRY OUR HOMEMADE BAKLAVA. THE BEST IN TOWN. FRESHLY PREPARED EVERY THURSDAY.

'Can we have free samples of the baklava, please?' the boys asked the baker eagerly.

'We don't give free samples any more,' he replied, shooing them out like flies.

Every Thursday, for three weeks in a row, Nasruddin and his friends unfailingly stopped by the bakery asking for free samples, and got the same negative reply. On the fourth

Thursday, when the boys appeared and asked for free samples, the baker lost his temper.

'I've told you repeatedly that we don't offer free samples of baklava any more. If I see you boys in my shop again next week asking for free samples, I will chase you out with a cane and then whip you on the street.'

The following Thursday, Nasruddin, with his pals in tow, went up to the bakery and asked: 'Do you have a cane and a whip?'

'No, I don't,' the baker replied, frowning.

'That's good,' Nasruddin smiled. 'Do you have any free samples of baklava?'

8

Opposite Ends

Throughout his childhood, Nasruddin drove his parents to despair by being disobedient and contrary. Any instruction given or request made to the boy, he would do the opposite: if asked to sit, he would stand; if told to assist his father with a household chore, he would immediately leave the house.

Eventually, his parents used reverse psychology to get Nasruddin to do what they wanted. If they needed him to go to the bazaar, they would prohibit him from going there; if they wanted him to pick up something that he dropped on the floor, they would urge him to let the object lie there. In this inverse way, they managed to get Nasruddin to 'obey' them.

On his son's thirteenth birthday, Yousef felt that Nasruddin was now old enough to help with household chores and decided to entrust him with the task of drawing water from the well. Summoning Nasruddin, Yousef told him: 'Son, I'd like to entrust you with an unimportant task. I want you to take a bucketful of water and climb down to the lowest level of the steps inside the well just above the level of the water. Then empty the water into the well and climb back up with the empty bucket.' Confident that his son would do the opposite of what he had been told, and thus not venture inside the well at all but use a bucket and rope to fill an empty bucket, Yousef lay down to have a nap. He was soon woken by muffled screams that seemed to be coming from the backyard.

'Help! Help!' came the cries from the well. Peering over the edge, Yousef saw Nasruddin standing waist deep in water, feeling very sorry for himself. 'The steps were so slippery that I fell into the water from the lowest one. Save me from drowning, Baba,' the boy begged.

'Don't be silly, Nasruddin. The water level is not deep enough for you to drown, so don't panic,' his father advised. 'I'll help you up the steps and make sure that you don't fall into the water again.' With his father's help, Nasruddin was soon standing on firm ground, soaked and shivering, with only his pride injured.

'You foolish boy!' his father scolded. 'All these years you've done the exact opposite of what you were told. What made you comply with my instructions today? Wasn't it obvious that I meant you to do the reverse of what I said? Why would I want you to climb down slippery steps with a full bucket?'

'Baba, today I became a teenager and can no longer be considered a child. To show you that I'm now grown up, I decided to obey your orders word for word. How was I to know that by following your instructions I would end up in cold water?'

9

An Unsuitable Boy

Nasruddin never really lost his childhood cheekiness, growing into a stocky youth with a large head and an equally big mouth. At the age of twenty, when he showed no signs of settling down, his doting aunt Mariam set about finding a suitable bride for her nephew, who was stubborn and no oil painting but still a paragon of virtue in her eyes. At this young age, her talented nephew had already tried his hand at various professions: he had worked as a miller, ferryman, trader, donkey driver, water diviner, and even taught at a local madrasa, where he was given the title of mullah.

'Doesn't he have a steady job or profession?' the families of prospective brides would ask.

'Steady job?' Mariam would exclaim indignantly. 'How can he have a steady job when he is being pulled in different directions by people? Whenever the townsfolk have a problem, they expect my nephew to solve it. He is very much in demand. In fact, he is the town's most eligible bachelor, and his bride will have to be equally talented and worthy.'

Despite the glowing testimonials from his aunt, the young women of Akşehir showed no interest, Nasruddin having gained a reputation for being temperamental and obstinate. Mariam therefore declared that the local ladies weren't good enough for her nephew and widened her search. Eventually, Fatima, a girl from a neighbouring village, described as kind, good-natured, and homely, met with Mariam's approval and the nuptials were hastily arranged lest the bride-to-be should change her mind.

For newlywed Fatima, short and pleasantly plump with a ready dimpled smile, large hazel eyes, and a tiny upturned nose set in a round face, there was no honeymoon period. Marriage instantly transformed her from a cheerful and happy-go-lucky girl to a miserable nag, having to contend with a husband who always replied to a question with a question, never gave her a straight answer, had no fixed occupation, and occasionally did not earn enough to put food on the table. Fatima tried cajolery, tricks, tears, and tantrums to get her husband to see sense—meaning her point of view—to no avail. 'I'm so unfortunate to have the most foolish and obstinate husband in the land,' she moaned to anyone who would listen.

Eventually, when feminine charms and wiles failed, Fatima decided to give Nasruddin the silent treatment. For several days, the couple did not say a word to each other. Fatima cooked and served meals in sullen silence, but her husband wolfed down his food without a word while she glared at him. He'll realize that I'm upset and angry and will soon come to his senses, Fatima thought to herself.

Not so, it seems, for after a week of non-communication with his wife, a beaming Nasruddin broke the silence for a moment to declare: 'Isn't it wonderful that we are finally beginning to get along?'

10

A Strong Stomach

Returning home from work one evening, the mullah found his young bride in tears, sobbing into her apron and wailing that something terrible had happened. 'My dear,' Fatima said, 'I tried out your aunt's recipe and grilled a piece of meat for you, but the cat jumped onto the table and ate it.'

Secretly grateful that their ill-tempered cat had spared him the trouble of putting on a charade of enjoying his wife's lack of culinary expertise, Nasruddin patted Fatima on the shoulder and said: 'Don't worry about it, dear wife. It's only a minor catastrophe. You see, cats have nine lives. He should survive long enough to stomach some more of your cooking. I'll get us some kebabs and lahmacun for our dinner.'

11

The Town Gossip

Nasruddin's neighbour Tariq stopped him on the street one day. Clearing his throat nervously, he said: 'Nasruddin, I need to discuss a rather delicate matter with you.'

'Go ahead,' came the response.

'It's about your wife,' Tariq began. 'She's a compulsive gossip and spends hours every day going from one house to another bad-mouthing and telling tales against everyone in the neighbourhood. People are getting annoyed with her. Often my wife can't get on with her household chores because your wife is prattling on for hours on end about the latest rumour or scandal.'

'I find that hard to believe,' said Nasruddin, 'because I have never known my wife to gossip about anyone to me.'

'Be that as it may, you should perhaps advise her to spend more time at home, minding her own business,' Tariq said firmly.

'I'm willing to talk to her, but I don't think it will make a difference,' replied the mullah. 'Because, you see, my wife is smart enough to know that the only way to ensure that people don't gossip about her, is by keeping them preoccupied by gossiping about others.'

12

Fear Factor

Nasruddin was slowly climbing a ladder with a sack of tiles slung over his shoulder to repair his roof when Tariq passed by his front gate.

'How's everything, Nasruddin? All well, I hope?'

'I'm fine, thanks,' Nasruddin replied, happy to stop for a chat, 'but I have some worries on the domestic front....'

'Is your wife unwell?' Tariq asked.

'Far from it,' Nasruddin replied. 'But I've discovered that she is such a terror that even the elements are fearful of her.'

'What do you mean?'

'It's like this,' the mullah continued, climbing down the ladder. 'This morning, before I'd even had breakfast, Fatima began nagging me to replace a few loose tiles on our roof. Although it was bright and sunny, my wife was convinced that it was going to rain and that our roof would leak. I told her that the rungs on our ladder were broken and unsafe, but she insisted I should borrow a ladder from a neighbour. I told her I had a backache, and it would be difficult for me to lug a tall ladder to the house. She told me to stop making excuses and then walked out of the room in a huff.

'I fixed myself some breakfast and then lay down on the divan for a bit of rest, hoping that my wife would calm down soon. After a while I began to feel hungry so I put on my coat and turban and was about to head to the bazaar to buy some lahmacun, when my wife appeared in the room. "Where do you think you are going?" she asked angrily. Before I could answer, there was a crash of thunder and it began to pour. I didn't want to go outside in bad weather so I went into the living room and sat down on the couch, listening to the rain pounding on our roof, while Fatima began banging pots and pans in the kitchen, presumably preparing lunch for us.

'A few minutes later, she stormed into the room to inform me that the rain was dripping into the kitchen. "Never mind your backache and never mind the rain, get up immediately and replace the broken tiles on the roof," she screamed. Before I could make any excuses and while my wife was still yelling at me, the downpour suddenly ended and the sun peeped out of the clouds. Now I have no excuse for not repairing our roof, but I'm convinced that it was the very sight of my wife that made the rain start and then stop!'

'That's amazing,' Tariq replied, then added slyly: 'In that case it shouldn't be too difficult for her to stop her torrents of gossip.'

'Oh, come now, Tariq! I think my wife is unfairly being called a gossip just because she points out other people's mistakes. If everyone behaved themselves then she wouldn't have any need to talk about them, would she?' Nasruddin said, sticking up for his wife for the first and only time in their marriage.

13

The Buffalo Throne

Nasruddin bought a buffalo to provide milk for his family. Noticing that the buffalo had a large, majestic head, Nasruddin had an insane impulse to perch on it, between its big, curled horns, which he could hold on to for support.

One day, finding the buffalo sitting on the grass in the backyard, Nasruddin hoisted himself onto its head. Taking it firmly by the horns, his legs dangling by its ears, Nasruddin called out proudly to his wife, who was watching the bizarre scene from the kitchen window. 'Look, Fatima. I have fulfilled my desire and now I feel like a king on his throne!'

The buffalo, startled by the sudden assault on its body, got indignantly to its feet, let out a series of deafening grunts and jerked its head violently, sending Nasruddin flying into the air and into a flower bed near the back gate.

'Don't worry,' he said to his wife, who came huffing and puffing to his rescue. 'This is not the first time a king has been rudely ejected from his throne.'

14

Burglar Alarm

Returning from a wedding feast, Nasruddin and his wife were surprised to find a group of neighbours gathered outside their front gate, who informed them that their house had been burgled. The door was wide open and furniture, kitchen utensils, foodstuff, clothes, and all moveable objects had been looted.

Turning angrily on Nasruddin, her large eyes brimming with tears, Fatima sobbed: 'It's all your fault that we are in this mess. Because of your indifference, we've lost everything we had! You don't lift a finger around the house nor do you care about your family's safety. You could at least have checked that the door was locked and bolted before we left.'

Before Nasruddin could think of a fitting rejoinder to his wife's accusation, his nosy neighbours began to berate him.

'Why did you leave the front door unlocked?' one of them asked angrily. 'And why didn't you shut the windows if you were going out? Weren't you asking for trouble?'

Another added: 'For weeks your wife has been complaining that the locks and bolts were faulty and that you needed new ones, so why didn't you replace them?'

A third busybody piped up: 'You must have been aware that there have been a number of thefts in the town in recent weeks. Why didn't you take any precautions?'

Tiring of this barrage of accusations, Nasruddin raised a hand to silence his critics: 'I think all of you are being very unfair to me. I am the victim, yet you are cross-examining me as if I were the criminal. Why blame only me? Don't you think the thieves should get their fair share of the responsibility? They seem to have got away with everything else.'

15

An Ideal Husband

Mullah Nasruddin and his wife were arguing, neither one willing to end the quarrel. 'I was a fool when I married you,' Fatima moaned tearfully.

'That's true,' replied Nasruddin. 'But being young and naïve, I didn't notice. Now that I'm older and wiser, I realize that you have been trying to change me from the day we were married. Thanks to you, I have improved so much and become such a good husband that I now feel that *you* are not good enough for me.'

Fatima stormed out of the room, aware that her husband couldn't see sense when he was in a rage, and even when he was not. A prolonged sulk ensued on both sides, and the bitterness and resentment worsened.

A few weeks later, on a hot summer afternoon, Nasruddin's neighbours were awakened from their siestas by loud shouts and screams from the street. Running out to check what the disturbance was about, the neighbours were alarmed to see their stocky mullah chasing his rotund wife down the street, brandishing a rolling pin and shouting: 'I've had enough of your insolence! I can't take it any more!'

Out of breath and running out of steam, Fatima darted through the front door of her friend Zehra's house, closely followed by an enraged Nasruddin. Zehra, the local matchmaker, who specialized in helping couples tie the knot or untie it should the need arise, was accustomed to handling domestic disputes. Arms akimbo, she formed a protective shield between the cowering wife and the glowering husband, urging them to calm down.

Divested of the rolling pin and appeased by Zehra's offer of tea and sweetmeats, Nasruddin's wrath seemed to diminish. The group of anxious neighbours gathered outside Zehra's front door dispersed when they saw their mullah and his wife seated side by side on the divan—a picture of domestic bliss—sipping tea and wolfing down the sweets.

When all the confectionery had been consumed, Nasruddin thanked Zehra for her hospitality and signalled to his wife that it was time to head home. As soon as they reached their house, the pair started bickering again. Unable to bear her husband's barbs and taunts, Fatima once again headed for the door to make her escape. Calling out to his tearful wife, Nasruddin said: 'I'm in the mood for something savoury, so this time head for the baker's house. He makes mouth-watering kebabs.'

'Get the kebabs yourself,' Fatima said angrily. 'I'll stay the night at Zehra's and leave for my mother's house first thing tomorrow. You can fend for yourself from now on.'

After spending a few days pouring her heart out about Nasruddin's many faults to her mother, Fatima began to feel better and regretted her hasty decision to leave her marital home. Her mother persuaded her to return to her husband, promising to accompany her and have a stern talk with her son-in-law.

Surprised to see his wife return so soon and dismayed to see who she was with, Nasruddin was on his best behaviour for the next few days. Finding him alone in the yard one afternoon, his mother-in-law began her counselling session. 'You must learn to be more tolerant, Nasruddin,' she advised. 'Marriage is a matter of compromise, of give and take. Don't forget that my daughter is giving you the best years of her life.'

'If that is so, I shudder to think what the worst years will be like,' the mullah muttered under his breath.

16

Passing the Buck

After dinner one evening, Fatima noticed that her husband seemed very tense as he paced up and down in their yard.

'What's the matter? What's worrying you?' she asked.

'I borrowed fifty akçe from Fayaz the barber a few months ago and promised to repay him in full on the last day of this month,' Nasruddin said. 'That's tomorrow, but I don't have the money. I don't know what to do.'

'There is only one thing you can do. Go and tell Fayaz that you're unable to repay him tomorrow,' said Fatima.

Following his wife's advice for once, Nasruddin went across to his friend's house and returned a short while later looking happy and relaxed.

'How did he react?' Fatima asked.

'It's hard to tell,' Nasruddin replied. 'He was pacing up and down in his yard when I left.'

17

Uneasy Rider

With a wife and three children to support, and frequently ending up in debt, Nasruddin realized that the time had come for him to settle down with a steady job or trade. Accustomed to walking a couple of miles to a nearby town to buy fresh vegetables and groceries for his household once a week, he decided that he would buy the items in bulk and then sell them for a small profit in Akşehir.

The townsfolk were happy with this arrangement and Nasruddin's business enterprise got off to a promising start. However, lugging home the sacks of fruits, vegetables, and grain was a back-breaking ordeal, so the mullah decided to buy a donkey to do the heavy lifting.

At the livestock market a sturdy, little grey donkey caught the mullah's attention. She had big black eyes with white circles around them, long ears, and a white muzzle-like band across her nose. As Nasruddin approached the donkey's owner to negotiate the purchase, she stopped grazing, lifted her head, twitched her ears, and followed Nasruddin with her unblinking gaze as he inspected her from front to back and side to side to ensure that she was in good condition.

The owner extolled the virtues of the donkey, claiming that she was strong, obedient, and sensible. 'Well, that is more than I can say about my wife,' Nasruddin quipped, 'but I didn't have a choice in her case.' After some animated haggling, Nasruddin set off for home with his new purchase, whom he named Akilli, which means clever in Turkish.

In a matter of days, the smart ass had the mullah well

trained. At the first sound of Akilli's braying, Nasruddin would head for the barn with armfuls of straw and hay to feed her. He even instructed Fatima to knit a blanket for Akilli to keep her warm on chilly nights.

Despite the mullah's dutiful devotion, going to the marketplace with Akilli posed unforeseen challenges, as lengthy bouts of tugging and pulling at the reins invariably ended with Akilli going her own way. Being almost as mulish as the four-legged beast, Nasruddin decided to chastise Akilli by riding her facing backwards.

Whether this strategy had a calming effect on Akilli we will never know, but it did attract a lot of attention from passers-by, young and old, all of whom were mystified by the sight of the mullah making an ass of himself. Stories about his bizarre behaviour soon spread far and wide.

'Why are you riding your donkey facing backwards?' baffled onlookers would ask, and each time Mullah Nasruddin would come up with ingenious explanations.

'Every time I want to go somewhere, my donkey insists on going in the opposite direction. To teach her a lesson, I insist on facing the direction I want to go. That way, we both win.'

Or he might say: 'It's not me who's looking in the wrong direction. My donkey is facing the wrong way.'

He'd even tell inquisitive strangers: 'I never know where my donkey's going but by riding facing backwards, at least I get some idea of where we've been.'

Despite the fact that he was now an object of ridicule thanks to Akilli's shenanigans, Nasruddin's bond with his four-legged friend grew stronger over the years and he was always attentive to her creature comforts.

One day, during one of their frequent squabbles, Fatima told her husband: 'You seem to care more for that smelly beast than you do for your children and me.'

'That's because Akilli doesn't nag or complain and never answers back,' Nasruddin explained.

18

No Shortage of Advice

The learned mullah liked to spend a lot of his time outdoors, not because he loved nature especially, but more to escape Fatima's ceaseless demands that he help her around the house.

The family member whose company he seemed to enjoy most was that of his son, Ahmed, a quiet and diffident boy who had been henpecked into docility by his domineering mother and two older sisters—quite the opposite effect that Nasruddin's mother and sisters had had on him. As soon as Ahmed was old enough, Nasruddin cajoled the boy into accompanying him on his eventful forays with Akilli to markets in neighbouring towns.

One warm summer's day, with Ahmed riding on Akilli's back and Nasruddin walking alongside holding the reins, the trio set off on their shopping expedition as fast as the little grey donkey's temperamental pace would allow. They were plodding along happily when they came across a troupe of dervishes, instantly recognizable in their flowing white robes, who were on their way to a cultural festival in Akşehir. The dervishes bowed their heads in respectful greeting to Nasruddin, but one member of the group glowered at Ahmed, shook his head disapprovingly, and said: 'You should be ashamed of yourself, young man. You are healthy and strong and yet you sit astride a donkey while your elderly father, who looks feeble and fatigued, is forced to walk! It is a sorry state of affairs that the youth of today show no consideration for their elders.'

'There's no need to get into such a whirl,' Nasruddin mumbled, deeply offended at being called elderly and feeble.

Ahmed, humiliated by this exchange, dismounted immediately and insisted that his father ride Akilli while he walked alongside.

Everything went well for a while and the threesome were trudging along at a fair pace with the father and son chatting casually when they came across a group of women sitting and gossiping by the roadside. The women's conversation died down when they spotted the father, son, and the little donkey. As the trio approached them, the women hastily covered their faces with their veils, tut-tutted in dismay, and one of them said loud enough for the passers-by to hear: 'Isn't it disgraceful that the father rides comfortably on the donkey and makes the young child walk in this heat? Parents have become so uncaring these days....'

Now it was Nasruddin's turn to be embarrassed. He lifted Ahmed up to ride along with him and they proceeded on their journey, hoping against hope that they would not encounter any more advice-givers on the way. Unfortunately, that was not to be.

At the very next village, several residents gave the father and son disapproving looks and bemoaned the fate of the poor donkey: 'What heartless and selfish people,' one of the villagers said. 'Father and son both look perfectly hale and hearty, yet they're both riding on one tiny donkey. The poor creature looks ready to collapse under their weight!'

On hearing this, father and son both dismounted immediately and decided to continue their journey on foot. 'That should put an end to all unsolicited advice,' fumed an infuriated Nasruddin, but he had spoken too soon.

They had gone only a short distance when a group of men laughed out loud at the sight of the father, son, and donkey walking past them. 'Just look at those buffoons,' they scoffed. 'They prefer to walk in the heat despite having a strong and sturdy donkey they could easily ride! It's clear that the most senseless of the three is not the one you'd expect it to be!'

Nasruddin was stung by the men's insults. I hadn't realized that Akilli had such a large family, with so many loud-mouthed supporters, he thought to himself. Then trying to make the best of a bad situation, he turned to Ahmed and smiled: 'Son, we've learned an important lesson today, which is that people have opinions—especially on matters that don't concern them—and seldom hesitate to voice them. They would have criticized us even if we had been carrying Akilli instead of the other way round! There's a saying that everyone has two eyes but no one has the same view. The point is that no matter how hard one tries, one can never ever please everyone.'

'If that's the case, Baba, were we wrong to let other people's opinions influence us?' the boy asked.

'No, we were not wrong nor were they right,' Nasruddin replied. 'But sometimes, for the sake of peace, it is better to heed other people's views. If we all choose to ignore everyone else and do as we please, there would be chaos in the world.'

19

A Smart Choice

Always one to find inventive ways of making money, Nasruddin took to standing at a street corner on market days to be pointed out as the village idiot. People would offer him a choice between a large and a small coin, and Nasruddin unfailingly chose the smaller piece of lower value, which he was allowed to keep, while onlookers sneered at his simplicity.

This public humiliation of her husband caused Fatima no end of grief. Even his children complained that their friends were taunting them about their father's foolishness. One day, his eldest daughter advised him: 'Baba, why don't you take the bigger coin which is worth more? You will not only make more money that way but people will no longer laugh and poke fun at you or at us.'

'My dear,' Nasruddin replied, 'I know that the bigger coin has higher value, but if I take the larger coin, the game will be over. People will stop offering me money to prove that I am more stupid than them. Then I would have no money at all. This way, I not only make a fool of them, but can buy provisions for at least a few days. Being laughed at is a small price to pay for making easy money and providing for my family. People who think they are smarter than me don't realize that the joke's on them: it is I who get to laugh at fools who are so easily parted from their money.'

20

The Mullah's Fall

Nasruddin was on his way to the bazaar, riding Akilli facing backwards, as usual, and fantasizing about expanding his business and buying a bigger house, when a group of young boys lit fireworks in the middle of the market square. Startled by the loud explosions, Akilli took off like a racehorse, causing the daydreaming mullah to violently jerk backwards and almost fall off, his turban slipping forward over his eyes and blinding him.

Trying desperately to get Akilli to stop, Nasruddin grabbed on to her tail with both hands, but the frightened animal continued her frenzied gallop around the marketplace, causing shoppers to run helter-skelter to get out of her way.

'Where are you going in such a hurry, Mullah?' one of the vendors called out.

'Don't ask me, ask my donkey,' Nasruddin gasped, sliding from side to side on Akilli's back as he struggled to sit up straight.

When Akilli slowed down to a trot after several laps round the market, Nasruddin let go of her tail with one hand to readjust his turban, but lost his balance and slipped off the donkey's back, knocking over a basket of peaches as he fell to the ground with a thud. Mayhem ensued as a few passers-by grabbed hold of the mullah's arms to help him to sit up, the fruit seller scuttled about trying to salvage any fruit that had not been crushed under the mullah's weight, Akilli scampered off to a safe distance, and the boys who had sparked the fireworks doubled over with laughter at the sight of the mullah sprawled on his back, his turban muddied, and his tunic stained with peach juice.

Struggling back to his feet, embarrassed at the spectacle he'd made of himself, Nasruddin faced his young tormentors and asked them angrily: 'What are you laughing at, you foolish boys? Does it not occur to you that I might have wanted to get off my donkey anyway?'

21

Tender Loving Care

Nasruddin had been working on his household accounts all morning and by midday he had a splitting headache. He was about to take a nap when he saw his friend Hussain pass by. Calling out to him, Nasruddin asked what he should do to ease the pain.

'I can tell you what I do,' Hussain said. 'Whenever I have a headache, my wife gently massages my forehead, rubs some soothing balm on my temples, puts her arms around me, and comforts me until I completely forget about the pain.'

Nasruddin cheered up instantly and said: 'That sounds wonderful. Is your wife at home now?'

22

The Rainmaker

When Akşehir faced a severe drought, the town council hastily convened an emergency meeting. The mayor and other senior officials turned up at the appointed hour, but there was no sign of Nasruddin, the town's official water diviner.

After waiting for half an hour, the meeting had to be cancelled but the mayor sent an emissary to find out why Nasruddin had failed to show up. On reaching the mullah's house, the mayor's aide was surprised to see Nasruddin bent over piles of wet clothes at his well, scrubbing them diligently.

'Mullah, instead of turning up at the mayor's meeting, you are washing your clothes! You do realize that we're facing a drought because there's been no rain for months, don't you?' the man said, a look of shock on his face.

'Calm down, my dear chap,' Nasruddin replied. 'I was appointed the town's water diviner for good reason, because I have a foolproof way of ending droughts. I don't need a divining rod or a forked stick to find water. All I have to do is to hang my laundry outside to dry, and it is guaranteed that the heavens will open and it will definitely rain. Do warn your wife, just in case she is planning to do her washing....'

23

Cha and Chat

Following a long and chequered career as a cleric, teacher, grocer, donkey driver, ferryman, water diviner, and marriage counsellor, Mullah Nasruddin decided that the time had come for him to give up full-time work and spend more time with his family. Within just a few days, he realized that being in a confined space with his wife and children was not good for his and more so their sanity. He therefore took to whiling away his time at the neighbourhood teahouse, much to his family's relief.

The teahouse, Time for Tea, was located on one of Akşehir's main thoroughfares and provided a convenient meeting place for the town's menfolk. A modest one-storey structure with a thatched roof, Time for Tea's owner had his living quarters and kitchen at one end of the house and had converted the hall and dining area into a tea room and eatery with long wooden tables and benches, where patrons spent hours in lively discussions on every subject under the sun. Three long tables and benches were arranged in a U shape against the walls, the seating arrangements facilitating conversation and interaction between customers. Visitors—regulars or strangers—happily sat at a table with other customers instead of choosing to sit on their own. In those simpler and friendlier times, people enjoyed each other's company and always made time for cha and chat.

Like Nasruddin, most of the patrons of the teahouse were in their dotage—that twilight zone in which each had less to look forward to and more to look back on—and derived great pleasure in debating the issues of the day or discussing their favourite topic: themselves. Most of the teahouse's patrons had grown up in and around Akşehir, and had known each other for more than four decades. Nasruddin was by far the town's most famous son, having gained a reputation for fearlessly questioning authority and outsmarting renowned thinkers. It was, therefore, not surprising that the mullah often did most of the talking and also featured prominently in his friends' nostalgic stories.

Over steaming cups of tea, Nasruddin's childhood friend Hussain was reminiscing about their schooldays. 'It's hard to imagine that the mullah, now considered a pillar of our community, was once the bane of our schoolteachers. He was defiant, disobedient, and completely unafraid of the punishments he received,' Hussain began.

'Although Nasruddin was famous for defying and outwitting our teacher, his biggest fightback was with a fellow student. I remember one incident as if it happened yesterday. We must have been around eleven years of age when a few of us, Nasruddin included, were being badgered and bullied by an older student named Talah, who was not only stronger than us, but also came from a much wealthier family. He scoffed at our worn, patched-up clothes and scruffy footwear, and said he felt sorry for us because we would never amount to anything in life.'

Pausing for a sip of tea, Hussain continued: 'Our first response to the bully was to ignore him, but he mistook our silence for fear, and troubled us even more. One day, Nasruddin decided to confront our tormentor....

'He went straight up to Talah and said: "You're a bully and a coward, picking on kids who cannot or won't fight back. Just because you wear smarter clothes and have more money than us doesn't make you better than us, nor does it give you the right to keep putting us down like this. If *you* had earned the money that enabled you to buy all your finery, your shameful boasting would be understandable, but still inexcusable." Talah just stood there, speechless, so Nasruddin continued even more confidently.

'"As I see it, my friends and I are better off being insignificant nobodies rather than an arrogant somebody like you. It's sad that the only way you can feel superior is by making others look inferior." And with that, Nasruddin turned and walked away, leaving the bully stunned, opening and closing his mouth like a fish out of water, still unable to speak. Needless to say, we had no problems with Talah from then on.'

The hushed silence at the end of Hussain's story was broken by cries of 'Vay be! Vay be! Well done! Well done!' from patrons of the teahouse.

'What I learned from that experience is that bullies are cowards and once you confront them, they're too scared to fight back,' Nasruddin said, openly delighted with the vocal acclaim for his bravery.

'I wonder what happened to Talah,' one of the townsfolk mused aloud.

'I heard that he fell into bad company,' Abdul, a local landowner and moneylender, spoke up. 'Talah squandered his father's wealth, got heavily into debt and borrowed money from friends and relatives, none of whom were paid back. When his creditors—myself included—began baying for his blood, we were told that Talah had abandoned his wife and family and run off to Constantinople. He has not been seen in these parts since.'

'Good riddance,' the learned mullah exclaimed. 'How people behave after they have borrowed money from you reveals a great deal about their character or lack thereof.'

'I agree with you completely, Nasruddin,' Abdul interjected. 'I'm amazed how many people seem to completely forget about the money they've borrowed from me, forcing me to remind them about the loan. When I ask them to repay me, they take great offence and get angry with me for asking them for my money!'

Nasruddin nodded and said: 'It's never a good idea to borrow money, and even worse to lend it. Sadly, whenever I've needed money, people have been most reluctant to lend me any. I often wonder why people seem more willing to dole out money to the greedy rather than the needy.'

24

Practice Makes Perfect

A neighbour knocked on the door of Nasruddin's house and found the mullah alone and talking to himself. 'I'm sorry to bother you, Mullah, are you busy?'

'No,' replied Nasruddin. 'Just rehearsing my sermon for Friday—practising what I preach.'

25

Preacher's Block

One of Nasruddin's regular preoccupations was to give religious discourses and lead the Friday prayers at one of the town's mosques. A recent addition to the town's landscape, the wooden-roofed mosque in the mullah's charge was a more modest structure than the ancient mosque with the imposing minaret that had so impressed him as a boy. The new mosque had a smaller dome and a shorter minaret but boasted a spacious prayer hall and wooden pillars adorned with intricately carved geometric designs.

Having grown immune to the mosque's aesthetic appeal and having preached there every Friday for years on end, the mullah was running out of original ideas for his sermons and yearned for a break. One hot summer's day, not having given any thought to the topic of his sermon, he climbed up to the pulpit, surveyed his congregation seated on the plush carpet on the tiled floor looking up at him intently, and asked: 'Do you know the subject I'm going to discuss today?'

'No,' came the honest reply, as his followers shook their heads in confusion.

'How can you not know, given all the major events that have occurred in the past week? I am not going to waste my time preaching to such an ignorant assembly,' said Nasruddin indignantly, then flounced out of the mosque and headed home for a siesta.

The following Friday, he climbed up to the pulpit and asked the same question: 'Oh, ye men of faith, do you know the subject of my sermon today?'

Fearful of offending the mullah and causing a repeat of the walkout that had been staged the week before, the congregation nodded their heads and replied: 'Yes, yes. We know what you are going to discuss today.'

'In that case, there is no point in my telling you what you already know,' said the mullah, making another hasty exit.

The next week, Nasruddin again climbed up to the minbar and asked the congregation: 'Do you know what I'm going to speak about today?'

This time, his followers had anticipated the question and were well prepared with their answer. 'Some of us know and some do not,' they said.

'That's good. Then those who know can tell those who don't,' said the mullah and left.

Tiring of their mullah's idiosyncrasies, the congregation agreed that something should be done. After some deliberation, they appointed a village elder to have a stern word with the mullah. Woken from his afternoon snooze by someone knocking at his door, Nasruddin was surprised to see the town's oldest resident. 'Please come in,' said Nasruddin, trying hard not to look as if he'd been asleep.

'No, thank you,' the man replied. 'I'm here merely to pass on a message from the members of your congregation. Having missed out on your enlightening sermons for three weeks in a row, the villagers are considering inviting a mullah from a nearby village to lead the Friday prayers for a couple of weeks to give you a bit of a break. I'm sure you will welcome their decision.'

Realizing that the townsfolk had seen through his trickery, and terrified of losing his job and his stature in the community, Nasruddin quickly replied: 'Please inform the villagers that there is no need to find a substitute mullah while I am alive. Assure them that I will be there next week and the topic of my sermon will be the importance of regularly attending Friday prayers.'

26

Over the Moon

At Time for Tea one afternoon, people who had travelled far and wide were recounting the wonders of nature they had seen in foreign lands: the exotic flora and fauna, majestic snow-capped mountains, breathtakingly beautiful blue seas, spectacular desert sunrises and sunsets, and so on. As Nasruddin had not ventured further than the towns and villages surrounding Akşehir, he felt a bit excluded from the discussion but butted in nevertheless: 'I think the moon outshines all other natural phenomena.'

'Why is that?' his listeners asked.

'Because the moon is more useful to us than the sun.'

'What makes you say that, Mullah?'

'There are two main reasons,' Nasruddin responded. 'First, the moon has the ability to regenerate itself. Each time an old moon dies, within a matter of days, a new moon emerges. Second, the sun disappears every evening when it gets dark, but then thankfully the moon appears and provides light at night, when we need it more. Anyone who doubts my claim should look at the sky on a starry night and see for themselves how the moon dispels the darkness when millions of stars do not.'

27

Nasruddin the Brave

A group of soldiers passing through Akşehir on their way to join their platoon stopped off at the teahouse and started bragging about their exploits in combat. Finding in the villagers a receptive and trusting audience, the soldiers' boasts about their heroic feats became more and more audacious.

A tall and muscular trooper twirled his impressive moustache and proclaimed: 'Even though we were outnumbered two to one, the enemy did not stand a chance against my platoon. With sword in hand, we charged towards them fearlessly, wielding our blades left, right, and centre until the majority of our opponents were decimated and a handful of them beat a hasty retreat, scattering like chickens in a barn escaping a fox.'

His awe-stricken audience burst into applause amid cries of 'Bravo!'

Unable to tolerate other people bragging, Mullah Nasruddin cleared his throat and said: 'Your bravery reminds me of the time when I was caught up in a fierce battle.' Time for Tea's regular customers looked at each other in surprise, never having known their mullah to have been anywhere near the front lines, as he added dramatically: 'The enemy soldiers were charging towards us, brandishing their swords in the air. When I was close enough to one of them, I gripped my sword firmly in both hands and with a downward swipe I cut off his arm. Chopped it off with one clean blow.'

'When it comes to dealing with an enemy, sir, it would have been better if you had cut off the enemy's head,' said the captain of the soldiers.

'That was actually my intention,' Nasruddin nodded, 'but I found that somebody had already taken care of that.'

Before anyone could question his heroism, Nasruddin continued: 'On another occasion, some years ago, I came to the rescue of an entire platoon. I was passing by a field where our king's soldiers were resting after a fierce battle in which they had slaughtered the enemy. As I knew the commanding officer and many of the soldiers, they asked for my assistance. Several of the men had been severely wounded and needed medical help.

'Their commanding officer requested me to ride back into town and ask the authorities to send doctors and medical supplies for the injured soldiers. Being a local and familiar with the terrain, he was sure I would be able to pinpoint their location,' Nasruddin said, pausing dramatically for a sip of tea.

'Did help reach them in time?' a soldier asked.

'Yes, eventually,' Nasruddin replied. 'The rescue party seemed to have some difficulty finding the platoon even though I had specified that the camp site was located directly under the moon.'

28

Honestly Speaking

A modest and soft-spoken young man introduced himself to Nasruddin in the marketplace. 'I have heard so much about you, Respected Mullah,' the youth said. 'My name is Adil, and I'm from the village of Hortu in Sivrihisar district. I have come to Akşehir to make an honest living.'

'You're in the right place and should do well,' Nasruddin replied. 'An honest man won't have much competition here.'

29

God's Way

Heading home from the market, Mullah Nasruddin came across four boys playing by the side of the dusty pathway. The boys stopped their game and skipped alongside the mullah—who was astride Akilli, facing backwards—and asked: 'What have you got in those sacks, sir?'

'I have lots of fresh fruits and vegetables,' the mullah replied, 'and in these bags I have the most delicious cherries from the best orchard in the land.'

'Can we have some cherries, please?' the boys asked eagerly.

As Akilli had already decided to make an unscheduled stop to graze in a nearby field, and being in a generous mood, Nasruddin dismounted. He carefully counted out twelve ripe cherries from a sack. 'I will share these sweet and juicy treats with you,' Nasruddin told the boys. 'But first you must tell me how you want me to distribute the cherries between the four of you. Should I divide them the way God would or the way a human would?'

'God's way, of course,' the boys said, without a moment's hesitation.

'Very well,' said the mullah and handed over five cherries to the first boy, four to the second, three to the third, and none to the fourth. The children were puzzled and gaped at Nasruddin in confusion.

The boy who had not been given any cherries spoke up: 'This is very unfair, sir. What kind of division is this?'

'It may seem unfair, but this is how God distributes gifts amongst people,' the mullah replied. Sensing the tense situation, Akilli stopped grazing and fixed her gaze on the group. The mullah continued: ‘We cannot always understand God’s mysterious ways but just look around and you will see that some people get a huge amount, others get a lot less, and many get nothing at all. That is the harsh reality of life: what God sees as fair and what men think is fair is not necessarily the same. Now, if you had asked me to divide the cherries as mortals would, each of you would have received an equal share.’

30

Age of Discontent

Having gained a reputation as a hub for animated discourse and debate, Time for Tea had become a popular platform for self-styled philosophers to propound their banal theories. One afternoon, Hamad, a local smart aleck, was holding forth to a captive audience: 'We seem to be living in an age of discontent. People never seem to be satisfied. They're always complaining, even though their complaints don't make things better. What's the point of endlessly grumbling about the weather, moaning that the winters are too cold, and going on about summers being too hot, when you cannot do anything about it?'

'I hear your complaint, Hamad,' Nasruddin said, stifling a yawn. 'But have you ever wondered why nobody grumbles about spring or autumn?'

Unwilling to be outsmarted by the canny mullah, Hamad persisted: 'At the end of the day, I suppose everything boils down to a person's attitude—their optimism or pessimism and whether they see a pitcher as half full or half empty.'

'I think that argument is redundant,' Nasruddin retorted. 'After all, if the pitcher contains poison, one would be glad that it is only half full. But if it is half empty and contains nectar, then it can always be refilled, can't it?'

31

Mr Right

'Respected Mullah, you have accomplished so much in your life and have had so many varied occupations and responsibilities. What has been the biggest challenge you faced?' asked a visitor from a nearby town.

Nasruddin thought for a moment and replied: 'Always being right has been a heavy responsibility to bear. Especially when it comes to domestic disputes. I never argue with my wife, but merely try to explain why I am right. Each time we have a disagreement—which is several times a day—I say to her: "I'm sorry if I upset you, my dear. Next time I'll try not to be right." For some reason, that seems to aggravate her no end, and we end up back where we started.'

32

Seeking Truth

A group of itinerant mystics visited Akşehir in the hopes of being granted an audience with Mullah Nasruddin, who had gained a reputation for coming up with inventive answers to the most vexing questions.

'What is truth?' they asked the mullah. 'How and where do we find it?'

'If you are seeking the truth, you will have to pay a high price for it,' the mullah told them.

Taken aback by this response, the leader of the mystics spoke up: 'With all due respect, Mullah, don't you think it is unreasonable to ask people to pay for something like truth?'

'My friend, truth is a rare commodity,' the mullah explained. 'Though the demand for truth may be high, supplies of truth are extremely low. As you know, it is the shortage of a commodity that determines how much it is worth.'

33

Vexing Questions

A group of overseas students stopped off at Time for Tea en route to their university in Italy. The young scholars were welcomed by the teahouse regulars and offered cups of tea and plates of sweetmeats. After the usual pleasantries and small talk, the discussion turned to more philosophical questions.

'There are so many difficult questions for which we do not yet have answers,' one of the young students said.

'Such as?' asked Nasruddin.

'Such as, what is the secret to finding happiness?'

'A wise man once told me that happiness is everywhere you find it, but never where you seek it,' the mullah replied.

'Is there an easy way to solve the problems we face in life?'

'Yes, the same wise man told me that the problem often lies in the way you see the problem. So the solution is to change your perception.'

'Sir, do you believe in the afterlife? And what is life like after death?'

'I find that life before death is difficult enough and have therefore decided not to worry about life after death. However, I'm convinced that the afterlife must be more or less like life itself, because I've observed that babies come into the world crying and most people leave the world in tears or in agony.'

34

Earning Respect

A preacher from a distant country was passing through Akşehir and stopped off at the teahouse, whose patrons were always welcoming to and curious about strangers. 'I am the most popular priest in my homeland,' the preacher claimed. 'In fact, attendance at my sermons has grown so much that we've had to construct a larger prayer hall to accommodate my followers.'

Turning to Nasruddin, the preacher asked: 'I hear that you are the local mullah. What has your experience been?'

'I haven't looked upon my calling as a popularity contest,' Nasruddin replied. 'I'm well aware that I'm disliked by people who don't like what I say. I've realized that people who never hesitate to voice the truth about others seldom like to hear it about themselves!'

'Perhaps you could be more tactful....' the visitor persisted.

'Being tactful is like telling a person to go to hell and then wishing them a pleasant journey. It is not for me. If people don't like my plain speaking, I hope at least that they respect my candour. Wouldn't you agree that it is better to be respected than to be liked?'

35

The King of Vegetables

Sultan Omar, the most powerful overlord in Anatolia, had gained a reputation for being a despot whose whimsical behaviour and short temper terrified most of his subjects. Like all bullies, the sultan had a grudging respect for people like Nasruddin, who stood up to him, so he often invited the mullah to be a guest at his palace.

On one occasion at a state dinner for a foreign delegation, the sultan's chef served up a delectable eggplant dish, which was much appreciated by the sultan and his guests. Suppressing a satisfied belch, Omar turned to Nasruddin and asked: 'Wouldn't you agree that eggplants are the most delicious vegetables in the world?'

'Indeed, sire,' said Nasruddin, 'eggplant is the king of vegetables. They are not only tasty but also nutritious and should be eaten every day.'

'Excellent suggestion, Nasruddin,' said the sultan and ordered his chef to cook eggplant for every meal. The chef, well aware of the harsh punishments meted out to his predecessors who had served up meals that were not to his master's liking, tried his best to concoct different eggplant recipes for lunch and dinner. For an entire week, the sultan and his guests, including Nasruddin, were served eggplants—in soups, salads, grilled, fried, roasted, stewed, sautéed, breaded, and curried.

By the end of the fourteenth meal, the sultan was sick and tired of eggplants. He summoned the chef and bellowed: 'Remove these disgusting vegetables from my sight immediately. I cannot bear to even look at them, never mind eat them.'

'You are absolutely right, My Lord. They are the most flavourless vegetables in the world,' Nasruddin concurred from his seat further down the table, despite having gorged himself at every meal.

Veering angrily to face the mullah, the sultan said: 'But Mullah, last week you were eulogizing the benefits of eggplants and advised all of us to eat them daily!'

'I remember doing so, but for once I may have been mistaken,' Nasruddin replied. 'I owe no allegiance to eggplants, but as Your Lordship's obedient subject, I must bow to your superior taste and judgement and agree that too much of a good thing can turn one's stomach.'

36

The Sultan's Breakfast

Sultan Omar and his attendants were on a hunting expedition when they decided to take a break in Akşehir. As none of the townsfolk's homes was large or grand enough to accommodate the august company, the sultan and his minions ended up at Time for Tea, where Nasruddin had been left in charge while the owner was away on business.

'What is your desire, sire?' Nasruddin asked respectfully.

'My desire is to conquer the world,' came the brusque response, 'but what I need is a good breakfast and I'm in the mood for an omelette.'

'Please make yourselves comfortable while I prepare the best omelette you have ever eaten,' said Nasruddin with his usual lack of modesty as he hurried to the kitchen. After several minutes of bustling about and noisily banging pots and pans, he served up fluffy omelettes, freshly baked simit, and hot tea for his guests, who hungrily tucked into their meal.

'That was an excellent breakfast, Nasruddin,' the sultan proclaimed. 'The omelette was delicious. How much do we owe you?'

'Sire, for you and your entourage the price for the breakfast will be twenty gold coins.'

Taken aback, the sultan exclaimed: 'Twenty gold coins! That's a very high price to pay for breakfast. Is the cost of eggs extremely high in this part of the country?'

'My Lord, the price of breakfast is determined by the simple economics of supply and demand,' Nasruddin replied.

'Is there a shortage of eggs in this part of the kingdom that I am unaware of?' the sultan asked with a deep frown.

'There is no scarcity of eggs here,' Nasruddin explained. 'But as visiting sovereigns are in short supply, the price has gone up.'

With a grunt and a nod, Omar gestured to one of his attendants to hand over the twenty gold coins. 'Here's one coin for the breakfast and the balance is for your quick wit, which merits a high price because it is so scarce in others,' said the sultan, with a hint of a smile.

37

No Complaints

Sultan Omar announced that he planned to set up a department to handle any complaints against his administration, and was seeking a qualified candidate to head the new unit. Nasruddin was among the applicants for the post.

'It has come to my attention that other rulers have established similar facilities in their kingdoms for people to air their grievances,' the sultan explained. 'As it is highly unlikely that any of my subjects will have any gripes against me, this will be a nice and easy job for the laziest man here. Raise your hand if you are the laziest.'

Everyone, except Nasruddin, raised their hands.

'Why haven't you raised your hand, Mullah?' the sultan roared.

'It was too much trouble, My Lord,' replied Nasruddin, thus clinching the cushy post as the sultan's complaints officer.

Nasruddin was assigned a small room near the administrative offices, outside which he placed a large sign that read: 'Spending today complaining about yesterday won't make tomorrow any better'. When reports reached the sultan that the mullah spent most of his working day dozing, the Complaints office was shut down permanently.

38

Your Cat Is Dead

Nasruddin's cousin Faisal left Akşehir to study at a university in Baghdad, leaving some of his possessions, including his beloved pet cat, in Nasruddin's care. One day, the cat suddenly died. Usually verbose, Nasruddin sent Faisal a surprisingly terse message saying: *Your cat is dead.*

Deeply distressed at his much-loved pet's demise, and more so by the curt message devoid of empathy, Faisal sent a reply to Nasruddin saying:

> Your message was very upsetting. I was deeply saddened by the death of my cherished pet, but more so by the insensitive way in which you passed on the news. Don't you know that you should be more sensitive when giving a person bad news? Instead of just telling me bluntly that my cat was dead, you should have let me know little by little. For instance, you could have started off by saying 'Your cat is acting strange', then said 'Your cat is not eating properly' or 'Your cat is missing', and finally broken the news and said, 'Your cat is dead'.

A month later, Faisal received another brief note from Nasruddin. It said: *Your mother is acting strange.*

39

Fate

'What is fate?' the mullah was asked.

'Fate is one of life's greatest mysteries, and means different things to different people based on their assumptions.'

'How so?'

'Well, when people assume things are going to go well but they don't—they deem it bad luck. When they assume things will go awry but they don't—they attribute it to good luck. When folks don't know for sure whether certain things are going to happen or not happen—they presume that the future is unknown. When the unexpected happens and people are taken by surprise—that is what they call fate.'

40

The Power of Silence

At Time for Tea one afternoon, a visitor asked: 'Respected Mullah, would the world be a better place if everyone spoke their mind?'

'Most definitely not. Very few people talk sense and, besides, no one has the time to listen.'

'In that case, do you believe silence is more powerful than speech?'

'That depends entirely on who is keeping silent and who is doing the talking,' the mullah replied. 'I personally enjoy the silences that I share with my wife much more than our conversations. I have explained to her time and again that I'm very busy with my various jobs and have requested her to talk to me only on a need-to-know basis. Unfortunately, she feels I need to know *everything* that happens to her in the course of any given day....

'But I digress. To answer your question: in my view a meaningful silence is better than meaningless words. A fool is known by his words and a wise man by his silence.' While the visitor nodded in agreement, regular patrons of the teahouse couldn't help wondering which category Nasruddin fell into, given his reputation for being talkative rather than taciturn.

41

Telling Right from Wrong

Having gained a reputation for his quick thinking and ready answers to perplexing questions, Nasruddin was appointed as a magistrate. Presiding over his first case, Nasruddin was so swayed by the plaintiff's forceful argument that he cried out: 'I think you are right!'

Taken aback by this proclamation, the clerk of the court cautioned Nasruddin to refrain from making any comments until the defendant had been given a chance to testify.

The defendant then presented his case so persuasively that Nasruddin was completely won over, so much so that as soon as the man had finished giving evidence, Nasruddin declared: 'I think you are right!'

The clerk of the court had to intervene once again. 'Your honour, they cannot both be right.'

'I think you are right!' exclaimed Nasruddin.

There was consternation in the court as the plaintiff, the defendant, and the court clerk stared at Nasruddin in dismay.

'Don't look at me as if I've committed a crime,' Nasruddin said defensively. 'Everyone knows that there are always more than two sides to a story—the plaintiff's version, the defendant's version, and the truth. I've heard the plaintiff and defendant's views. Now I'll have to determine the truth.'

42

Where God Is Not

Nasruddin was asked to join a mayoral delegation to Baghdad. He happily accepted the invitation hoping that he could stay with his cousin Faisal, whom he hadn't seen for more than three years.

Faisal was happy to host the mullah, provided he abided by the house rules. After leaving Akşehir, Faisal had not only become extremely studious but also excessively devout. Ushering Nasruddin into the spare room, Faisal explained why the bed had been placed at an odd angle in the tiny space. 'I have positioned it so that your head faces towards Mecca,' Faisal said. 'I hope you will be comfortable.'

Tired from his long journey, Nasruddin had an early dinner and went up to his bedroom, but tossed and turned for hours in the unfamiliar bed before finally falling asleep. The next thing he knew, Faisal was shaking him awake and looking very distressed. 'Nasruddin, I didn't expect this of you,' his cousin said. 'I'm upset and disappointed.'

'What have I done to upset you?' Nasruddin asked, not feeling too bright after his disturbed night.

'You have slept with your feet facing Mecca, which is most disrespectful,' Faisal said angrily.

'I'm sorry, Faisal, I meant no disrespect. I didn't sleep very well last night and must have moved in my sleep.'

That night, Nasruddin was restless again and when he woke, he found his feet on the pillow and his head where his feet should be. What was worse, Faisal was standing in the doorway, glaring at him disapprovingly.

'I take a dim view of your behaviour, Nasruddin,' Faisal said sternly. 'Being a mullah, you should know that all good Muslims sleep with their feet pointing away from Mecca. You must point your head towards God and your feet away from him. If you cannot do that, then I shall have to ask you to leave my house.'

Not wanting to move out of his free lodging, Nasruddin decided to have a talk with his fastidious cousin. 'Can I ask you something, Faisal? Doesn't God rule over everything?'

'Of course, he does.'

'And isn't God present in every part of his creation?'

'Of course! You know full well that he is!'

'So, if God is everywhere—in humans, in birds, and beasts, in mountains, rivers, and deserts—then, Faisal, please show me some place to point my feet where God is not!'

43

Planning Ahead

Nasruddin took up a part-time job as assistant to a trader who ran a prosperous business in Akşehir, but the mullah's absentminded and erratic behaviour sometimes proved too much for his employer. One day, the trader lost his temper.

'Nasruddin,' he yelled, 'why don't you try using your brains once in a while? Why must you make three trips to the market to buy three eggs? Why can't you buy all three eggs in a single trip? You've made a habit of not completing your tasks in one go. You're wasting your time and my money because of your foolish ways. Is it too much to ask that you complete all your errands in one trip?'

Realizing that his employer was at the end of his tether and that he might lose a lucrative job, Nasruddin acknowledged his mistake. 'Please forgive me, sir. From now on, I will follow your instructions and not waste time going back and forth to complete my assigned tasks. All my jobs will be completed in one trip, I assure you.'

A week later, the trader suddenly took ill and instructed Nasruddin to fetch the hakim as soon as possible. Nasruddin bustled off on his bandy legs and returned a short while later at the head of a small procession of men. Walking briskly behind Nasruddin was Arif, the local hakim, and behind him came a man carrying a wooden box full of tiny vials of medicine, followed by four men, one of whom was carrying a white shroud and another a wreath.

Perplexed at the sight of this parade, the trader asked weakly: 'What is the meaning of this, Nasruddin? Who are all these people?'

Nasruddin replied: 'I fetched the hakim as you requested. I also asked the apothecary to come along so he can provide whatever medication Arif prescribes. I hope and pray that you recover after his treatment. But in case you don't get better and the worst happens, I have made arrangements for these pallbearers to take you to the cemetery. I followed your instructions and completed all tasks in one trip.'

Nasruddin's employer was dazed and dumbstruck but felt too ill to argue against his employee's undeniable logic.

44

Nobody's Business

Invited to a formal reception by the mayor of a nearby town, Nasruddin reached the venue before any of the other invited guests and dignitaries. With his usual overconfidence, he strode up to the podium and sat down on one of the plush chairs covered in velvet.

Not recognizing Nasruddin as one of the local luminaries, a senior aide went up to him and politely whispered: 'Excuse me, sir, these seats are reserved for the guests of honour.'

Looking the man straight in the eye, Nasruddin replied: 'Oh, but I am more than just an honoured guest.'

'Pardon me for asking, but are you a diplomat?'

'I am far more than that!'

'Really? Then you are probably a minister?' the bewildered aide persisted.

'No, much more important than that.'

'Is that so? In that case, you must be the sultan himself, sir,' the aide said sarcastically.

'Higher than that!'

'That's impossible!' the aide exclaimed. 'Higher than the sultan! Nobody is higher than the sultan in this town!'

'You've got it at last! I am nobody!' Nasruddin declared. He then got up from the chair and headed to a table laden with food to help himself to the snacks. He wangled invitations to these pretentious events solely for the free banquets, which he thoroughly enjoyed despite being a nobody.

45

Teaching a Horse to Sing

During a visit to the capital, a small crowd gathered to hear Nasruddin's views on a variety of topics. A bystander called out: 'Mullah, do you think it is right that people should pay with their lives when the sultan embarks on military campaigns one after the other?'

'Whenever a monarch errs, it is his people who pay the penalty,' Nasruddin replied.

Word of this jibe immediately reached Sultan Omar through his lackeys. Taking offence at the taunt, the sultan had Nasruddin arrested and imprisoned on charges of heresy and treason. Nasruddin apologized profusely and begged forgiveness, which made the sultan so angry that he decreed that Nasruddin should be beheaded the following day.

On the morning of his execution, Nasruddin made a final appeal. 'Your Lordship, may God grant you a long and healthy life! You have known me for many years and are aware that I am a great teacher. It will be a huge loss to your kingdom if I am executed and my vast reserves of knowledge die with me. I appeal to you most earnestly to delay my sentence for one year, during which time I will teach your favourite horse to sing.'

Sultan Omar did not believe that such a thing was possible, but his anger had cooled and he was amused by the audacity of Nasruddin's claim. 'Very well,' he said, 'I will grant your request. You can move into the stablemen's quarters right away but if at the end of the year you have not taught my horse to sing, believe me you will wish you had been executed today.'

When Nasruddin's friends visited him later that evening, they found him in high spirits, humming happily to himself. 'How can you be so cheerful?' they asked. 'Surely you do not believe that you can teach the sultan's horse to sing?'

'Maybe, maybe not,' Nasruddin replied. 'But now I have a whole year, which I did not have yesterday, and a lot can happen in that time. It is possible that the sultan might forgive me and order my release. It is possible that he could die in one of his frequent battles or succumb to illness. It is possible that the horse might die or I could die too. But I'm not going to lose heart. I've heard that in some western countries, people have managed to teach horses to dance to music. So, if horses can dance, maybe this one can be taught to sing.'

46

Needs Assessment

Nasruddin was heading home from the mosque after Friday prayers, when a beggar squatting on the pavement asked him for money. The man looked fit and clean, and the mullah's curiosity was aroused.

'Are you a big spender?' Nasruddin asked.

'Yes,' came the reply.

'Do you like sitting around drinking tea and smoking?'

'Yes, I do.'

'I guess you like to go to the public baths every day?'

'Yes, I do.'

'And do you gamble and drink occasionally?' asked Nasruddin.

'Yes, I do.'

Nasruddin tut-tutted disapprovingly and handed the beggar a silver coin.

A short distance away, another sickly-looking and scruffy beggar who had overheard the conversation, also appealed to Nasruddin for alms.

'Are you a big spender?' asked Nasruddin.

'No, far from it,' replied the second beggar.

'Do you like sitting around drinking tea and smoking?'

'No, I don't.'

'Do you go to the public baths every day?'

'No, I can't afford to.'

'Do you gamble and drink occasionally?'

'No, never. I live frugally and devote my time to prayer,' replied the second beggar, whereupon Nasruddin handed him a small copper coin.

'Mullah,' the disappointed man wailed, 'I am a thrifty and pious man, but you give me a mere copper coin, yet you gave that extravagant fellow a coin of far greater value!'

'My friend,' replied Nasruddin, 'according to my assessment, his needs are greater than yours.'

47

Frankly Speaking

Despite his foolish and erratic behaviour in many aspects of life, Nasruddin had gained a reputation for being a frank and astute marriage counsellor, whose advice was often sought by couples about to tie the knot and also those who found themselves in a knotty situation after taking the plunge.

A shy young girl approached the mullah for guidance, revealing that her parents had found her a prospective groom who was educated and rich.

'So what's the problem?' the mullah asked.

'I don't know what I should do—I've found that he is not always honest,' the girl sobbed. 'Do you think I should marry a man who lies to me?'

'Yes, unless you want to remain single forever,' Nasruddin advised.

On another occasion, a pompous young man newly returned to Akşehir with a college degree from a university in Baghdad, sought Nasruddin's guidance.

'What would you advise me to do?' the youth asked. 'I have two options: should I marry a sensible girl or a beautiful girl, Mullah?'

'Has it occurred to you that you might not be able to do either?' the mullah countered.

'Why not?' asked the surprised graduate.

'I think women have good instincts and are often shrewder than men,' Nasruddin replied. 'I am sure that before giving you her heart, a girl would use her head. If that is the case, I think the beautiful girl could do better and the sensible girl would know better.'

48

Just One Question

A visiting scholar dropped in at Time for Tea hoping to meet Nasruddin and engage in serious debate. Being market day, a messenger was dispatched to intercept the mullah requesting him to stop off at the teahouse on his way home.

Nasruddin was beginning to tire of these futile encounters which invariably entailed the visitor posing mystifying questions—'What is the depth at the deepest point of the ocean?' or 'What is the distance to the moon?'—to which there were no verifiable answers. Visibly exhausted, Nasruddin entered the teashop, flopped on to the bench next to the visitor, and beckoned for a cup of tea.

'Respected Mullah,' the visitor said, 'I have heard so much about your sharp wit and originality of thought and was keen to see for myself if you are as clever as people say. You appear to have had a tiring day so I will give you a choice: would you like to answer a hundred easy questions or just a single difficult one?'

'Just one question, please.'

'That's fine,' said the scholar. 'Please tell me which came first, the chicken or the egg?'

'The chicken,' Nasruddin replied confidently.

'How can you be so sure?' asked the scholar, hoping to ambush the mullah.

'I agreed to answer just one question and you have already asked it,' said Nasruddin as he finished his tea and walked out of the teashop, leaving the scholar speechless.

49

Dressing for a Feast

Hearing that an iftar banquet was being held at the home of the wealthiest man in town, to which everyone was invited, Nasruddin made his way to the feast after a full day's work on his farm. Arriving at the host's palatial estate, Nasruddin's stomach was rumbling, his mouth parched and dry, and he was looking forward to breaking his fast, but the guards, noting his bedraggled condition and sweat-stained clothes, ushered him to a corner a long distance away from the head table at which the mayor and other important townsfolk were seated.

The tables were laden with large platters of dates, pistachios, cashew nuts, dried fruits, olives, freshly made bread, piping hot dishes of falafel, kofte, kebabs, lamb and chicken pilaf, and an array of desserts—halva, date rolls, stewed figs, and baklava.

Scores of people, all dressed in their best, were already seated at the tables, tucking into the food, but nobody made room for Nasruddin, no one offered him anything to eat or drink and everyone behaved as if he wasn't even there. Deeply offended by the host's neglect and the other guests' behaviour and unable to enjoy his meal, Nasruddin decided to leave.

Hurrying home, he had a quick wash, changed into a magnificent embroidered coat and silk turban, and returned to the feast. This time the welcome he received was completely different—the guards bowed and showed him to a seat nearer the top table. The host greeted him warmly, and many of the townsfolk waved and beckoned to him from all corners of the room to sit with them.

Nasruddin sat down quietly. Picking up a handful of dates, he carefully placed them in his coat pocket, saying: 'Eat, coat, eat.' Next, he took a handful of nuts and put them into another pocket, repeating: 'Enjoy your meal, coat, eat your fill.' Grabbing handfuls of food, he shovelled some of it into his coat's pockets and rubbed the rest of it on his turban.

The guests seated around him stopped eating as they watched this strange behaviour. Everyone in the room was staring at Nasruddin, wondering what he was doing. The host hurried over. 'Nasruddin, what's the matter? Why are you putting food in your coat pocket and rubbing it on your turban?'

'Well,' replied Nasruddin, 'when I first came to this banquet in my old work clothes, I was not welcome. No one would even speak to me. But, when I changed into this coat and turban, suddenly I was greeted warmly. So I realized it was not I that was welcome at this party, but my clothing. Therefore, I am feeding my coat and turban, making sure that they are well nourished and content, because without them I would have gone hungry.'

50

Grey Matter

Fayaz the barber was trimming the mayor's hair at the mayoral residence. When he had finished, Fayaz casually remarked: 'Your hair is starting to turn grey.'

Infuriated at the barber's audacity, the mayor ordered that Fayaz be put in jail for six months. He then turned to a court attendant and asked: 'Do you see any grey in my hair?'

'Not much,' the man replied.

'Not much!' the mayor exclaimed. 'Guards, take this man to jail and keep him there for two months!'

He then turned to another attendant and asked the same question. 'Sir, your hair is completely black,' the man replied.

'You liar!' the mayor yelled. 'Guards, give this man ten lashes on the back, and put him in jail for three months.'

Finally, the mayor turned to Nasruddin and asked: 'Mullah, what colour is my hair?'

'Sir,' Nasruddin replied, 'I am colour blind, and therefore cannot answer that question with any degree of accuracy. But I cannot help thinking that to a bald man like me, hair of any colour would be a blessing.'

51

The Bigger Share

A renowned philosopher was passing through Akşehir and invited Nasruddin to join him for dinner and stimulating conversation. Ever ready to enjoy a good meal at somebody else's expense, Nasruddin accompanied the scholar to a nearby restaurant, which was renowned for its cuisine.

Showing them to a table, the waiter announced: 'I would strongly recommend today's special—fresh fish fillets cooked to perfection and served with steamed vegetables!'

'Bring us one portion each, please.'

A short while later, the waiter emerged from the kitchen with a large platter on which were two pieces of fish, one medium-sized, the other much larger, surrounded by steamed vegetables. As soon as the platter was placed on the table in front of them, Nasruddin helped himself to the larger fillet, leaving his host gaping at him in stunned disbelief.

'I cannot believe my eyes,' the scholar sputtered, as Nasruddin reached out to help himself to a large portion of vegetables. 'What you have done is not only selfish but also goes against the principles of moral and ethical conduct and basic etiquette. I have not witnessed such uncouth behaviour ever before.'

When the philosopher ended his tirade, Nasruddin asked: 'Well, sir, what would you have done?'

'Having been taught good manners and knowing how to behave in polite society, I would have taken the smaller piece of fish for myself.'

'Well then, here you are,' said Nasruddin, and placed the smaller fillet on his host's plate, still wondering what the fuss was all about.

52

Falling on Deaf Ears

Nasruddin was at the teahouse one afternoon when Arif the hakim walked in.

'How are you, Mullah? I hope you and your family are well,' Arif asked politely.

'I'm fine, thanks, Arif, but I'm worried about my wife, who seems to have become very hard of hearing. Is there any cure for her problem?' asked Nasruddin.

'Well, some degree of age-related hearing loss is normal,' Arif said. 'If you bring your wife to my dispensary, I can check her hearing and prescribe the necessary treatment. But before you do that, you can try this simple test. When you go home this evening, call out to your wife from the gate and see if she hears you. If not, then try speaking to her from the front door and keep reducing the distance until she responds. This way you will be able to gauge how serious her hearing deficiency is.'

Nasruddin thanked the doctor for the free medical advice and headed home. Calling out to Fatima from the gate in the front yard, Nasruddin said loudly: 'I'm home, dear. What are we having for dinner?'

Getting no reply, Nasruddin opened the front door and yelled: 'I'm home, dear. What are we having for dinner?'

Still getting no response, Nasruddin pushed open the kitchen door and repeated loudly: 'What's for dinner, dear?'

Fatima, who was stirring a large pot on the stove, turned to face her husband. 'Are you deaf, Nasruddin?' she said angrily, wiping her hands on her apron. ‘For the third and last time I repeat: we are having fish stew and pilaf, followed by apricot halva for dessert.’

53

A Title for the Sultan

The sultan sent an aide to Nasruddin with a request. 'Respected Mullah, the sultan needs your help in thinking up an honorary title for him. His Lordship wants his new title to have the word "God" in it, similar to the labels other conquerors have given themselves in the past, such as God Given, God's Gift, God's Grace, and so on. Do you have any suggestions that I could pass on to the sultan?'

'How about God Forsaken?' Nasruddin replied.

54

God's Servant

Mullah Nasruddin was sitting at a roadside café, eating a frugal meal of rice and beans, which was all he could afford. Idly watching people walking past the café, Nasruddin noticed a tall, well-built, and stylish man who stood out amongst the crowd. Sporting a purple velvet turban, tastefully embroidered vest, finely tailored silk shirt, baggy satin trousers, and a gold scimitar tucked into a broad gold belt, the stranger was making heads turn as he strutted down the street.

Pointing to the immaculately dressed man, Nasruddin asked the restaurateur: 'Who is that?'

'He works for Sultan Ali in Beyşehir,' the restaurant owner replied.

Mullah Nasruddin sighed heavily, turned his eyes heavenwards, and said: 'Dear Lord, I hope you are noticing the difference in the lifestyle of Sultan Ali's servant over there and your own servant here! Don't you think that poverty is a high price for your followers to pay?'

55

Running for Mayor

Mullah Nasruddin put himself in the race for the hotly contested post of town mayor. After making a rousing speech at a rally, he asked the crowd if they had any questions.

'I have one question for you, sir,' said a man. 'Do you drink alcohol?'

'That depends,' replied the mullah, 'on whether my answer leads to disqualification or an invitation....'

On the day of the election, Nasruddin was bitterly disappointed to learn that his opponent had won the post by a small margin.

'I am a victim,' he complained to his friends, 'a hapless victim.'

'A victim?' a friend asked. 'Of what?'

'A victim of accurate counting.'

56

God's Wisdom

One hot summer's day, Nasruddin was relaxing in an orchard under the shade of an apricot tree. Looking around him, and marvelling at nature's bounty, he wondered why apples, cherries, and other small fruit grew on trees, while large melons and pumpkins grew on vines at ground level.

Sometimes it is hard to understand God's ways, he pondered. Imagine letting apricots, cherries, and apples grow on tall trees while large melons and pumpkins grow on delicate vines!

At that precise moment, the mullah's reverie was interrupted by an unripe apricot falling from the tree and bouncing off his bald head. Roused from his musings, Nasruddin stood up, raised his hands and face towards heaven, and said humbly: 'Forgive me, God, for questioning your wisdom. You are all-knowing and all-powerful. I would have been in a sorry state now if melons grew on trees.'

57

No Stomach for Meat

Mullah Nasruddin stopped off to visit Fayaz at the barber shop to announce that he had recently become a vegetarian. Fayaz, who had eaten meat all his life, was very upset by Nasruddin's decision and tried to make the mullah change his mind.

'Vegetables are for weaklings. You get strength and vigour from meat, not vegetables. By becoming vegetarian you will be sure to lose the few hairs that remain on your head. And I am sure you will miss your kofte and lamb stew and shish kebabs.' When the mullah could not be dissuaded, the exasperated barber asked: 'What has brought about this change in you? Why have you stopped eating meat?'

'I'm not trying to deter you from eating anything you like, Fayaz,' Nasruddin said. 'But slaughtering animals for food causes them intense pain and suffering and I cannot bear to cause the discomfort, distress, and death of innocent creatures.

'A few months ago, I was invited to a feast by a tribe who live in the hills some distance from Akşehir. When I reached there, the tribesmen welcomed me and offered me tea and sweetmeats. They then told me that, according to their tribal ritual, their honoured guest had to slaughter a lamb for the evening meal. They brought in a sharp knife, glinting in the sunlight, and a few seconds later a fat lamb with a rope tied tightly around its neck was dragged outside the tent in which we were seated. The knife was placed in my hands and the men and I walked out of the tent.

'Knowing instinctively that it did not have long to live, the lamb was wriggling, kicking, and struggling to get its head out of the noose-like rope. For a fleeting second, it looked straight into my eyes, and all I could see was its fear and despair. My hands began to tremble so violently that I dropped the knife. I knew that my hosts would consider me a coward, but I picked up the knife and handed it to one of the tribesmen. I told them that I did not have the heart to slaughter an innocent animal, and also—from that point on—would never be able to stomach meat, even if it came from an animal that had been slaughtered by someone else.'

'That's all very well, my friend,' Fayaz retorted, 'but aren't vegetables innocent, too? Think of a poor cabbage or a pumpkin. What have they done wrong? They are probably as innocent as a goat or a lamb!'

'You are right,' said the mullah.

'And can you be sure that plants don't feel pain? Isn't it possible that they suffer more than animals do?'

'It's possible,' Nasruddin agreed.

'So, are you ready to give up this no-meat nonsense?'

'On one condition,' said Nasruddin. 'We can make a final decision after you spend a day at the slaughterhouse, while I spend a day at the pumpkin harvest.'

58

Praying for Change

Sitting with his friends in the teashop, Nasruddin was in a pensive mood. 'Looking back on my life, I see that when I was young, I was so full of enthusiasm that I used to pray to God to give me the strength to change the world.

'When I was in my fifties, I woke up one day and realized that my life was half over, and I had changed no one so I prayed to God to give me the strength to change those close to me who so much needed it.

'Nowadays, I observe that everyone gets older, but not necessarily wiser. At this age, my prayer is simpler. Now, the only thing I ask is for God to give me the strength to at least change myself. Unfortunately, that requires more fortitude than I am able to muster.'

59

Two in One

Nasruddin was taking a shortcut home through the cemetery, where a burial was in progress. As he walked past the group of mourners, he overheard one of them saying: 'Today is a sad day for us all. We have buried an honest man and a politician.'

A sad day indeed, Nasruddin thought to himself. I didn't realize that the situation was so dire that they are now compelled to bury two people in the same grave!

60

Nasruddin's Will

Aware of the passage of time, and the harsh reality of attending more funerals and fewer birthday or anniversary celebrations of friends and relatives, Nasruddin decided to make a will. He wrote:

> I declare that this will has been made out of my free volition and without any coercion. The law stipulates that my worldly possessions and money must be divided amongst my dependants or designated heirs. Let it be duly noted that I have few possessions and no money, but my last wish is that these should be divided equally amongst my wife and three children. Anything left over is to be distributed to the poor.

61

The Last Laugh

With age finally catching up with him, Mullah Nasruddin began to make all the necessary arrangements for his funeral. His wish was to be buried in his home town, in a tomb that he designed himself, which would be unlike any other in the world.

His grave was to be fronted by a large, heavy wooden door, secured by a huge padlock. 'Bury the key to the padlock in my grave with my body so that no one can open the door except me,' he instructed his family members. 'I'd like to get out once in a while to get some fresh air.'

Word of Nasruddin's whimsical request became the talk of the town and eventually reached the sultan, who dismissed it as yet another of the mullah's attention-seeking eccentricities. But one of the sultan's advisers pointed out: 'I don't think the mullah's strategy will work. Because if he is buried behind the padlocked door along with the key, how is he going to get outside to unlock the door?'

The mullah was summoned and the flaw in his plan was pointed out. 'Wait and see,' was his enigmatic reply.

Nasruddin died in his early seventies and was buried in a grave behind the imposing padlocked door. It was impossible to gain access to the tomb through the door but visitors wanting to pay their respects to the deceased could do so despite the grave's forbidding portal, because the mullah had ordered that his tomb should have no roof nor any walls around it.

Thus, in death, Mullah Nasruddin Hodja had the last laugh, making sure that people laughed with him, not at him.

PART II

AN EMPEROR AND HIS WISE WAZIR

Jalaluddin Muhammad Akbar was born in 1542 and came to the throne as head of Hindustan's Mughal empire before the age of fourteen, following the death of his father, Humayun. With his father's military commander, Bairam Khan, appointed as regent, the teenaged emperor quickly mastered his challenging new role, maturing into a popular sovereign, whose progressive thinking and liberal attitude during his forty-nine-year rule earned him the title of Akbar the Great.

A curious amalgam of extreme bravery and deep compassion, Akbar's tolerant and broad-minded religious policies won the support of his non-Muslim subjects, thus laying the foundation for a truly multicultural empire. Under his leadership, the arts, literature, and 'mental sciences' such as logic, philosophy, and theology flourished, even as his empire expanded through military conquests under Bairam Khan's guidance. By the time of his death in 1605, Akbar's empire extended from Afghanistan in the north to the Godavari River in the south, and from Sindh in the west to Bengal in the east.

A man of eclectic tastes and diverse interests, Akbar was said to have had at least eleven wives, some from Hindu royal families. Most of these unions were politically inspired: local princes were eager to send one of their daughters to the imperial palace, thus acquiring family status and access to the emperor. Historians have noted that the ladies of the imperial palace were quite influential and played an active role in society.

All references to the consort in the anecdotes that follow are to the emperor's Hindu wife, Harkha Bai, daughter of Raja Bharmal, ruler of Amer. Referred to as the queen mother of Hindustan, Harkha Bai was officially recognized as the chief Hindu Mughal consort and also given the title Mariam-uz-Zamani (Mary of the Age) after giving birth to Akbar's eldest surviving son, Prince Salim, the future Emperor Jahangir. Harkha Bai was said to be a shrewd businesswoman, who ran a highly successful international trading empire and was wealthy in her own right.

Unlike other military conquerors who preceded and succeeded him, Akbar won the loyalty of the people he conquered. Though not much of a reader—there is speculation that he may have been dyslexic—he insisted on being read to every day and had a powerful memory. Despite a lack of book learning, he was intellectually curious and put together an able administration, rewarding talent, loyalty, and intelligence regardless of the ethnic background or religion of his courtiers and aides. He sponsored some of the brightest minds of the era—including poets, musicians, artists, philosophers, and engineers—in his courts around the kingdom.

The elite group of Navratnas or nine gems of Akbar's court consisted of singer and minister of culture Miyan Tansen, historian Abul Fazal, poet and scholar Faizi, military commander Raja Man Singh, financial expert Raja Todar Mal, minister of home affairs Mullah Do-Piyaza, mystic and religious adviser Fakir Aziao-Din, poet and astrologer Abdul Rahim Khan-i-Khanan, and last but certainly not least, the emperor's closest confidant and adviser, Raja Birbal, whose counsel and guidance to his emperor became legendary.

The Boy King

Prince Akbar had greatness thrust upon him while still a young teenager, when he came to the throne following his father Humayun's death. Being too young to shoulder the burden of kingship, Bairam Khan, the commander of his father's army, was appointed as regent and adviser to the untried boy king.

The kingdom Akbar inherited consisted of scattered fiefdoms, but a series of successful military campaigns spearheaded by Bairam Khan brought unity and power to the realm. As guardian, guru, and trusted ally, Bairam Khan became a father figure for the boy king, and groomed his young charge to shoulder the responsibilities that weigh heavily on crowned heads.

Of average height and build, with a wide forehead, bright sparkling eyes, dark hair and, in later years, a pencil moustache, Akbar's most majestic feature was his booming voice, which he used to good effect. The fledgling monarch set up courts in Delhi, Agra, and eventually in Fatehpur Sikri, and as he came of age and gained confidence, he sent shock waves through the realm by dismissing his mentor Bairam Khan. Swiftly thereafter, he took full control of the government and its military strategy.

But when one door closed—or was forcibly shut as in Bairam Khan's case—another opened for the young monarch....

63

Lost and Found

Passionate about horse riding from an early age, Akbar had become an expert horseman and enjoyed hunting in the forests around Agra. One day, while on a hunt with his entourage, the young king and three of his courtiers became separated from the rest of the hunting party. With their horses tiring, and all of them hungry and thirsty, they realized that they were lost and had no way of finding the rest of their group.

Trotting along through the deep, shadowy forest, with only a few hours of daylight left, Akbar and his courtiers eventually came to a junction of three roads, one of which would surely lead to the capital. But which of the three was the road to Agra? No one knew. While they were trying to figure out which path to take, they saw a lean and wiry man, with sharp features and a long, thin face, dressed in a coarse but clean homespun kurta and pyjama, walking down one of the roads, swinging a lantern and humming happily. Spotting the four horsemen, the man, who appeared to be in his mid-twenties, stopped at the junction and stared at them curiously.

'Kind sir, please tell us which of these roads goes to Agra?' Akbar asked.

The man looked at the young but haughty and expensively dressed rider, rolled his large, dark eyes and wiggled his head. 'Sir, you should know that roads are incapable of moving. So how can these roads go to Agra or anywhere else?' he said in a soft voice, sniggering at his clever riposte. Taken aback by the man's impertinence, Akbar and his courtiers were speechless. Observing their confusion, the man persisted: 'It is *people* who go to places, not roads. All three of the roads in front of you will lead to Agra, but two of them will get you there in a more roundabout way. I assume that you need to know the shortest and most direct way of reaching the city. Am I right?'

Akbar laughed and said: 'You are indeed correct.' Then asked: 'What is your name?'

'My name is Mahesh Das,' the man replied. 'And who are you, sir? What is your name?'

'I am Jalaluddin Muhammad Akbar, emperor of Hindustan. My men and I have become separated from the rest of our riding party. Can you please show us the quickest way to get to Agra?'

Bowing respectfully to his monarch, Mahesh Das pointed out the road leading to the capital. 'Your Majesty, it will be dark soon so please take my lantern to guide you on your way home,' he added.

'Thank you for the kind offer, but you will need it more than us, because you are on foot. Now that we know which path to take, we will swiftly reach the palace,' the monarch said. 'I am proud to have intelligent and helpful young men like you in my kingdom.' Then taking off his gold ring bearing the royal insignia, Akbar handed it to Mahesh Das, saying: 'If you come to my court with this ring, I will recognize you instantly. Thank you for your assistance.'

As he watched the emperor and his courtiers ride off into the sunset, Mahesh had a strong feeling that he had not seen the last of the monarch and that this chance meeting would be a turning point in his life.

Over the years, Mahesh's belief in hidden forces shaping his life and destiny grew stronger. How else could one explain an encounter deep in a forest with the mighty emperor of Hindustan that led to a bond that lasted over three decades and brought a lowly peasant great fame and fortune?

64

Royal Welcome

Unable to forget his meeting with the sovereign, Mahesh Das bade goodbye to his ageing parents a few months later, and set off on foot for the emperor's palace in Agra. It was a hot day and the journey took several hours. When he finally reached the palace, the tall sentry at the imposing main gate, noticing the scrawny visitor's simple clothes and dishevelled state, refused him entry. 'Unless you have an appointment, you cannot get an audience with the emperor so easily,' the guard said curtly.

'Will this be enough to gain admission to the durbar?' Mahesh asked softly, holding out the ring with the royal emblem that the king had given him.

The guard's eyes widened. Sensing an opportunity to share in the largesse that the monarch evidently bestowed on this ordinary young man, the sentry declared: 'I'll let you enter on one condition—that you give me half of whatever reward you receive from His Majesty.'

Agreeing to the sentry's terms, Mahesh entered the glittering great hall in which the emperor held his weekly durbar. The large high-ceilinged room, with its marble floor, red sandstone walls with elaborate carvings and lattices, gleaming candle holders, and colossal jewel-encrusted columns, felt refreshingly fragrant and fresh, cooled by ornate punkahs that were suspended above the arched windows. Walking down the length of the long room, Mahesh had his eyes fixed on the dignified figure sitting on the dais on an oversized throne. Bowing deeply to his monarch, Mahesh held out the ring in his cupped hands, and Akbar immediately recalled their encounter in the forest.

'Young man,' said the king, 'I am so happy to see you. Tell me, what can I do for you?'

'Most Benevolent of Benefactors,' Mahesh Das replied, 'I humbly beseech you to give me fifty lashes with a whip as a reward.'

Everyone at the durbar was stunned by this strange request. They looked from Mahesh Das to the emperor and at each other, wondering whether they had misheard the young man. Akbar too was taken aback by Mahesh's wish and asked him for the reason behind it. 'I will reveal my motive after I receive my reward,' Mahesh replied. Sensing that there was method to the clever young man's madness, Akbar signalled to his guards to proceed with the flogging.

After twenty-five lashes had been painfully administered on his bare back, Mahesh called out to the guards to stop and requested that the sentry at the main gate be summoned to the durbar.

The sentry strutted into the great hall, barely able to conceal a smug smile at the thought of the bounty that awaited him. Mahesh Das stepped forward and said: 'Jahanpanah, your sentry allowed me into the palace on the condition that I would share half of my reward with him. As I am a man of my word, I request that the remaining twenty-five lashes be given to him.'

The emperor and his courtiers were impressed by the clever way in which Mahesh was settling the score with the greedy sentry, and a loud cheer went up in the durbar. Akbar doubled the sentry's punishment to fifty lashes and sentenced him to a year in prison.

Then turning to Mahesh Das, Akbar announced: 'My good man, from this day onwards, you shall be known as Birbal, meaning brave of heart, and I am pleased to offer you a permanent place in my court as a counsellor.'

And that is how a humble Brahmin became a valued guide and confidant to the most powerful man in Hindustan.

Appointed to the emperor's special committee of advisers known as the nine gems, Birbal's brilliance and clarity of thought soon made him not only the most treasured jewel in Akbar's court, but also the most resented and envied.

65

The Brightest Gem

Emperor Akbar matured into a sagacious and broad-minded ruler with a passion for arts and culture, equally adept at statecraft as at warfare. His greatness lay not only in his wide interests and yearning for knowledge but in his sound judgement in appointing men of genius as his advisers. The fame of the nine gems of the Mughal crown spread far and wide, and Akbar basked in the reflected glory that the men—each a master of his craft—brought to his court.

The presence of these luminaries inevitably triggered intrigue and jealousy amongst Akbar's courtiers, but the emperor's fondness for and dependence on Birbal was resented not only by the courtiers but also his family members. Among the latter, the main opposition came from Akbar's wife Harkha Bai, the beautiful, petite, and feisty Rajput princess.

The queen's brother, Raja Jaimal, often voiced his displeasure over Akbar's partiality to Birbal. 'Your favouritism is making him arrogant and big-headed,' Jaimal complained to his brother-in-law. 'Birbal is not even a tenth as clever as everyone thinks he is. I'm sure that there are many questions for which Birbal will not have answers. Why don't we put him to the test?'

Akbar agreed to the challenge and Birbal was summoned to the durbar. Jaimal strutted to the front of the hall, twirled his moustache, looked down his hooked nose, and addressed the gathering haughtily: 'I will put two questions to Birbal, questions that no man has yet been able to answer. Let's see whether he can solve the mysteries.'

Turning to face the favoured adviser, he said in a stentorian voice: 'Here's my first question to you. Can you tell us how many stars there are in the night sky?'

Birbal replied instantly but so softly that the entire durbar leaned forward to catch every word; being soft-spoken was a clever way to get people's attention and Birbal used it to great effect for years to come. 'The number of stars in the night sky is the same as the number of grains of sand in that hourglass,' he said, pointing to a jewel-encrusted hourglass on the table next to the throne. 'My friend can get the answer to his question by counting the grains of sand.'

'We don't have time for that,' Jaimal said dismissively. 'So, let's move on to the second question. Can you pinpoint the exact location of the centre of the earth?'

'That's an easy one,' Birbal replied. 'The exact location of the centre of the earth is directly under the throne of our glorious Shahenshah Akbar.'

'What proof do you have to support your answer?' Jaimal asked loudly.

'There's no need for me to prove it because I know it to be true,' came the calm reply. 'If you have any doubts, you can easily prove it yourself. You must first head west, carefully counting each step until you reach the end of the world, then return to this spot and repeat the process heading east, north, and south. In each case, you will find that the distance will be exactly the same.'

Shaking his head in disapproval, Jaimal turned to his brother-in-law for support. Walking up the steps of the dais, he approached the emperor and whispered: 'Huzoor, can you not see that Birbal is nothing but a charlatan who lives by his wits and dupes people by giving unverifiable answers to serious questions?'

'My dear brother-in-law,' Akbar replied, loud enough for all to hear, 'you are the one who posed the questions that Birbal has answered. If you disagree with him, the onus is on you to disprove his responses. I will reserve my judgement on his character until such time as you are able to prove him wrong. Meanwhile, let's proceed with the rest of the day's business.'

66

Appointing a Judge

When a vacancy for a judge opened up in the royal advisory council, Birbal was Akbar's first choice for the post. The emperor's blatant preferential treatment towards Birbal caused considerable displeasure among his courtiers and aides, each of whom wanted the position to go to a relative or friend for their own selfish reasons. Birbal had the intelligence and the integrity required for the job, but found no backers in the royal court.

The strongest opposition to his appointment as a judge came from Harkha Bai, who confronted her husband bluntly: 'Don't you think it will be extremely foolish to appoint Birbal as a judge? Do you expect people of noble birth and high ranking to heed the decisions of a man from such a lowly background? Do you think he is even capable of delivering the right verdict? Who is going to accept the judgement of an emaciated Brahmin from a poor family who doesn't have enough strength in him to speak loudly and clearly?'

'His humble background doesn't seem to have impeded his discernment as far as I can tell. And unlike some other members of my court, Birbal does not feel it necessary to shout to make himself heard,' Akbar responded calmly, oblivious to the irony of possessing the loudest voice in his court. 'My people will have no choice but to follow my command to accept Birbal's decisions.'

'That is absurd,' the queen said with a haughty toss of her head. Then pouting prettily, she added: 'If you are considering appointing a Hindu to such a coveted position, I think the most suitable candidate would be my brother.'

'Your brother?' Akbar asked, unable to disguise his bewilderment.

'Why do you sound so surprised? My brother would be the perfect candidate for the post. He has the right background—he is a blue-blooded Rajput prince and as brave as they come.'

'One must admit that Jaimal is a competent soldier,' Akbar said, choosing his words carefully.

'A fearless and heroic warrior,' the queen pointed out.

'Maybe so,' Akbar continued. 'But a judge needs wisdom more than fearlessness and heroism. I'm not sure if your brother has the knowledge and understanding that is required of a judge.'

'Well, put him to the test and decide for yourself,' the queen said confidently. 'That's the only way to get those foolish ideas about your blasted Birbal out of your head. Let my brother prove his mettle.' Akbar smiled and stroked his chin, an unconscious habit when he was in deep thought.

That afternoon, he summoned his courtiers to the durbar. 'I have an important announcement to make,' he told the assembled dignitaries. 'I have narrowed down my choice for the new judge of the royal court to two candidates: my distinguished brother-in-law Raja Jaimal and my trusted aide Birbal. To determine which one is better suited to the job, I will present three cases to the two candidates over the next few days. The one who resolves the cases or hands down the fairer sentence, will be appointed judge.'

As Birbal bowed respectfully to his monarch, his rival Jaimal, with his aristocratic nose in the air, glanced around at the gathered assembly with a disdainful smirk, confident of getting the coveted post.

Observing the two men, Akbar couldn't help noticing the glaring difference between them. The one from the humble background conducts himself with dignity and decorum, he thought, while my nobly born brother-in-law has too many airs but no graces.

The emperor had no doubts as to which one of them would pass the tests.

67

The Mango Tree

The first case presented itself a few days later. Two farmers, Arjun and Raju, turned up at the palace seeking justice in a property dispute.

'Please state your complaints,' Akbar told them kindly.

Arjun confidently stated: 'Your Majesty, our quarrel is over a mango tree that stands between our two farms. My neighbour claims that all the fruit belongs to him, even though I have nurtured and watered the tree for many years.'

'What do you have to say?' Akbar asked Raju, who looked terrified and uneasy.

'Sire,' Raju began nervously, 'I planted that tree shortly after my marriage and have tended it for thirty years. But for many years, my neighbour has been taking the fruit from the tree and even selling some of it. When I requested him to stop, he laughed at me and continued helping himself to the mangoes.'

Akbar, stroking his chin, turned to his brother-in-law and asked: 'What is your verdict in the matter, Raja Jaimal?'

Having no patience with snivelling peasants and their petty complaints, Jaimal replied: 'In my considered opinion, this is a pointless dispute because, after all these years, there's no way of proving which one of them planted the tree and which one tended it. Besides, I'm sure the tree provides enough fruit for both of them, so I'd recommend punishing them for wasting everyone's time.'

The courtiers nodded in agreement at Jaimal's sagacity.

Turning to Birbal, the emperor asked: 'What do you have to say on the matter?'

'Jahanpanah, in my humble opinion, I don't think the dispute can be dismissed lightly because it will continue to cause friction between neighbours. I therefore propose that all the mangoes should be gathered from the tree and divided equally between Arjun and Raju. Then the tree itself should be chopped down, the branches and trunk should be hacked into smaller pieces, and divided equally between the two complainants for use as firewood. That should put an end to all disagreements.'

Rubbing his hands in glee, Arjun said: 'That decision is fair to both of us, sir. I agree with your suggestion.'

Raju appeared to be in deep thought and looked disappointed. Akbar leaned forward and asked: 'Do you accept my adviser's decision?'

'No, Jahanpanah. It will be difficult for me to see the tree destroyed,' Raju replied. 'It has provided my family shade in the hot summers, and since their childhood my sons have enjoyed climbing up to its lower branches to pluck the fruit. It has been so much a part of my life that I would sooner hand it over to Arjun than see it cut down.'

A hush fell upon the entire durbar as the truth dawned on everyone present. Birbal broke the silence: 'I sentence Arjun to pay his neighbour thirty silver coins, one for each year that he has taken fruit from a tree that did not belong to him. If he cannot pay that amount, he should be given thirty lashes for his greed and dishonesty.'

There was a murmur of approval throughout the durbar at Birbal's verdict and the emperor was visibly pleased. The queen and her brother were the only ones who looked as dissatisfied as the culprit.

Birbal had clearly won the first challenge.

68

The Real Mother

The next case was also an ownership dispute, but of a different kind.

Two well-dressed and prosperous-looking women were ushered into the durbar, followed by a maidservant of the palace, who held a baby in her arms. Each of the women claimed that the boy was hers and accused the other of stealing him. Both women had worked themselves up into a frenzy, were weeping loudly, and beating their chests hysterically. Those present in the grand hall were greatly puzzled and could not tell which of the two was telling the truth.

Turning to his brother-in-law, Akbar said: 'Well, Jaimal, how would you resolve this matter?'

Jaimal, seeing similarities with the dispute over the mango tree, decided to test the women in the same way. 'My decision is to cut the child in two and give half to each woman. That should settle the dispute.'

Expecting the baby's real mother to come forward and strongly object to any harm being done to her son, Jaimal was taken aback when both women prostrated themselves before the emperor, protesting at the judgement and begging for mercy. They beat their fists on the marble floor and sobbed so loudly that everyone in the room felt sorry for them both, not knowing how to ease their anguish. Watching from the gallery above, the queen looked deeply distressed at the women's suffering.

'What is your view, Birbal?' the emperor asked. 'Can you resolve this matter?'

'Of course, Jahanpanah. First, I need to question each of the ladies, but separately, if I may.'

As one of the women was led away by an attendant to wait in an antechamber, out of earshot of the durbar hall, Birbal turned to the other standing in front of him and asked: 'You claim that the boy is yours. Tell me, does he have any birthmarks or moles or other distinguishing features?'

'Huzoor, in my eyes, my son is perfect in every way. When he was born, he had no hair but there was a brown birthmark on his head above the left ear. Now that his hair has grown, the birthmark is not visible but it is still there.' Birbal walked over to the maidservant who was holding the baby in her arms, inspected the child's head and returned to his seat on the dais, signalling to the attendant to lead the woman out of the durbar.

The second woman was brought into the hall, and Birbal asked her the same question about the child. The woman was quiet for a while and then replied: 'By God's grace, my son was born without any blemishes. When he was born, I wept in gratitude at the sight of his flawless little hands and feet. He is a good baby and gives me no trouble at all.'

A hush fell over the court as the first woman was summoned back into the hall. Walking over to the maidservant, Birbal took the baby from her arms and handed him to the first woman.

'You are right,' Birbal told the woman. 'Your son does have a birthmark above his left ear. Take your child home and love and cherish him.'

Turning to the second woman, Birbal said: 'Someday when you have a child of your own you will realize what pain you caused to a mother with your fraudulent claim. A child is a woman's greatest treasure and you are guilty of trying to steal one from its mother. You have also wasted the court's time. As it was an easy matter to resolve, I will let you off with a small fine. You must pay the child's mother twenty silver coins for the distress you caused her. And beware of making false accusations in future.'

While the courtiers applauded the judgement, Raja Jaimal seethed inwardly and stole a glance upwards at his sister, who had been watching from the balcony and looked utterly dejected. That wily Birbal had outsmarted them once again.

69

Unequal Rights

A third case presented itself a few days later.

A wealthy businessman died, leaving all he owned to his two sons. Both men received an equal share of the father's property and business, but as there was no record or proof of the exact value of the inheritances, each of them thought that his sibling had received the larger share, and came to the emperor's court to resolve the dispute.

'Your Exalted Highness,' the older brother began, 'despite my being older, and having looked after my father far more than my younger brother did, he has received the greater share of my father's assets. I beseech you to rectify this injustice and make sure that I receive my rightful equal share of my father's legacy.'

The younger brother spoke up angrily: 'Your Majesty, my older brother's claim is baseless and unsupported. He was always our father's favourite, and tricked him into bequeathing him the larger portion of his property. I hope that justice will be done and that I will be compensated for the unfair assets that my brother has taken.'

'What do you have to say on the matter, Jaimal?' the emperor asked.

Deep in thought, trying to anticipate Birbal's line of questioning, Raja Jaimal finally said: 'Huzoor, the only way of resolving the dispute is by getting an impartial accountant to ascertain how much each brother's assets are worth, and then divide the difference, if any, equally between the two.'

Turning to Birbal, Akbar asked: 'Do you agree with Raja Jaimal's suggestion?'

'In my humble opinion, Your Majesty, we don't need to involve an accountant to resolve this dispute. The brothers are both agreed on one point: each wants what the other has, so the solution is quite straightforward. All that needs to be done is for the two siblings to swap their inheritances.'

Satisfied with Birbal's decision, the two brothers were ushered out of the court.

When they had left, Akbar addressed the assembled courtiers: 'Each of you has to make difficult choices every day, decisions that impact you and your family. But the choices made by kings have an impact on families throughout their kingdom so it is vital to have the right man in the right job.' Turning to Raja Jaimal, the emperor added: 'My dear brother-in-law, you are descended from a distinguished family of warriors and are a fearless soldier yourself. I, therefore, put you in charge of a battalion of five thousand soldiers.'

A cheer went up in the court from Raja Jaimal's servile supporters. Signalling for silence, Akbar continued: 'After my coronation, I came to realize an important truth: kings need the advice of wise men far more than wise men need the counsel of kings. Bearing that in mind, I hereby appoint Birbal as judge of the royal court.'

70

The Well

Two neighbours came to the durbar for resolution of a property dispute. Iqbal, a trader by profession, and Firdaus, a farmer, shared a common garden in which stood a well that had formerly been owned by Iqbal.

Firdaus told the court that he approached Iqbal to buy the well from him because he needed the water to irrigate his fields. Iqbal agreed to the sale, and signed a deed handing over ownership of the well to Firdaus for a price of five hundred mohurs. Despite the official transaction, Iqbal continued to draw water from the well, which Firdaus claimed was unlawful. 'I, therefore, approach the royal court seeking justice,' he said to the assembled dignitaries.

Akbar asked Iqbal why he continued fetching water from the well even after selling it to the farmer. Iqbal replied: 'The sale agreement states that I sold only the well to Firdaus, not the water inside it.'

Stumped by this response, Akbar turned to his judge to resolve the dispute. Birbal stepped forward and addressed the trader: 'According to your claim, Iqbal, you have sold only the well to the farmer, implying that the water is still yours. If that is the case, you have two options—you can empty all the water from the well to store elsewhere, or you must pay rent to Firdaus for storing your water inside his well. You will have to calculate how much water was stored, and for how long, and pay the accrued rent in arrears and then also going forward.'

Realizing that both alternatives would be time-consuming and nigh on impossible, Iqbal begrudgingly said he would stop drawing water from the well if the case were dropped. Firdaus happily agreed to do so.

71

A Lesson for the Emperor

At an age when most men toil day and night to support their families, Akbar found himself at the helm of one of the greatest empires of the period. He lived a maharaja's existence in a luxurious palace with magnificent gardens, attended to by a retinue of loyal servants, surrounded by kowtowing courtiers who revered him as if he were a deity. Having already been blessed so much by God, the young sovereign became obsessed with collecting material things—jewellery, art, Persian carpets, Arabian horses—anything his heart desired and that money could buy. Things were getting so out of hand that Birbal decided that it was time for the mighty emperor to face a few home truths.

One evening, as the emperor was heading back to the palace after a leisurely stroll through its magnificent gardens adorned with a hundred fountains and abloom with colourful and fragrant flowers, he noticed a sadhu who appeared to be fast asleep on the floor of a gazebo. Wondering how the man had entered the palace grounds, and making a mental note to have his guards punished for this trespass, Akbar walked over to the sadhu and nudged him with the tip of his pearl-embedded velvet slipper.

'Hey, you,' Akbar exclaimed. 'What are you doing here? This is private property so get out of here immediately!'

Sitting up slowly and rubbing his eyes, the sadhu adjusted his turban and asked: 'Huzoor, is this your garden?'

'Yes, it is,' said the emperor. 'This garden, the rose bushes, the jasmine, the mogras, the champaks, the fountains beyond that, the courtyard, the palace, the staff quarters, the stables, they all belong to me!'

The sadhu, whose face was almost completely hidden by the end of his turban and a thick white beard, stood up slowly. 'What about the river, huzoor? And the city, the country, the empire? Do they all belong to you?'

'Yes they do. They are mine, all mine. I order you to leave immediately!'

'I see,' said the sadhu, giving no indication of leaving. 'And before you, huzoor, who did the palace and the garden and the city belong to?'

'Everything belonged to my father, of course,' the emperor replied, becoming a bit impatient at the man's persistence. Despite his dishevelled appearance, the sadhu appeared to be a learned man, and Akbar was admittedly intrigued by his questions.

'And who was there before your father?' the sadhu asked.

'My father's father.'

'Oh, I see. So the flowers, the fountains, the palace only belong to you during your lifetime. Before that they belonged to your father, and in years to come they will belong to your son, and then to your son's son?'

'Yes,' Emperor Akbar replied, wondering at this line of questioning.

'So each one is only temporarily in possession of all these things, is that right?'

'That is correct,' Akbar replied slowly.

'In that case, aren't you merely a custodian?' the sadhu continued. 'Everything you own is transitory. Someone took care of it before you and someone will always be there after you have gone. Is that not so?'

'It is,' the emperor said softly.

'Your garden, your palace, your city, your empire...these are only places you will stay in for a short while, for the span of your lifetime. When you die, they will no longer belong to you. You will depart, leaving them in the possession of someone else, just as your father and grandfather did.'

Emperor Akbar, stroking his chin, considered this revelation. 'I see what you are trying to explain to me: worldly possessions do not belong to a single person permanently, because each person is only passing through this earth and must die one day.'

The sadhu nodded solemnly. Then, bowing respectfully, he removed his white beard and saffron turban and said: 'Jahanpanah, please forgive me! I was only trying to get you to think about the transient nature of life. If you focus too much on material things, you may lose sight of the more meaningful things....'

'Birbal, dear Birbal! Thank you for teaching me a valuable lesson. Life is a journey, be it long or short. Everyone—whether prince or pauper—comes into this world empty-handed and must depart from it with nothing.'

'Most Blessed of Men, do not get too attached to worldly possessions,' Birbal added. 'Instead, strive to be remembered for your good deeds. Let your actions become your monuments, built with memories instead of stone.'

72

The Dishonest Magistrate

A magistrate in a town some distance from Agra had held the post for several decades and had become complacent and deceitful, believing he was above the law. One day, Yusuf, a local shopkeeper, came to the magistrate's court to seek his help.

'Sir, my wife passed away recently, after a sudden illness,' Yusuf explained. 'We were married for twenty-eight years, and I've still not recovered from the shock of her passing. I have no children and am nearing the end of my days. Before it is too late, I would like to go on a pilgrimage to Mecca. I would be very grateful if I could leave this pouch with you for safekeeping while I'm gone.'

'What's in the pouch?' the magistrate asked brusquely.

'My savings, sir, in gold coins. Everything that I have earned and set aside for my old age. My plan is to close down the shop when I return from my pilgrimage and start a school for young children. I'm afraid to take the coins with me on my journey because the caravan may be looted anywhere along the way. I also cannot leave them hidden in my house or shop because a determined thief is bound to find them. Therefore, I appeal to you to safeguard my property while I'm away.'

Furrowing his brow, the magistrate replied: 'Your plan to set up a school is commendable. But I must point out that it is not customary for an officer of the imperial court to become a caretaker of people's personal property.'

'I understand your position, Your Honour, but I approached you because I have no family and no one else that I can turn to.'

Throwing up his hands in a gesture of resignation, the magistrate said: 'All right. I will look after your property in your absence but, to make sure there are no problems later on, please have the pouch sealed.'

'I have already done that, sir,' Yusuf replied, pointing to a wax seal on the cloth pouch, which secured the top of the bag to its body.

'That's good. Have a safe journey and may God be with you.'

A few days later, Yusuf set off on his perilous journey by bullock cart from his home town to the port city of Kolachi*, by dhow across the Arabian Sea to the east coast of Arabia, then on camel back across miles and miles of undulating golden sands and winding mountain roads before reaching the holy cities of Mecca and Medina, where he worshipped and rested for several months.

Almost a year later, Yusuf returned to claim his property from the magistrate, who made a great show of retrieving the pouch from a locked cupboard and handing it back to its owner. Yusuf bowed to the magistrate and said: 'Sir, please allow me to make some recompense for looking after my property. Please accept ten gold coins as a token of my gratitude.'

'No, no, that's not at all necessary,' the judge said hastily. 'But, before leaving, please check the seal and make sure that it is not broken.'

Holding the pouch up to the light, Yusuf peered at the red wax. 'The seal is as it was. It is undamaged. Thank you very much, Your Honour.'

'You are welcome. Peace be with you.'

Yusuf headed home, clutching his valuable property. Once there, he opened the cloth bag but was shocked to find it filled with copper coins instead of gold. Despite being tired from his long walk to see the magistrate, he headed back to

---

*Present-day Karachi.

the court and held out the pouch of copper coins to explain why he had returned.

The magistrate was outraged. 'Are you accusing me of stealing your gold coins?' he shouted. 'Did I not return the pouch to you, with its seal intact, less than an hour ago? You confirmed that the seal had not been damaged, but now here you are implying that I've duped you by replacing gold coins with copper. Your accusation is baseless and highly insulting! Get out of my sight!'

Disappointed by the magistrate's belligerent response, Yusuf decided that his only recourse was to take the matter to the highest court in the land—to Emperor Akbar and his wise wazir Birbal.

The next day he headed to Agra and patiently waited for his turn to present his case at the durbar. After listening to Yusuf's story about the loss of his life savings with which he had hoped to set up a school for children, Birbal asked the shopkeeper to show him the money bag. Closely inspecting the pouch and its now broken seal, Birbal said to Yusuf: 'Leave the pouch with me. I will settle the matter in a few days.'

With Akbar's permission, Birbal dispatched an aide to the town where Yusuf lived. His mission was to find the seal maker whose shop was closest to the magistrate's court and summon him to the durbar the following day. The seal maker didn't know what to make of the royal summons but hoped it would lead to business from the imperial palace. Appearing at the specified time, he bowed low to the emperor and his council of nine advisers.

'Tell me, are you often approached to make copies of seals?' Birbal asked.

'On occasion, yes, huzoor. Sometimes customers may have lost the seal stamp, so if they show me the seal, I copy the design, and make a new stamp for them. I didn't know it was wrong to do that....'

Showing him the broken seal on the money bag, Birbal asked: 'Have you seen this seal before?'

The nervous seal maker immediately recognized the seal that he had made for the local magistrate. Terrified by the wazir's stern tone, and worried that instead of being hired by the palace he might end up losing his livelihood, the seal maker replied: 'Y-yes, sir, I have seen th-this seal before because I am the one who made it s-some months ago.'

'Who was it made for?' the emperor asked.

'It was for our local magistrate. He is well known in our town,' came the reply.

'Send orders for the magistrate and the complainant to attend the durbar at eleven o'clock tomorrow morning,' Akbar ordered, and turning to the seal maker, he instructed: 'Make sure that you are here too.'

At the appointed hour the next morning, the magistrate strode in confidently, but the ingratiating smile on his lips disappeared as soon as he saw Yusuf and the seal maker standing in front of the dais on which the emperor and his advisers were seated.

'Do you recognize this bag?' Akbar asked icily, as the magistrate fell to his knees.

'Forgive me, Jahanpanah,' the magistrate pleaded. 'It was an error of judgement on my part. I broke the seal of the bag and had a new seal made after substituting copper coins for the man's gold coins.'

'An error of judgement?' Akbar spluttered. 'It was far worse than that. You have not only disgraced your office and betrayed the trust imposed in you but have also been disloyal to your monarch. You are dismissed from your office with immediate effect. You are hereby ordered to repay this man twice the amount that you stole from him. Your remaining property and ill-gotten gains should then be distributed to the poor.'

Turning to Yusuf, Akbar said: 'I'm delighted to hear your plans to put your life savings to good use by setting up a school for children. I would like to contribute five hundred gold coins towards that worthy project.' Overwhelmed by the emperor's generosity, Yusuf bowed and headed home. For the first time since his wife's death, he had a smile on his face.

73

Birbal and the Shah

The royal courts of Persia and Hindustan had shared close ties for several generations. In fact, shortly before Akbar's birth, his father Emperor Humayun had lost his throne after being defeated in battle by Sher Shah, founder of the Suri empire. The Mughal royal family fled to Persia accompanied by a few trusted friends, where they were given refuge by Shah Tahmasp. In exile for nearly fifteen years, Humayun eventually reclaimed the throne thanks to the help of his Persian allies and the military acumen of his army commander Bairam Khan.

When Akbar came to the throne, Shah Abbas, his counterpart in Persia, never let him forget the good turn his predecessors had done Humayun and his family. The shah patronizingly referred to Akbar as his 'younger brother' and went so far as to claim that Akbar owed his eminence to the magnanimity of his Persian benefactors.

Envious of Akbar, and keen to discover the secret of his success, widespread fame, and glory, Shah Abbas dispatched a letter to Akbar inviting him to send an emissary to Persia. He wrote:

> I have heard nothing but praise about your kingdom from my countrymen who have travelled its roads. I would like to learn more about your wondrous country from someone who has actually lived there.

Akbar promptly selected Birbal as his emissary. Preparations for the long and perilous journey began, and caravans loaded with gifts, precious stones, and treasures headed for Persia.

After weeks of travel by road and by sea, Birbal arrived at the Persian king's opulent palace in Isfahan, with its magnificent and awe-inspiring architecture. Entering the grand hall with its high ceiling, tiled marble floor, and pillars encrusted with turquoise and gemstones that sparkled in the luminescence of a hundred candelabra, Birbal was surprised to see six identically dressed men seated on thrones on the dais at the end of the spacious room. Each of the men was elegantly dressed in splendid jewelled robes, all wore crowns, and all looked alike.

Realizing that he was being put to the test, Birbal looked from one to the other and then confidently strode up to one of the men, bowed to him, and introduced himself, adding: 'It is an honour to be in your august presence, Your Majesty.'

'Birbal, the reports of your wisdom have not been exaggerated. How did you figure out that I am the king?' the puzzled monarch asked.

Birbal smiled: 'You were the only one of the six men who looked completely at ease on the throne. The five other kings looked self-conscious and kept glancing at you now and then. You alone looked as if you were to the manner born.'

The king of Persia was deeply impressed by Birbal's powers of observation. The visit was off to a promising start.

After a good night's rest, Birbal was ushered into the shah's presence the next day. 'Wazir Birbal,' the shah said, 'I am told that you are Akbar's most trusted adviser. Wherever I go, whoever I meet, everyone sings the praises of my younger brother, the great Akbar. What is the secret of his success?'

'His progressive thinking and humility,' Birbal replied confidently. 'He is wise enough to know that he doesn't have all the answers and humble enough to seek advice from those who do. Though he is surrounded by yes-men, he knows that minds are not stimulated by heads nodding in agreement. His greatest strength is that he bows to wisdom and never hesitates to seek guidance from his advisers.'

'That is indeed an admirable quality,' Shah Abbas said. 'I am deeply impressed by your candour and intelligence, Wazir Birbal. I know you have travelled far and have met many rajas and rulers, so I have one more question for you. Tell me, how do I compare with other kings?'

'Other kings may shine briefly but are unable to hold a candle to you. You are as majestic as the full moon.'

Suitably flattered, the shah smiled. 'And now you must tell me honestly, how do I compare with my younger brother, Emperor Akbar?'

'Emperor Akbar is the new moon,' Birbal replied.

Delighted with Birbal's response, the shah loaded him with gifts for his return journey. But news of Birbal's compliment to the shah had preceded him to Hindustan. Akbar was hurt and upset. Ignoring the piles of gifts from Isfahan, the emperor turned on his aide angrily and said: 'Birbal, you have betrayed and offended me! In open court you praised the shah of Persia as the full moon and compared me to the tiny sliver of a new moon?'

'Most Sublime Radiance,' Birbal replied calmly, 'what I meant was that, like the full moon, the shah's powers will gradually wane, but like the crescent moon, you will continue to grow and glow until you reach your destined glory. You will be a shining light for years to come.'

With a laugh, Akbar embraced his friend. 'Welcome home, Birbal. I don't think anyone will be able to match your brilliance and sparkle. You outshine us all.'

74

Catching Thieves

Birbal had become so adept at solving petty crimes, that whenever a theft took place anywhere near the capital, the victims usually headed for Akbar's court rather than to the police to solve the case.

A rich merchant turned up at the durbar one day claiming that he had been robbed. His wife's jewellery and a bag of gold coins were missing and the merchant suspected that the theft had been carried out by one of his four employees. Birbal accompanied the merchant to his house and questioned the employees, all of whom swore that they were innocent and denied any knowledge of the theft.

Birbal had anticipated their denial. 'I will give each of you a stick of equal length,' he told the four men. 'These sticks have magical properties. By tomorrow morning when I come to inspect them, the thief's stick will have grown by two inches.'

The next morning, when Birbal inspected the sticks that he had handed out the day before, he found that one of them was two inches shorter than the others. Pointing to the employee with the shorter stick, Birbal said: 'This is your thief, merchant. The guilty man has cut the stick at night fearing it would grow by two inches.'

On another occasion, one of the emperor's ministers complained that his house had been robbed and all his gold coins had been stolen during the night. Akbar was shocked to hear about the theft because the area surrounding the palace, where all his ministers lived, was believed to be the safest in the kingdom. How could anyone have broken into the house at night to steal the coins? It could only be one of his ministers who had carried out the theft.

The emperor turned to Birbal to solve the case. Birbal asked for a cow to be tethered to the gate leading to the ministers' quarters. He told the puzzled ministers: 'This sacred cow has extraordinary powers. Each of you must lift its tail and loudly declare, "I did not steal the gold coins". If you are lying, the cow will moo loudly. Once you have undergone the test, please come straight back to the durbar.'

The ministers did as they were instructed and trooped into the durbar in the evening. When all of them were present, Birbal asked each one to hold out their hands, palms facing upwards so that he could inspect them. All the men had streaks of black on their palms, except for the minister who had stolen the coins. Birbal had applied a semi-permanent dye onto the cow's tail knowing that the guilty party would not touch it, fearing he would be found out. He had managed to catch the thief using his usual unconventional methods.

75

Unlucky for Some

During Emperor Akbar's reign, there lived a poor man called Saad in Fatehpur Sikri. Although his name meant 'happiness', the unfortunate Saad was widely believed to bring people bad luck. He had earned the reputation of being a bad omen following a string of personal disasters: while still in his teens, Saad's parents, two sisters, and three brothers had died of smallpox, and Saad often felt he was cursed to have been left to fend for himself at such a tender age.

Eking out a meagre living as a woodcutter, he lost his job when a man working nearby was felled by a falling branch. Saad was nowhere near the scene of the accident, but rumours began to spread that somehow he was to blame, because bad luck seemed to follow him wherever he went. People were convinced that if he crossed their path in the morning, they would have a bad day. 'Get out of our sight. One glance at you and our day is ruined!' some would say. 'You bring nothing but misfortune, so cover your face before you kill someone with your evil eye!' others would add.

Saad's undeserved reputation had reached the emperor's ears and Akbar expressed a desire to meet him: 'I want to see for myself if what they say about this accursed man is true.' Long-suffering Saad, who had never harmed anyone in his life, was ushered into the emperor's presence, shaking with fright and not knowing why he was being summoned. Akbar glanced at Saad briefly and asked him to return in the evening.

As luck would have it, it turned out to be a tiring day for the emperor, who had to contend with urgent correspondence, tedious affairs of state, troublesome courtiers, and a steady stream of supplicants. It was such a busy day that the emperor did not even take a break for his lunch. Hungry, tired, and irritable, the situation worsened when a messenger brought an urgent summons from the queen informing Akbar that Prince Salim had been taken ill.

What a dreadful day it has been, Akbar thought, as he rushed to his beloved son's bedside, and then suddenly remembered that he had seen the face of the 'unlucky' man that morning. The emperor instantly jumped to the conclusion that the problems he had faced throughout the day were somehow Saad's fault.

When Saad returned to the durbar in the evening, Akbar ordered his guards to arrest him immediately and put him in prison for life, where he could not bring misfortune to others. The courtiers nodded approvingly and seemed to be in full agreement with the emperor's decision, all except Birbal, who let out a short but audible laugh.

'Do you find my decision amusing, Birbal?' the emperor asked haughtily.

'Forgive me, O Fount of All Wisdom,' Birbal replied. 'I couldn't help noticing the irony of the situation. You claim that this man brought you bad luck because you had to go without lunch since you saw him this morning. But let's consider his misfortune: yours was the first face he saw today and he has been sentenced to a lifetime in prison because of it. I couldn't help wondering who brought bad luck for whom.'

Akbar immediately withdrew his rash order and instructed his aides to hire Saad as an assistant to the palace gardeners. At long last, Saad's luck had changed.

76

Monkey Business

Raja Jaimal was holding forth on a quiet day at the durbar. 'I'm sorry to say,' he declared in a tone that did not sound at all apologetic, 'that God's ways are truly mysterious and incomprehensible. Just look at the indiscriminate manner in which he chooses to bestow his blessings.... When endowing somebody with a sharp mind and exceptional shrewdness, one would expect that God would choose someone from an aristocratic background, well-bred, and good-looking. Birbal may be smart, but he looks like a monkey!'

As several courtiers and dignitaries present in the durbar tittered at this insult, Jaimal smirked at having demeaned the emperor's favourite. Akbar was visibly annoyed at his brother-in-law's disrespect, but before he could voice his disapproval, Birbal spoke up: 'Your Majesty, I firmly believe that while insults can be freely given, they need not necessarily be taken.'

Then, turning to face Jaimal, Birbal continued: 'My honourable friend, you have actually paid me a compliment by likening me to a monkey. In several ancient cultures, monkeys are considered so astute that they see no evil, hear no evil, speak no evil, and do no evil. Therefore, I don't think there is any shame in looking like a monkey or in acting like one. In fact, some people in this noble assembly could learn a trick or two from apes.'

Akbar was the first to applaud Birbal's rejoinder and the rest of the audience clapped wholeheartedly. Only Jaimal sat in sullen silence, wondering whether Birbal's parting shot had been aimed at him.

77

Qissa-e-Akbar

One of Akbar's favourite pastimes was to have his courtiers and advisers read or relate stories to him. The emperor especially enjoyed mythological tales from ancient lands and cultures. Summoning Birbal to his chambers one morning, Akbar told him: 'My chamberlain recently read the Mahabharata to me, which I thoroughly enjoyed. It got me thinking—if such a memorable classic was written about the Pandavas and the Kauravas, shouldn't a similar epic story be written about me and my accomplishments?'

'That's something we could think about, Your Majesty,' Birbal replied non-committally.

'Yes,' replied the sovereign. 'I *have* been thinking about it and have even come up with a title. We will call it *Qissa-e-Akbar*. I want you to begin writing it immediately.'

'Certainly, Jahanpanah, your wish is my command,' Birbal replied, wondering what hare-brained challenge the emperor would foist on him next. 'But please give me at least three months to enable me to do full justice to your extraordinary life story.'

'Of course,' said the emperor. 'Take all the time you need.'

Three months later, not having written a word, Birbal appeared at court carrying a thick stack of blank pages resting between elaborate covers.

'Well,' the emperor asked eagerly, 'is the book ready?'

'Most Noble of Monarchs, I have nearly completed the book, but need to include some minor details. With your permission, I would like to have a short meeting with the queen so as to get a feminine perspective about your family life. It will enable me to paint a more complete portrait of Your Majesty for future generations.' Akbar immediately agreed and Birbal was granted an audience with the queen.

Harkha Bai, who disliked Birbal, and had not forgiven him for depriving her brother of the judge's position, greeted him frostily when he was ushered into her presence and did not invite him to sit down. 'What is it that you want to know?' she asked icily, sitting stiffly on the edge of a large throne-like chair, her posture indicating her displeasure, her big brown eyes flashing brighter than her diamond nose-ring and earrings.

'Begum Sahiba, as you are aware, His Exalted Majesty has instructed me to write his life story in a style similar to that of the Mahabharata. In my story, His Majesty is Yudhishthira, the embodiment of truth, courage, and honour. And you are Draupadi, beautiful and spirited. I have even dedicated my book to you.'

Mollified by Birbal's praise, the queen visibly relaxed and requested him to read the passages in the manuscript that were about her. 'Your wish is my command, Your Majesty. I have devoted several pages in the book extolling your beauty, elegance, and grace, but will read you the parts that refer to Your Majesties and the Mahabharata,' said Birbal, making a great show of turning the blank pages of the book until he found the passage that he wanted.

He read:

> Yudhishthira loses everything—all his possessions, his half of the kingdom, his brothers, himself, and Draupadi in a gambling match against his wicked cousin Duryodhana. All the senior members of the court of King Dhritarashtra, Duryodhana's father, watch as Draupadi is dragged into the hall. Duryodhana and his allies spit on her, call her a slave, a loose woman, and a slut, rip off her veil and attempt to strip her naked....

'That's enough,' cried the queen, as she sprang up from her chair flushed with rage. 'How dare you use such language and write such filthy things about me! The king may have a lot in common with Yudhishthira, but I am nothing like Draupadi! This book is a meaningless exercise and I will not tolerate such falsified fiction.' With that she snatched the book from Birbal's hands and threw it into the fire. As the pages and the cover crinkled and turned to ashes, Birbal bowed to the queen and made a hasty exit.

Returning to the durbar, Akbar greeted him warmly. 'Is it done? Is *Qissa-e-Akbar* ready to take the world by storm?'

'Not really,' Birbal shrugged. 'The queen must have deemed it unworthy of you, so she tossed the whole thing into the fire.'

'But why would she do that?' asked the bewildered monarch.

'I cannot say for certain, Light of the World. I read her a short excerpt from the book and she became angry and upset. She then destroyed all the effort that I put into the manuscript for the past three months.'

'So what happens now? Will there be no *Qissa-e-Akbar*?'

'Most Munificent of Monarchs, you are making history every day,' Birbal replied. 'It will be impossible for any writer to capture all these memorable moments. Be content that tales of your wise rule and good deeds will be spread far and wide by your citizens and will convince more people of your greatness than words in any book.'

The emperor smiled and thought: As always, Birbal is right. It is better to have news of my accomplishments spread through word of mouth because not everyone reads books, and those who do, may not believe everything that they read.

78

A Way With Words

Finding the emperor in a mellow mood, following his army's success in a recent battle, his aides decided to speak to him about his bias in favour of Birbal. 'You indulge Birbal too much, Your Majesty,' they complained. 'Even when he gives you bad news, you accept it graciously, whereas you are impatient and curt with the rest of us. We cannot comprehend why Birbal has such a hold over you.'

Akbar stroked his chin and replied: 'Hmmm.... I can see why you think I favour Birbal. But haven't you noticed that he always finds a tactful way of breaking bad news?'

'Flattery and sweet talk have enabled him to reach the top,' the courtiers persisted.

'Not so,' the emperor replied. 'I will show you what I mean when the opportunity arises.'

A few weeks later, after attending to the day's matters in the durbar, Akbar addressed his courtiers. 'Before we disperse, there is a personal matter I wish to discuss with you. I had a strange and worrisome dream last night. I dreamt that the stable door was wide open and all my precious Arabian horses had escaped, except for my favourite stallion. How would you interpret this nightmare?'

The court's mystics and shamans discussed the question for a few minutes and the head priest delivered their verdict: 'The dream indicates that all Your Majesty's kith and kin will die before you.'

'That doesn't bode well for my empire and lineage,' said Akbar with a deep scowl. Noticing that Birbal had been silent throughout, Akbar turned to him and asked: 'Birbal, how would you interpret my dream?'

'Let me put it this way,' Birbal said thoughtfully. 'I think it means that of all your family members, you will be blessed with the longest and most fulfilling life.'

Turning to the envious courtiers, the emperor addressed them: 'Now do you see what I mean? Isn't that the better way to give bad news? Birbal truly has a wonderful way with words.'

79

A Taste for Tobacco

Tobacco was introduced in Hindustan by the Portuguese during Akbar's reign. Hoping to make it a lucrative item for importing into the country, the Portuguese liberally handed out seeds to farmers to encourage them to grow the plant and gave free samples of chewing tobacco to anyone willing to give it a try. People quickly became addicted to the nicotine-rich plant.

Strangely, Akbar, who had many other addictions, did not take to the new fad of chewing tobacco and thought it a filthy habit. He found its taste and narcotic qualities as revolting as the habit of spitting the chewed leaves into spittoons. Stranger still, Birbal, a man of simple tastes, had developed a weakness for tobacco, which he carried around with him in a pouch, helping himself to pinches of it throughout the day.

Having been told that donkeys and several other animals wouldn't go anywhere near a tobacco plant, Akbar devised a plan to try and make his adviser kick the habit. He ordered an aide to arrange a visit to a tobacco farm and to bring a donkey there too.

Accompanying the emperor in the carriage, Birbal realized something was afoot when Akbar refused to reveal any details of their outing or tell him where they were heading. When they reached the tobacco farm, Akbar asked for the donkey to be let loose in the field. The donkey took one sniff at a tobacco plant and trotted out of the field as fast as possible.

'Did you see that, Birbal? Even a donkey doesn't go anywhere near tobacco. He runs as far from it as possible because it is a nasty thing.'

Birbal knew that the emperor was right, but he had to have the last word: 'Your Majesty's observation is correct: donkeys don't chew tobacco, but people do. However, as donkeys are not known for their discernment or judgement, maybe it would be more accurate to say *only* a donkey wouldn't take a liking to tobacco.'

80

A Miser's Trial by Fire

In a town neighbouring Fatehpur Sikri there lived a man who had gained notoriety for his mean spirit and stinginess. Kanhaiya had never done a charitable act in his life, was tight-fisted with his family members and servants, had hoarded his earnings and bought pearls, diamonds, and expensive gemstones with his savings. He stored his collection of several hundred gems in a metal box which he kept hidden under his bed. Every night before going to sleep, he would open the box to admire its contents. Running his fingers through this treasure, he would polish the gemstones with a soft cloth before replacing them in the box, exulting in his good fortune to possess such immense wealth.

One day, Kanhaiya's house caught fire and the leaping flames soon enveloped the entire wooden dwelling. While his servants rushed out onto the street in a panic, Kanhaiya thrashed about in a frenzy, flailing his arms helplessly against the flames, trying desperately to retrieve the treasure chest from under his bed. A small crowd gathered to see what the ruckus was about, and while the miser's servants forcibly dragged him from the burning house, his neighbours tried to douse the blaze with buckets of water.

Having inhaled a considerable amount of smoke, Kanhaiya beat his chest and rasped: 'My box, my precious box. Please, please, help me to get my box. Anyone who salvages my priceless collection will be handsomely rewarded.'

A young jeweller who lived in the neighbourhood had always been envious of Kanhaiya's riches. Noticing the clouds of black smoke billowing skywards, the youth had rushed to the blazing house, sensing a golden opportunity to make some money. Running up to Kanhaiya, the jeweller said: 'I will brave the flames, and retrieve your box, on one condition.'

'Name your price,' Kanhaiya gasped in sheer desperation.

'If I am able to salvage your valuables, I will give you from it only what I like. Agreed?'

With time running out, and the fire raging, Kanhaiya hastily agreed, assuming that the jeweller would be satisfied with a few gems from his hoard. 'The box is stored under my bed, which is through the door and to the right. Hurry, please hurry!' he cried.

The fearless jeweller removed his turban and handed it to Kanhaiya to hold, poured a bucket of water over himself, and ran towards the house. Somehow managing to dodge the flames, he crawled into the burning house, found the box, and carried it out triumphantly. Kanhaiya was unconcerned that the young man's eyebrows and hair were singed and he was covered in soot, but overjoyed to see that the fire had not damaged the box containing his life's earnings. As the crowd cheered the brave young jeweller's heroism, Kanhaiya joined in the jubilation.

His rapture was short-lived: the jeweller knelt to place the heavy box on the ground by his feet, grabbed his turban from Kanhaiya's hands, shovelled the contents of the box into his turban and his pockets, then stood up and handed the empty box to its owner.

'Wh-what is the meaning of th-this?' Kanhaiya croaked, his head spinning at the thought of losing his fortune.

'Our agreement was that I would give you what I liked. So here we go—I'd like to give you this box,' the jeweller replied.

'Please, sir, I know that you've endangered yourself to save my fortune and I will gladly give you a fitting reward. You have risked your life so you can take half of the pearls and diamonds,' Kanhaiya said, reduced to tears. The jeweller was unmoved by Kanhaiya's distress, but several bystanders felt sorry for the miser and spoke up in his defence: 'It doesn't seem fair that you take all the contents of the box,' they said to the jeweller. 'Don't you think he is being more than fair by offering you half of his gems?'

Turning on them angrily, the jeweller said: 'Certainly not! It was not worth risking my life for half of his gems! All of you heard him agree, didn't you? He agreed that I could give him whatever I like. I have done exactly what I said. So why this uproar?'

'It is theft, brazen theft,' Kanhaiya sobbed. 'Only Birbal will be able to resolve the issue.'

To the jeweller's dismay, the crowd began to chant: 'Yes, yes! Birbal! Birbal! Only Birbal can resolve the matter.' He had no choice but to follow them to the durbar.

Birbal gave both sides a patient hearing and asked: 'Tell me once again what was decided between the two of you?'

The jeweller said: 'We agreed that if I recovered the box from the flames, I would give him only what I like.'

Turning to Kanhaiya, Birbal asked: 'Is the jeweller telling the truth?'

'Yes, huzoor.'

'Then why are you here?'

'Huzoor, he has taken all the pearls and diamonds and given me only the empty box,' Kanhaiya wailed.

Turning to the jeweller, Birbal asked: 'Which do you like between the two?'

'Sir! The pearls and diamonds, of course!' the jeweller declared.

'In that case,' said Birbal, 'you must hand over the pearls and diamonds that you like and keep the box for yourself.' Seeing the surprised look on the jeweller's face, Birbal added: 'It was you who laid down the terms and conditions, so you must abide by them.'

The jeweller realized that he had been outwitted and shamed. After a few seconds he said: 'Sir, I am willing to share the gems with this man. After all, I did risk my life to save his fortune.'

'I leave it to the owner of the gems to decide whether he owes you anything at all,' said Birbal.

As the jeweller reluctantly returned the gems to their rightful owner, Kanhaiya, having returned to his miserly senses, bowed to Birbal: 'Huzoor, thank you for sorting out the matter. I'd be happy to reward this brave young man by giving him twenty of the finest diamonds from my collection.'

Kanhaiya then headed back to the smouldering ruins of his house, thankful that he still had nearly all of his priceless gems with which he could rebuild his home. The jeweller walked away dejectedly with twenty sparkling diamonds in his pocket but deeply regretting not accepting Kanhaiya's offer of half of his precious gems. I must never let greed get the better of me again, he thought.

81

The Queen's Treasure

Like all couples, Akbar and his consort were not exempt from the occasional marital tiff over some trivial issue, which invariably ended with his wife in tears and him in a foul mood. One evening, after a long and tiring day dealing with petty disputes, mulish foreign ambassadors, and grovelling favour-seekers, Akbar was already in a bad temper when the queen began nagging him to accompany her to visit her parents who lived some distance from Fatehpur Sikri.

'I don't have time for holidays,' he snapped. 'In case you hadn't noticed, I have an empire to run. If you're so keen to spend time with your family, you can leave immediately and stay as long as you like. Don't bother coming back unless I send for you.'

Stung by his harsh tone, the queen burst into tears and apologized profusely, but Akbar was adamant. 'Nothing you say will make me change my mind. You must leave the palace as soon as you're packed and ready.' And with that, he stormed out of the room.

While her handmaidens set about packing trunks of clothes and jewellery, the dejected queen summoned Birbal to request his help to resolve her predicament.

The next morning, the queen entered the king's bedchamber, her head bowed and her eyes brimming with tears. 'Light of My Life,' she said, 'I have come to bid you farewell. But before I leave, will you kindly grant me one request?'

'What is it?' the emperor asked sullenly.

'Will you permit me to take something that is precious to me with me when I leave the palace?' she asked softly, tears streaming down her flushed cheeks.

'You can take what you want but then leave immediately.'

'My Precious One, it is you that I wish to take with me to my parents' house. You are my treasure, dearer to me than all the wealth in the world, and because I love you more than life itself, I wish you to accompany me.'

Moved by his wife's tender words, the emperor immediately regretted losing his temper and banishing her from the palace. Taking the queen's hand in his, he raised it to his lips and then ordered his aides to make the necessary arrangements for him to accompany his wife to her parental home. After spending a few days with his in-laws, Akbar returned with his queen to Fatehpur Sikri, where Birbal was richly rewarded for coming up with the strategy that restored domestic harmony.

82

A Matter of Faith

One morning, when the durbar had dispersed, Akbar turned to Birbal and said: 'I've been giving a lot of thought to a matter that has been troubling me for a long time. Although born into a Muslim family, I am married to a Rajput princess who is the mother of my son and heir, and the majority of my people are Hindus. I believe that God is in everything and everywhere, and though the paths may be different for Hindus and Muslims and Christians and other faiths, ultimately they all lead to the same place. I was therefore considering following a few Hindu rituals so that my subjects could relate to me better and have more confidence in me.'

'O Keeper of the Faith, you have always been a good man and a just and wise king. Is that not enough for you?'

'You are not going to talk me out of this, Birbal,' Akbar said. 'I have made up my mind. I would like to go to Varanasi to take a dip in the holy Ganga and wash away my sins. We can leave as soon as all preparations for the pilgrimage have been made.'

Birbal bowed respectfully and made arrangements for the journey. A large contingent of courtiers, spiritual advisers, and attendants, travelling by day and setting up camp at night, headed out on horseback from the dusty plains and hills of North India heading east to the lush green valleys that housed the mighty river.

One evening, after a hot and tiring day, when the king's large and cumbersome entourage had halted before nightfall at a quiet spot on the banks of the river, Birbal invited Akbar to join him for a stroll while they waited for the evening meal to be prepared. The pair walked in silence for a while, admiring the vivid pink and fiery orange hues with which the setting sun was painting a cloudless blue sky. A short distance away, they saw two peasants, one pulling and the other pushing a donkey towards the river.

The donkey, which had a garland of marigolds around its neck, was putting up strong resistance against entering the swirling, ice-cold water. Noticing the animal's distress, Akbar called out to the men: 'What are you trying to do to the poor animal? It looks scared out of its wits.'

'Sir, we are trying to change this donkey into a horse,' one of the men replied.

'And how do you propose to do that?' Akbar asked in disbelief.

The second man replied: 'We were advised by a wise man that if we dipped our donkey into the waters of the holy river and made appropriate offerings to the gods, he would become a horse by the end of the day.'

'That is the silliest thing I have ever heard,' Akbar laughed.

'Really?' the first peasant said indignantly. 'Then you have not heard about our Muslim king who thinks he can change his religion merely by having a dip in the holy waters of the Ganga at Varanasi? If he can do that, then I think we have an equal chance of ending up with a horse.'

Guessing that Birbal might have instigated these bizarre events, Akbar cast a sideways glance at his adviser, who was gazing admiringly at the sky and seemed enchanted by the glorious sunset. Turning to the two peasants, Akbar asked: 'Was the wise man who gave you this advice Wazir Birbal by any chance?'

'Yes, sir,' the peasants replied.

Smiling at his adviser's craftiness, Akbar said: 'You've made your point, Birbal. I realize that I have as much chance of becoming a Hindu as that donkey has of becoming a horse. Let's turn around and head home,' Akbar said.

'O Noblest of Men,' Birbal replied, as they walked back to their camp, 'you have proved to your entire kingdom that you are a tolerant and benevolent ruler. You are known for rewarding talent and merit regardless of the individual's religion or background. You will be remembered throughout history for your open-minded approach to other faiths, where religious scholars—be they Muslim, Hindu, Christian, or Zoroastrian—are welcome. You have proved yourself a keeper of all faiths and have earned the loyalty and respect of your subjects...so these man-made rituals are not required of you.'

Akbar nodded silently and said: 'You are the best adviser a king could have, Birbal. You don't force your views on me but test me enough to compel me to figure things out for myself. I am very lucky to have you as my guru.'

Birbal smiled. 'The good fortune is mine, O Fount of Perception. Not many kings have the level-headedness to accept that there are some things that they cannot change, the valour to change the things that they can, and the discernment to choose the right option.'

83

A Test of Love

The durbar was in session one morning when the proceedings were disrupted by the pitter-patter of tiny feet as Prince Salim toddled into the room to show his father the new clothes that his mother had gifted him for his third birthday. The emperor was usually a stickler for discipline but as this was a special occasion, Akbar visibly relaxed as his son clambered onto his lap and put his plump little arms around his father's neck. A faint susurrus swept through the durbar as the courtiers murmured their approval of this touching scene and showered blessings and good wishes for a long life on the endearing child.

'For a parent, there can be nothing more precious in the whole world than the life of his or her child,' the emperor said, rocking his son gently from side to side.

'You are absolutely right, huzoor,' several of his courtiers agreed in unison. Only Birbal was quiet.

'Do you not agree with my observation, Birbal?' the emperor asked.

'Your observation is not borne out by facts, Jahanpanah,' Birbal replied softly. 'For nearly all living things, their own life is much more precious than the life of their child.'

'I think most parents would disagree with your view,' Akbar replied, while his son tugged playfully at the pearl and ruby necklace around his father's neck. 'I remember an elderly courtier telling me a story about my grandfather, Babur, who sacrificed his life to save my father, Humayun,' Akbar said, lifting his son off his lap and handing him to an attendant to take back to the queen's quarters.

'The story goes that my father had fallen seriously ill in his childhood and the doctors had given up hope of him surviving. My grandfather was devastated and began to pray fervently for God to spare my father's life. A holy man advised my grandfather to sacrifice his most precious possession—specifically, the Kohinoor diamond—to save my father's life. My grandfather replied that the Kohinoor did not belong to him but was his son's property. He told the holy man that he would sacrifice his own precious life instead. Throughout the night, my grandfather circled my father's sickbed, praying for God to take his life but to spare his son. Almost miraculously, my father began to recover, but my grandfather fell critically ill and died soon after.'

Turning to Birbal, the emperor asked: 'Doesn't my grandfather's story prove my point?'

'What your grandfather's case proves is that when asked to sacrifice his most precious possession, he gave up his own life, not Humayun's,' Birbal answered.

'You are just being perverse and distorting the tale,' the emperor said. 'Can you prove your theory?'

'Certainly, Jahanpanah. But I will need help from the palace gardeners.' The gardeners were summoned as Akbar and his courtiers followed Birbal to the magnificent garden, fragrant with the scent of a thousand roses. When they came to a small tank of lotuses, Birbal ordered a gardener to empty the tank. Then he ordered another gardener to go to the private zoo that Akbar had set up in the palace grounds for Prince Salim's amusement, and fetch him a female monkey with her infants.

Returning a few minutes later carrying a chattering and screeching monkey with two infants clinging to her chest, the gardeners were ordered to place all three animals inside the drained tank. 'Now start filling the tank with water,' Birbal instructed.

The emperor and his courtiers watched the unfolding scene in amazement. As the water level in the tank began to rise, the mother moved her infants onto her back to save them from drowning. When the water reached chest level, she stood on her hind legs and moved them onto her head.

'Look, Birbal,' the emperor called out triumphantly. 'She puts her children's needs above her own.'

'Wait until the tank is full,' Birbal replied calmly.

As soon as the water level reached the mother's mouth and began getting into her nostrils, the monkey screeched and jumped out of the tank leaving her infants behind. Birbal immediately instructed one of the gardeners to leap into the tank and rescue the floundering infants. As soon as the infants were on dry ground, their mother gathered them up and scurried up a nearby tree with her wet and miserable offspring clinging to her for dear life.

Turning to the emperor, Birbal said: 'Our children are indeed dear to us, Jahanpanah. But not all parents are completely selfless—most living things value their own life above all else. I think my small experiment here has proved my point.'

'How can you possibly equate an animal's behaviour with that of a human?' Akbar said sharply. 'I'm sure most mothers and fathers would strongly object to your argument. I don't think we can make broad generalizations on such a sensitive and personal subject. On this matter, Birbal, we shall disagree.' The courtiers were quick to note that this was the closest the emperor ever came to rebuking his close confidant, who never brought up the subject again.

84

Punishment Fit for a Prince

The best part of the emperor's day was when he returned to his private apartments in the palace to spend time with his family and have some semblance of a normal family life.

One evening, Akbar had settled down on a velvet divan to have his tea on the palace veranda overlooking a pond awash with lotuses, when Prince Salim ran in, clambered onto his father's lap and announced: 'Abba, I'm hungry. I want to eat makai.'

An attendant was summoned and instructed to bring roasted corn for the prince. A few minutes later, a bowl of lightly buttered, steaming golden corn was placed in front of the prince.

'I don't want this,' the prince whimpered, turning his face away from the bowl. 'I want to eat it from the bhutta.'

'Very well,' the king said with a sigh, and issued instructions to roast a fresh piece of corn on the cob for the prince.

'I don't want another one, I want the same corn put back on the cob,' the prince demanded, beating his fists on his father's chest.

'That cannot be done,' the king said sternly, triggering a tantrum and tears from the little prince. His mother's indulgence is turning the boy into a spoilt brat, Akbar thought to himself, but trying to distract the wailing child, he said: 'Abba cannot put the corn back on the cob, my precious one. But instead he will give you something else, something even better. If you stop crying, you can have anything you like.'

Salim's tears stopped immediately and he turned his attention to choosing something he liked. Standing up on his father's lap, the prince reached out to touch the gems on his father's turban, knocking it askew. Akbar immediately handed the turban, encrusted with priceless gems, to an attendant and gestured to him to take it into the sitting room, away from the prince's clutches. The prince had now turned his attention to the multiple strands of gem-studded necklaces that hung around his father's neck.

'I like these white beads, they're so pretty,' said the prince, pulling at a strand of flawless pearls.

'Be careful with it, my precious one,' the emperor said, trying to extricate the necklace from his son's fingers. 'These are not toys to be played with, they are very expens....'

Before he could finish the sentence, the prince gave another tug at the necklace, breaking it and causing the pearls to fly to the floor, where they landed with a faint tinkle and then bounced and rolled off the veranda, straight into the pond.

'That does it!' Akbar yelled in annoyance, as Prince Salim burst into another loud bout of wailing. 'You must be punished for your carelessness. That necklace was one of the finest in my collection. It has been in our family for three generations and now you've destroyed it in a few seconds, you naughty boy!'

Hearing the commotion, the queen swept majestically into the room and the prince, still howling, ran up to her and buried his tear-stained face in her voluminous ghagra.

'Do you have any idea what your spoilt son has gone and done?' Akbar asked angrily, and recounted the entire saga to his wife.

'Why did you let him play with the necklace?' the queen asked loftily. 'You cannot hold him responsible for the loss. He is only a child, not yet four years old.'

'He is a prince,' Akbar said sharply, 'and he has to be taught to behave like one, and to take responsibility for his actions. He must be disciplined and punished.'

'If you are determined to punish the child, please don't do it now when you're angry. Wait until tomorrow, when your anger has cooled.'

Akbar grunted, marvelling at his wife's ingenuity in always getting her way. I may be emperor for the rest of the world, but in my home, I am slave to the queen, he thought as he watched his wife walk away with Prince Salim clutching her hand.

That night, the queen had no option but to send an urgent message to her nemesis Birbal, telling him about the king's rage and his intention to punish their son. 'Don't worry, Begum Sahiba, I'll handle it,' Birbal said reassuringly.

The next morning, as Akbar was taking his morning walk in the garden, revelling in its dewy freshness and the refreshing spray from the fountains, he saw Birbal and Prince Salim seated on the grass by the side of the pond, with a small jewel box placed between them, into which the child was rummaging happily, occasionally removing a gem from the box with his pudgy little fingers and laying it carefully on the grass.

'What's going on here?' the emperor asked.

'Your Majesty, I heard about the mishap that the prince caused yesterday and how angry it made you. So, I thought I would bring him here and let him play with my own small collection of gems to determine whether yesterday's incident was deliberate or merely an accident, and whether he needed to be punished,' Birbal explained, whispering the last word, lest it trigger tears from the prince. 'He has been playing contentedly with my gemstones and has been careful not to let a single one roll into the pond. I have therefore concluded that what happened yesterday was an accident, and leave it to you to decide how you wish to proceed.'

Akbar sat down on the grass and lifted his son onto his lap. 'You are right, Birbal,' he said, hugging his son. 'It would be unfair to punish him for something that he did not do on purpose. Salim is indeed too young to know about the value of things.... As he grows older, I hope that you will always be around to guide him and teach him the difference between right and wrong.'

85

Bedtime Stories

Akbar was a remarkable monarch whose interests went beyond statesmanship and policymaking. Despite his inability to read, his enquiring mind was like a sponge, keen to soak up the arts, sciences, culture, religion, and philosophy. The king's overactive mind and eclectic pursuits proved to be a nuisance for his attendants and courtiers—and especially his wives—all of whom were called on to provide round-the-clock attention to their monarch, who slept only four hours each night.

The emperor's insomnia was giving everyone around him sleepless nights. Remedies and potions prescribed by his doctors did not seem to help. Eventually, his counsellors were forbidden to discuss politics or matters of state with the monarch after sunset, but instead urged to tell him relaxing and soothing stories that would ensure a good night's sleep.

'That's an excellent idea,' said Akbar. 'From now on, every one of my courtiers must take it in turn to come to my bedchamber every evening to tell me a different story.'

This royal decree caused Akbar's courtiers to lose even more sleep. First of all, they had to find time to consult with each other to ensure that no one repeated a story that had already been told by someone else. Second, storytelling not being their forte, they had to rack their brains to come up with fresh ideas. Worst of all, each time they went through the ordeal of recounting a story to the emperor and were longing to head home to go to bed, he would ask: 'What's next?' The hapless and drowsy storytellers would then tell one tale after another until their throats became dry and they were utterly exhausted.

Fearing that they would fall ill from lack of sleep and stress, the courtiers decided to consult Birbal to resolve their predicament. 'Don't worry. It will be my turn to tell His Majesty a story tonight,' Birbal said, much to the courtiers' relief.

Reclining on his bed against a mountain of pillows, Akbar was delighted that Birbal, a masterful wordsmith, would be providing the evening's entertainment. Birbal settled on a chair next to the royal bed and began his story:

> Most Gracious Majesty, tonight I will recount a story from the *Panchatantra*, an ancient collection of wisdom that is relevant to this day.
>
> A long, long time ago there lived a lion in a dense forest who was as brave as he was strong and all the animals in the forest accepted him as their king. The lion was also very kind-hearted and hunted only when he was hungry, which made the other animals feel safe.
>
> With hundreds of animals to take care of in his kingdom, the lion decided to appoint a fox, a leopard, and a crow as his assistants. The fox, being crafty and shrewd, was appointed as the king's chief adviser. The leopard, known for his speed and strength, became the king's bodyguard. The crow, who could fly to great heights and knew the forest well, was assigned the role of messenger, who would notify the king where to find food, water, and shelter.
>
> All three took oaths to serve their king loyally, and the lion, in turn, vowed to provide food for all three of them and protect them from harm. The arrangement worked well: the three courtiers followed their leader everywhere and fulfilled his demands, and the lion provided enough leftovers for his assistants after each kill.
>
> One day, the crow asked the lion if he had tried camel meat. 'I ate it once in the desert at the edge of a forest. It was delicious,' the crow said, licking his beak.

'I have never eaten camel meat,' replied the lion, 'but I like the idea of trying something new for a change. Where can I find a camel for our dinner tonight?'

'There are no camels in the forest, Your Majesty,' the crow replied. 'They live in the desert. On my way here, I spotted a large one ruminating in the desert some distance from our forest. If we set off right away, we might be able to catch it.'

Never having been in the desert, the lion consulted the fox and the leopard whether they should proceed. The fox and the leopard had not been in the desert either, but didn't want to admit it to the lion. Instead the fox said: 'I think it would be a good idea to hunt for the camel. If it is as big as the crow says, then we might not need to hunt for the next few days.' The leopard nodded: 'I think the crow should lead us to the camel right away.'

The four of them set off in search of the camel. When they reached the desert, the lion, the fox, and the leopard were shocked at how hot and barren it was, with no water or shade. The sand below their feet was heating up like coal, but the dogged trio plodded on in pursuit of a good meal. Suddenly the crow called out to them that he had spotted the camel a short distance away. But by then, the soft pads of the lion's paws were burnt and sore because of the hot sand and he did not want to proceed.

He said: 'Let's rest for a bit and then head back to our forest. I'm not that keen on camel meat after all.' His advisers were dismayed by this announcement. They could see that the lion was in no position to make the long trek back to the forest, but all of them were tired and hungry. They needed to get some food.

The clever fox came up with a plan. He told the leopard to wait with the lion and asked the crow to lead him to the camel. When he reached the camel, the fox said: 'Greetings to you, my friend. I bring you a message from the king of the forest. He is unwell and unable to walk and needs your help. If you carry him back to the forest on your back, you will be richly rewarded.'

The guileless camel immediately agreed to help and accompanied the fox to the spot where the lion lay, panting heavily. The lion, the fox, and the leopard then leapt onto the camel's back and headed back to the forest with the crow guiding them overhead.

The three advisers were pleased that their plan had succeeded and waited eagerly for the lion to provide their lunch. Instead, the lion turned to the camel and said: 'Thank you for saving my life. As your reward, I offer you a position in my court and promise to protect you from danger.' Turning to his courtiers, the king asked them to find some food for him as he would not be able to hunt until his paws healed.

Upset by the king's decision, his three courtiers set off into the forest and began to plot their next move. The fox came up with another plan to kill the camel, and the crow and leopard agreed to go along with it. The trio headed back to the king.

The crow said: 'Your Majesty, we were unable to find any food. But I offer myself to you—you can eat me and fill your stomach.'

The fox scoffed: 'There is no more than a mouthful of you.... I have more meat on me than you, so let the king eat me instead.'

The leopard snarled: 'I am bigger than both of you put together, so the king should eat me.'

The camel had been listening silently, but finally spoke up: 'I am the largest of all, Your Majesty, so you should eat me. Do not harm your three companions because they will be more useful to you than I am.'

> The three courtiers moved in for the kill but the lion had other plans. 'Very well,' he said, turning to his aides. 'I will eat all of you in the order that you offered yourself. First, I will eat....'
>
> Before the lion could finish his sentence, the crow flew away, and the fox and the leopard ran off as fast as they could. Only the camel stood his ground, watching the fleeing figures with a puzzled look on his face. The lion laughed out loud. He turned towards the camel and said: 'You're the only one who has been loyal and true. From this day forth, we shall be friends.' And that was the start of a great alliance between two of God's creatures who each used their strengths to help the other.

As the tale ended, Birbal stood up to leave but the emperor stopped him: 'I think I'd heard that story before when I was a child. So, what's next?' he asked, eagerly anticipating another story.

Birbal had no choice but to sit down and come up with another yarn. 'There's an interesting legend surrounding a great king from the West,' he began.

> A few centuries ago, there lived a great king called Canute, who ruled over Denmark, England, and Norway. Canute was a renowned warrior and one of the most powerful men of his time. As his fame grew, so did the fawning of his courtiers and officials. Aware that flattery was an occupational hazard for a monarch, Canute felt particularly ill at ease when members of his entourage tried to outdo one another in singing his praises.
>
> 'Historians will note that you are the greatest ruler the world has ever known,' one of his acolytes would say.
>
> Another would add: 'Your reputation as a fearless fighter on land and at sea has spread beyond your kingdoms to the rest of the world.'

A third would declare: 'You have been sent to us by heaven and we are blessed to be your subjects.'

To top it all, the fourth would point out: 'Even our highest praise does not do justice to your towering achievements. The world and everything in it is at your command.'

'It all sounds so familiar,' Akbar smiled, stroking his chin. 'But please continue.'

Being a confident and sensible man—aware of his strengths and weaknesses—Canute became increasingly annoyed by these shallow words and decided to teach his sycophantic supporters a lesson.

On a warm summer's day, he set off for his castle by the sea, accompanied by his guards and courtiers. With his entourage following him, the king walked along the sandy shore in deep thought. Watching the waves of the incoming tide gently lapping against the golden sand leaving lacy frills of white foam in their wake, Canute ordered his attendants to place his chair on the sand near the water's edge. Walking briskly towards it, the king turned to his followers and asked: 'Do all of you agree that I am the most powerful man in the world?'

'Without a doubt, Your Majesty.'

'There is no one who can compare or compete with you.'

'Powerful and invincible,' came the replies.

'And nothing in the world dares to disobey me?'

'The entire world respects and honours you, O Mighty King,' his followers said. 'And there is nothing that dares to disobey you.'

'Will the great ocean obey me?' the king asked, looking down at the rings of frothy surf being washed up by the tide at his feet.

His courtiers looked confused, but they did not dare give him an honest answer. Finally, one of them spoke up: 'If you command the sea, Your Majesty, it will certainly obey.'

'Let's give it a try then.... O Mighty Sea!' cried the king, 'I, Canute the Great, command you to come no further! Tide, I order you to recede. Waves, I demand that you stop advancing and do not dare touch my feet or wet my shoes.'

Though the wind carried his words out to the deep blue sea, the tide continued its slow and determined advance onto the shoreline. Once again, the king repeated his command to the incoming tide to halt and not wet his feet and robes, but to no avail. Wave upon wave made its graceful forward-and-back dance upon the sand and the water level began to rise. The encroaching waves lapped gently around the legs of the king's chair, then splashed around the king's shoes with gentle slurps, wetting his feet and the hem of his robe. The king's officers stood by, not knowing how to react and wondering why their monarch continued to sit on his chair instead of stepping away from the water's edge.

After a few moments, Canute stood up, lifted the crown from his head and tossed it onto the dry sand. 'I shall never wear this symbol of my grandeur and might again,' he declared. 'My good men, it seems that I do not have quite as much power as you would have me believe. I hope all of you have learned an important lesson from what you witnessed today. No monarch, however mighty, can compare with the all-powerful King of Heaven, who commands the land, the sea, and the sky. You should be singing his praises and serving him above all earthly kings.'

They then headed back to the castle, the king sadder, but his followers wiser and deeply impressed by their monarch's humbleness and piety.

'That's a good story,' Akbar said. 'It's very important for monarchs to be reminded now and again that they are not all-powerful, especially against the forces of nature. So, what's next?'

Birbal sighed wearily and launched into another tale.

Once upon a time there lived a prosperous farmer in a hilly kingdom in the north of Hindustan. The farmer owned several acres of land and had divided up his farm into separate sections: one for poultry, another for cows and dairy farming, a third for goats, a fourth for sheep, and so on. The farmer had many shepherds working for him, and each supervised his section without much interference from the farmer.

One day, the shepherd in charge of the flock of sheep reported to the farmer that a few were missing when the herd returned after grazing in the hills. The shepherd suspected that the sheep had either been stolen, or carried off by a mountain lion or other predator. There were more than a hundred sheep in the flock who all looked alike, so it was difficult to keep track of them, he said in his defence.

'So, what did the farmer do?' Akbar asked eagerly, still wide awake even though it was nearing two o'clock in the morning.

The farmer immediately instructed that numbers be written in coal on the sheep's haunches. That would make it easier for the shepherd to keep track of the flock. But the farmer's strategy didn't work as planned. For one thing, it was impossible to keep count of the sheep as they all rushed into the pen in the evenings; and once they were inside the pen, they kept moving about, making it difficult for the shepherd to keep an accurate tally. Another problem arose after a day or two when the numbers marked on the sheep's white fleece got washed off in the rain. The farmer was forced to devise a new approach.

He built a high wooden fence around the sheep's enclosure and put up a narrow adjustable wooden gate at the entrance to the pen. The only way the sheep could get into the pen was by jumping over the low gate, and once they were all in the pen, the gate could be raised to the height of the fence. The shepherd in charge of the flock was instructed to position himself at the gate and count each sheep as it jumped over the barrier and into the pen.

On the day that the gate was inaugurated, the first white sheep jumped over it and ran to a distant corner of the pen. The shepherd counted aloud: 'One.' No sooner had the second white sheep vaulted over the gate and settled down to sleep, the shepherd called out: 'Two.' There was a short scuffle as two white sheep tried to jump over the narrow fence at the same time, but the shepherd was quick to note: 'Three and four.' Next, a fifth white sheep....

Akbar interrupted: 'I get the drift of your story, Birbal. How many of these white sheep are still to be counted?'

'We have only counted five so far, Your Majesty. I believe there are one hundred and fifteen still waiting to jump over the gate and be counted.'

'My goodness! When is this story going to end?' Akbar asked testily.

'Jahanpanah, it can end only when you stop asking "what's next?"' Birbal replied.

The emperor smiled. 'You've made your point, Birbal. Please let my courtiers know that the storytelling sessions are cancelled with immediate effect. Your tale about jumping fences has made me feel drowsy so I bid you good night. I will continue counting the remaining sheep until I fall asleep.'

86

Condemning All Sons-in-law

As he aged, Akbar became more petulant and cantankerous, occasionally passing hasty and imprudent judgements against anyone who upset him, including members of his family.

One day, it was his son-in-law's turn to incur the emperor's wrath. Akbar's eldest daughter had been married for more than a year and had moved from Fatehpur Sikri to Delhi. Missing her terribly, the doting father sent repeated requests to his son-in-law inviting the couple to visit him, but his daughter's lazy husband always made some excuse to avoid the long journey to his father-in-law's palace.

Having received another negative response from his son-in-law that very morning, Akbar was in a rage. When Birbal asked him what the problem was, Akbar explained: 'My wretched son-in-law is the problem. I haven't seen my daughter for more than a year, and the arrogant scoundrel comes up with all kinds of excuses to prevent me from meeting her. He uses his business or health or family issues as a pretext to avoid coming to Fatehpur Sikri, so I've sent him messages saying that if he cannot come himself then at least he could let my daughter visit. But he refuses. Can you believe that he has the audacity to disregard my requests?'

'Don't worry, Your Majesty,' Birbal said. 'I will arrange for your daughter to be brought here.'

'I've already tried to do that several times, Birbal. What makes you think that you can succeed where I have failed? My son-in-law is stubborn and possessive and flatly refuses to let my daughter travel without him. His behaviour is inexcusable.

I think there is only one way to resolve the situation, Birbal. I want you to arrange for gallows to be erected in all available open spaces across my realm, because I am issuing an edict for all sons-in-law in my kingdom to be hanged!' Akbar announced, thumping his fist on the table in front of him.

Stunned by the emperor's rash decision, Birbal tried to dissuade him from taking such a drastic and unwise step, but Akbar was adamant. When attempts to pacify him only made him angrier, Birbal gave up and issued instructions for gallows to be set up across the kingdom. Meanwhile, word of the emperor's edict had spread throughout his empire, causing panic among the populace. Entire delegations approached Birbal in secret, pleading with him to persuade the emperor to change his mind. 'I'll try my best,' Birbal promised, even as the building of gallows continued apace.

A week later, Birbal invited the emperor to inspect the gallows that had been erected all over the city and even in the palace grounds. Akbar was pleased that his instructions were being followed. 'Well done, Birbal,' he said. 'It will be a big relief when all the sons-in-law in my kingdom are eliminated.'

Turning a corner in the palace grounds, the emperor spotted two magnificent gallows, one made of gold and the other of silver. 'Who has given orders to put up those gallows in gold and silver?' Akbar asked angrily. 'It is a senseless waste of money.'

'It seemed the proper thing to do,' Birbal said softly.

'Proper?' Akbar thundered, flushed with rage. 'We are hanging sons-in-law here, not heads of state. For whom have you had these wastefully lavish gallows made?'

'The golden gallows is for you, Jahanpanah, and the silver one is for me,' Birbal replied.

'Golden gallows for me? Who has the audacity to send me to the gallows?'

'It is by your own order, O Supreme Commander. After all, you are also someone's son-in-law, as am I. How could we exempt ourselves from your decree? Tomorrow, as the most distinguished of sons-in-law in the realm, you must be the first one to be hanged, followed by your son-in-law, and then the others.'

Akbar was silent for a few moments. Turning around to walk back to the palace, stroking his chin pensively, he muttered: 'On further reflection, I think it will be very unfair to penalize all the innocent sons-in-law in my kingdom just because one has turned out to be a rascal. You can inform my people that I have decided to cancel the executions.'

News of Birbal's intervention and the emperor's change of heart led to great rejoicing across the realm as gallows were gleefully demolished. In the meantime, the emperor's son-in-law, feeling terribly guilty for having triggered panic and dread for all the innocent sons-in-law throughout the empire, immediately agreed to accompany his wife to visit her father.

87

A Rumour Quashed

One day, while Birbal was walking in the city, keeping his ears open to pick up any rumours floating around about the emperor and his court, a stranger came up to him and said: 'Greetings, huzoor. It is such a pleasure to encounter you in this splendid city. May you and our benevolent emperor be blessed with a long life!'

Birbal thanked the stranger and tried to walk on, but the man grabbed him by the sleeve and began relating his tale of woe. 'I have trudged more than twenty miles from my village with the sole desire of meeting you,' the stranger continued. 'All along the way, everyone I met was singing your praises, saying you are as generous as you are wise.'

Realizing that the stranger's fawning would inevitably lead to a request for money or a favour, Birbal extricated his sleeve from the man's grip and said: 'On your way home, please make sure to strongly deny those rumours about my generosity.'

88

The Right Answers

Birbal was taking a stroll in a garden near his house when a stranger approached him. 'Kind sir,' the man began, 'I'm told that the wise sage Birbal lives in this vicinity. Could you please tell me where I can meet him?'

'In a park,' Birbal replied.

'Where does he live?' the stranger persisted.

'In his house.'

'Why don't you give me his address?'

'Because you haven't asked for it,' Birbal said curtly.

'Isn't the information I need obvious to you?'

'No, it isn't,' Birbal said and walked away.

There was no one else to ask so the stranger followed Birbal. 'Sir, can you at least tell me if you know Birbal?'

'Yes, I do.'

'What is your name?'

'Birbal.'

'What a strange man you are!' the stranger said, visibly annoyed. 'Why couldn't you have told me who you are when I kept asking about you?'

'I based my answers on your questions,' Birbal said. 'But why were you looking for me? Do you need my help?'

'Yes, I do,' the stranger said. 'I need your help to resolve a family dispute. I've heard that you always give the fairest answers....' Birbal immediately agreed to help, being more forthcoming with his assistance than he had been with his replies to the man's queries, now that the questions were more challenging.

89

Birbal Helps His Arch-rival

As Birbal's reputation for being a just and wise arbitrator spread far and wide, Emperor Akbar began to rely on him more and more, much to the annoyance of his brother-in-law Raja Jaimal, whose ambition outstripped his abilities.

'Birbal has been a judge and adviser for several years now,' Jaimal complained to Akbar one day. 'Don't you think it's high time someone else took his place?'

Unable to deny his brother-in-law's request outright, Akbar said vaguely: 'I'll think about it.'

When news of Raja Jaimal's demand and the emperor's ambiguous reply reached Birbal, he immediately made up an excuse to take an extended break from his duties at the palace. Akbar had no choice but to appoint his brother-in-law as his principal adviser. While Jaimal was gloating over his success in getting rid of Birbal, Akbar summoned him and said: 'Jaimal, to welcome you to your new position, I hereby present you these three hundred gold coins. I want you to spend them in such a way that I get a hundred gold coins in this life, another hundred gold coins in the next world, and the last one hundred coins neither here nor there but somewhere in between.'

Jaimal was utterly stumped by the emperor's demand and cursed his brother-in-law's propensity for playing mind games with people. Struggling for days and sleepless nights to crack the riddle, he had no recourse but to turn to Birbal for help.

As Jaimal explained his dilemma, Birbal said: 'Give me the gold coins and let me handle the matter.'

With the bag of gold coins hidden in his cloak, Birbal began to patrol the city streets and formalize his plan. Turning into a wealthy neighbourhood with its tree-lined avenues, spacious brick houses, and large gardens, Birbal came across a lavish wedding celebration. Going up to the rich merchant who was celebrating his son's nuptials, Birbal handed him one hundred gold coins and said: 'Please accept this gift from Emperor Akbar along with his blessings and felicitations for your son's wedding.' Flattered and honoured that the king had sent a special envoy with such a generous gift, the merchant invited Birbal to join the wedding feast but when Birbal politely declined, the merchant instead presented him with several expensive gifts and a bag of gold coins for the king.

Birbal then headed for an area of the city where the poor lived. From the local grocers and shopkeepers, he bought food and clothing worth a hundred gold coins and distributed them in the name of the emperor. A grateful crowd gathered around him and showered blessings on the monarch and his emissary.

Heading back to the city, Birbal organized an impromptu music recital, free for the audience but where the performers were paid one hundred gold coins.

When Birbal walked into the durbar the next day, Akbar was overjoyed to see him. 'I'm so glad that you are back, Birbal,' the emperor said, rising from his throne to welcome his adviser. Bowing respectfully, Birbal announced that he had completed the tasks that had been assigned by the emperor to his brother-in-law.

'How did you manage that?' Akbar asked, settling back on the throne.

Birbal recounted the events of the previous day, adding: 'Jahanpanah, the money I gave to the merchant for his son's wedding has been repaid to you in this life. The money spent on food and clothing for the poor have been converted into blessings that you will get in your next life. The money that

I spent on the music concert—though enjoyed by many—was only a fleeting occurrence, so you won't get it back either here or there.'

As the courtiers burst into applause, Raja Jaimal resigned from his post and Birbal was reinstated as the emperor's official right-hand man.

90

The Art Competition

Renowned for being a patron of the arts, Akbar's court was an open house for writers, poets, musicians, dancers, sculptors, and artists. Now and again, the emperor would issue a challenge to each of these groups and present a lucrative reward to the winner.

To appease his brother-in-law, who was still sulking for being deposed from his post as adviser, Akbar decided to hold an art competition, and appointed Raja Jaimal and Birbal to judge the works of art and select one entry each. Akbar would decide the winner and award a purse of gold coins to the artist who painted the best picture depicting peace.

Artists from the emperor's courts in Delhi, Agra, and Fatehpur Sikri submitted an extraordinary array of paintings—blissful portraits of mothers and children, sleeping babies, priests at prayer, people meditating, doves flying, swans gliding in lotus ponds, flowers blooming, idyllic landscapes, and so on.

Jaimal scrutinized the submissions and finally picked his favourite. It was a serene depiction of a peaceful lake, whose crystal-clear waters perfectly mirrored the towering mountains surrounding it. Above the majestic forested peaks was a pale-blue sky dotted with fluffy white clouds. Everyone who saw it thought it was a perfect representation of peace. It appeared to be the top choice of the courtiers.

The painting selected by Birbal was also a landscape of mountains, but these were craggy and bare. Above them was a sky covered with dark clouds from which rain fell accompanied by bolts of lightning. In the forefront of the painting there was a cascading waterfall that ended in swirls of foam. It wasn't exactly the kind of picture one would think of as depicting serenity. When the emperor and his courtiers looked at the painting more closely, they saw a tiny shrub growing out of a crevice in the rock beside the waterfall. A bird had built her nest in that bush, and within a few feet of the angry torrent of water pouring down beside her, the mother bird was sitting on her eggs in the nest in perfect peace.

Puzzled by Birbal's choice of painting, Akbar thought it best to give both judges a chance to explain their selections.

For once, Raja Jaimal was brief: 'I chose this landscape because it is an embodiment of peace and tranquillity. One feels calmer merely by looking at it. Need I say more?'

Now it was Birbal's turn. 'Most Serene Majesty,' he began, 'I picked this painting because I have a different philosophy about peace. To my mind, peace does not imply a place where there is no noise, no danger, no discord. Real peace means being in the midst of all these things and still having the ability to be calm at heart. True peace comes from within us. That is the real meaning of peace. That tiny bird sitting serenely in her nest despite all the turmoil around her is a true embodiment of peace.'

Akbar awarded the prize money to Birbal's choice, and the fickle courtiers applauded. All except Raja Jaimal, who had got it wrong once again.

91

Just Imagine

A few weeks after the art contest, Akbar turned to Birbal and said: 'I was very impressed to note that you have a keen eye for art, Birbal. I'm sure you must be a good artist yourself. I want you to create a painting for me on any subject of your choice.'

'But, huzoor,' Birbal objected, 'I have never drawn in my life and have no artistic talent. How can I possibly create a painting for you that will meet your high standards?'

'No excuses, Birbal.' The emperor, who was never refused anything by his courtiers, was adamant. 'Bring me a painting in a month's time or face the consequences. Use your imagination.'

A few weeks later, Birbal entered the durbar carrying a medium-sized frame covered with cloth. Akbar was delighted that Birbal had obeyed his orders but his smile disappeared when he unveiled the canvas. Three-fourths of the painting was of a blue sky with daubs of white cloud and the rest was of mud-brown ground with a few blades of green grass sticking out here and there.

'What is this amateurish painting supposed to depict?' Akbar asked angrily, much to the delight of the courtiers.

'Most Discerning Majesty, it is a landscape of a herd of cows grazing in a field,' came the calm reply.

'Where are the cows and where is the grass?'

'As instructed by you, I used my imagination and allowed the cows to eat the grass and return to their shed.'

Akbar laughed and said: 'Your artwork leaves a lot to be desired but I cannot fault your witty clarification!'

92

A Tax on Fools

When not attending to affairs of state or waging wars to extend his empire, Akbar had a tendency to concoct bizarre assignments to keep his courtiers busy.

Thinking aloud, the emperor said to Birbal: 'I've come to realize that we have to bear the cost of other people's foolishness, while the fools get away without paying anything. It is most unfair that sensible people should have to pay the price for the stupidity of others. I think the only way to redress the balance is to initiate a tax on fools. In order to impose this tax, I will need a list of all the fools in my kingdom. Please start preparing the list right away.'

Birbal sighed and began drawing up the longlist of every fool in the empire. While he was preoccupied with this time-consuming challenge, a pearl trader from Bahrain stopped by at the royal court and was granted an audience with the emperor, who had a penchant for collecting precious gems from around the world.

From a pocket in his thobe, the trader fished out a small cloth bag containing pearls of various shapes, sizes, and colours. An oval pearl, the size of a quail's egg, caught the emperor's eye.

'O Most Discerning of Men,' the pearl trader began, 'you have picked out the most prized gem in my collection. If you hold this beauty up to the light you will see its subtle lustre and rarest of rare pink hues. I call this pearl Blushing Bride because of its glowing tint.'

'It is indeed an exquisite gem. I have never seen another like it,' the emperor said, turning the pearl around and admiring its beauty.

'O Jewel among Men,' the trader said, 'I have been diving for pearls for more than fifteen years and have a few more priceless gems identical to this one at my shop in Bahrain. If you are interested in adding them to your legendary collection of gems, I will consider it an honour to sell you ten of my largest pearls, this one included, for a hundred gold coins each. As I have to make the long journey by road and sea to Bahrain and back, I would be grateful if full payment could be made to me in advance. You may keep the Blushing Bride and I assure you that her nine equally stunning bridesmaids will be in your possession within the month.'

Akbar signalled to his treasurer to hand over a thousand gold coins to the pearl trader, who was so overjoyed at receiving this bounty that he walked the entire length of the large durbar hall to the exit backwards, bowing all the way.

When Birbal heard about this impulsive transaction, he decided to speak to Akbar about it.

'Huzoor, is it true that you gave the Bahraini trader one thousand gold coins for ten pearls after seeing only one sample?'

'Birbal, you know I have a keen eye for jewellery and am something of an expert. The pink pearl he showed me was so exquisite, it will be one of the most prized gems in my collection. I think I struck a good deal with the trader today,' Akbar replied.

'Did anyone at court introduce this man or recommend him to you? Isn't it risky to trust someone who walks in off the street?'

'Birbal, unlike you, I am not suspicious of everyone I meet. I don't think people cheat you if you put your trust in them,' Akbar said, not noticing Birbal rolling his eyes in disbelief. 'And by the way, how is the register of fools coming along? Is it nearly ready?'

'It is almost ready, huzoor, I only have to add one name.'

The following day, Birbal presented a lengthy scroll to the emperor. Taking a while to unfurl the bulky parchment, the emperor was shocked to see the name Jalaluddin Muhammad Akbar heading the list of fools in the kingdom.

'What is the meaning of this, Birbal?' Akbar yelled. 'How dare you add my name to this list?'

'Most Revered Monarch, far be it from me to cause you any distress. But you have entrusted one thousand gold coins to an unknown person from a far-off land whom you don't know and may never see again. Isn't that foolish?'

Gritting his teeth, Akbar replied: 'The man has promised that he will be back within the month.'

'Well, if he does turn up, I will remove your name from the list and replace it with his,' Birbal replied.

Suppressing a smile, Akbar said: 'On second thoughts, I think we should give up the idea to collect a tax from fools. Nobody will want to be assessed in that category.'

'That is a sensible decision, Exalted Leader,' Birbal replied. 'I think it would be easier and more beneficial for us to collect revenue if we call it a tax for the wise. Even the fools in your empire will be delighted to pay a wisdom tax.'

Akbar rubbed his chin and nodded as he considered Birbal's suggestion.

'If all the foolish people in the land come up with what they think are clever ways of avoiding the fools' tax, it will only make more work for us all,' continued his adviser. 'One should always be wary of fools who think they are too smart.'

93

For the Best

While hunting deer in a dense forest several miles away from Fatehpur Sikri, Akbar and Birbal somehow became separated from the rest of the hunting party. After riding for several hours, calling for help in the vain hope that the royal entourage was within earshot, the emperor and his trusted adviser had to accept that they were hopelessly lost.

Tired and thirsty, their mashq empty, the duo decided to give their horses a rest in a shady spot under a canopy of trees. Akbar was incensed that his attendants had failed to keep up with him. 'This is the height of incompetence,' he fumed. 'How on earth did my courtiers manage to lose sight of me?'

'Everything happens for the best, huzoor,' said Birbal calmly. 'Don't you recall that about twenty years ago you were in a similar predicament in a forest near Agra where we met for the first time? There are always hidden forces at work that steer us on the right path. Let us ride on further until we reach a river or lake.'

'What is the use of ruling an empire that boasts a hundred rivers if I cannot get a drink of water when I need it?' Akbar muttered as they rode on.

'Be patient, My Lord, it will be for the best,' Birbal repeated.

Irritated by Birbal's optimism, the emperor rode on in stony silence, his wazir by his side, until they suddenly spotted a small well a short distance away. Reining in their horses, Akbar ordered Birbal to get him a drink of water from the well.

'Your wish is my command,' Birbal said, dismounting and heading for the well with his mashq. Behind him, Akbar dismounted from his steed and started to follow Birbal, but tripped on a small rock and fell headlong, managing to break his fall with both hands. Hearing the emperor calling out in pain, Birbal rushed to his assistance. Akbar's palms were badly grazed and bleeding, and the only thing Birbal could do to help was pour water from his mashq to clean and soothe the emperor's injuries.

'What a calamitous day this is turning out to be,' Akbar grumbled, dabbing at his bleeding palms with the edge of his silk turban, which had come undone when he fell.

'Everything happens for the best. I'm certain some good will come out of these mishaps,' Birbal said.

'Birbal, that is a ridiculous and insensitive thing to say when you can see that I am hurt and in pain. This is neither the time nor the place for your platitudes. Take your horse and get out of my sight,' Akbar said angrily. Thinking it best not to argue, Birbal took his horse by the reins and walked off into the dense forest ahead of them.

As Akbar raised the mashq to his lips to take a sip of water, he heard a rustling sound behind him and realized that he was not alone. Veering around, he saw four fierce-looking tribesmen with white streaks painted on their faces and across their bare chests, pointing their sharp spears at him.

The leader of the tribesmen approached Akbar slowly and said: 'I am Zofar, chief of the cannibals. You have trespassed into our land. Now we must sacrifice you to our god and then feast on you.'

Holding up his hands with palms facing outwards, to keep the cannibals at bay, Akbar said: 'I am Emperor Akbar of Hindustan. All this land belongs to me, so it is you who are trespassing. I can order my soldiers to execute each one of you.'

The painted tribesmen did not pay much heed to the emperor's threats but were staring at his bleeding hands. Zofar took a step back and said: 'It would be an affront to our god to offer you as a sacrifice. It is forbidden to sacrifice injured persons or animals to the gods. Your bleeding hands have saved your life. We'll have to find something else for our dinner.' All four men turned around and vanished into the thick forest.

Relieved at his narrow escape, Akbar waited until the tribesmen had moved out of earshot, and began calling out to Birbal, who had hidden behind a tree and witnessed the emperor's encounter with the tribesmen. Apologizing profusely for banishing him, Akbar added: 'Birbal, as always, you were right. At least in my case, everything did happen for the best.'

Birbal replied: 'Hidden forces were at work for me too, Jahanpanah. Your injured palms saved your life, and being banished into the woods saved mine. If I had been here with you, I would have ended up being the cannibals' dinner.'

Akbar looked shocked at the thought of Birbal ending up in a cauldron, and started to feel a little better about evicting him. 'Ultimately,' concluded Birbal, 'it is fate that determines whether one man's good fortune should mean misfortune for another.'

94

Breaking a Friendship

Prince Salim's childhood had been very different from that of his father's, who had spent his early years living in exile and in the care of aunts and other relatives. Salim, on the other hand, had been brought up in the lap of luxury, his every whim indulged by his parents and everyone around him.

At seventeen, the age at which his father had already been emperor for three years, Prince Salim shouldered no responsibilities but preferred whiling away his time with his best friend, Harivansh, the son of a wealthy merchant. Both teenagers spent hours in each other's company, ignoring their tutors and duties, playing cards or chess instead.

One day, Harivansh's father approached Birbal for help. 'Huzoor,' the merchant said, 'my only son and Prince Salim are very close friends. I am not opposed to their friendship but feel that it should not be my son's main focus. The prince will one day become the ruler of Hindustan whether he has learned anything or not. But my son will have to work for his living, and he will not succeed if he doesn't learn how to manage the business. My wealth won't last forever, and I'm worried about my son's future if he doesn't master my trade.'

'Don't worry,' Birbal reassured the merchant, 'I'll sort things out.'

When Birbal mentioned the merchant's concerns to the emperor, Akbar said: 'The queen and I too are worried about their friendship. The queen thinks Harivansh is a bad influence on Salim and should be banished from the kingdom. She wants to send Salim to live with her parents for a few months, but I don't think that will help. Salim needs to stay here and learn the art of statecraft. Harivansh is only required to manage his small business, which anyone can do. But Salim will have to govern an entire kingdom and must do so wisely and well.'

'Huzoor, what is your hukum? Do you want me to try and end their friendship?'

'I know it is never a good thing to break up a friendship, but I think in this case it will be the best thing for them both,' Akbar said, rubbing his chin.

That evening, Birbal dropped in to Prince Salim's quarters, and found the two friends lounging on a divan playing cards. Birbal made small talk with Salim for a few minutes and then turning to Harivansh, he said: 'Come here, Harivansh. I need to talk to you about something highly confidential.' Birbal put an arm round Harivansh's shoulder, led him to a distant corner of the room and whispered something in the boy's ear. Harivansh looked puzzled but before he could speak, Birbal walked out of the room, saying: 'Please don't tell anyone what I told you.'

Salim was overcome with curiosity. 'What did he say? Tell me what he said,' he urged his friend.

'I couldn't make any sense of what he said,' Harivansh replied.

'How dare you lie to me! With my own two ears I heard Birbal say that he was telling you something in confidence. I'm supposed to be your best friend, and this is how you treat me?' Salim said indignantly.

'You are my dearest friend, Salim, but please believe me—I couldn't make any sense of what Birbal mumbled in my ear. I think he said something like "even the smallest river flows into the mighty ocean". It made no sense at all.'

'Liar! You are making this up and hiding the truth from me,' Salim yelled angrily. 'Why would Birbal tell you something so idiotic and ask you not to tell anyone? If you cannot confide in me, it means that I cannot trust you and we cannot be friends.'

'You're an arrogant fool,' Harivansh shouted back, 'because you don't believe the truth. I cannot be friends with someone who doesn't trust me.'

Prince Salim and Harivansh never spoke to each other again, and while the merchant's son went on to master his father's trade, the prince eventually ascended the throne as Emperor Jahangir, but was unable to attain his father's glorious heights.

95

What's in a Name?

It had been a trying day at the durbar, during which Akbar had presided over a long and petty dispute between two watchmen. After the petitioners and supplicants had left, the emperor said to Birbal: 'I have often observed that people who have the words "wan", and "baan" appended to their professions—such as gadiwan[*], kochwan[†], and darbaan[‡]—are invariably very quarrelsome by nature.'

Without a moment's hesitation, Birbal exclaimed: 'As always, you are absolutely right, meherbaan.[§]'

As the courtiers struggled to suppress their laughter, the emperor was silent, stumped by Birbal's swift comeback.

---

[*] cart driver
[†] coach driver
[‡] watchman
[§] one who is merciful

96

A Test for Husbands

During the stifling summers, when temperatures soared and the palace punkahs, sprinkled with scented water, waged a losing battle against the dry heat, the regular afternoon durbar sessions were invariably cancelled. While most of his courtiers were enjoying their afternoon siestas, Akbar would summon Birbal to the palace to discuss affairs of state and other matters.

Discussing his army's latest conquest, Akbar was singing the praises of his commanders' bravery when Birbal observed: 'I am certain that all of these men though assertive and in command on the battlefield, meekly follow orders from their wives at home.'

'I would never let my wives order me around,' Akbar said confidently and then hastily added: 'But I do humour them sometimes and let them have their way, for my peace of mind. I therefore strongly disagree with you that all men are controlled by their wives.' With that, the emperor and his wazir decided to put the matter to the test.

All the married courtiers were summoned to attend the evening durbar, at which Birbal announced:

> His Majesty has invited you here to try to resolve a timeless mystery. He wants to know how many of you comply with your wives' commands and how many of you command your wives. You are urged to respond to the emperor's question honestly, bearing in mind that the penalty for those who do not reply truthfully will be harsh. Now let us proceed.... All those who follow their

> wives' instructions are ordered by the emperor to gather on the left side of the hall. Those who are head of their households and not under their wife's control should move to the right of the hall.

A few minutes of chaos ensued as the courtiers, perspiring from the heat and perplexed by the instructions, shuffled about the durbar hall in confusion, none of them wanting to be the first to move to the left. A few of them headed to the right of the hall and then swiftly did an about-turn, fearing they would be penalized for being untruthful. Eventually, realizing that most of the assembly was veering towards one side, they all stood in a line on the left side of the hall. Satisfied that they had all made the correct choice, the courtiers were astonished to see one solitary young man standing bravely on the right-hand side of the hall.

Akbar smiled and clapped his hands in delight at the sight of the lone figure. 'I am delighted to note that I have at least one brave heart among my courtiers, a strong young man who does not let his wife dictate to him. His valour shall be rewarded.'

Before Akbar could issue instructions to his treasurer, Birbal hastily whispered in his ear: 'Huzoor, let me first find out why he is the only one in this august assembly who is standing on the other side of the hall. He may have misunderstood the question.'

'You are too cynical, Birbal. You shouldn't be so distrustful of the human race,' Akbar said.

'It is actually the opposite, O Wise One. It is because of my study of human nature that I would like to question this young man.' Walking up to the youth, Birbal asked him why he had not joined the rest of the men on the left of the hall.

The young man replied: 'Sir, it's like this.... My wife comes from a family of scholars and is wise beyond her years. The other day I asked her what would be the best way for me to impress our revered emperor given that I am merely one amongst hundreds of his courtiers. My wife said that the best way to impress our mighty monarch is to stand out from the crowd and not follow the majority. She believes that the majority opinion is often wrong. When you posed the question to the court, I remembered my wife's advice and decided not to go along with the majority decision.'

Loud applause rang out in the court as the emperor bestowed a handsome reward on the honest youth, saying: 'Well, young man, you have certainly succeeded in making me notice you.'

Birbal added, with just a hint of a smile: 'I'm sure His Majesty has also noticed that behind every outwardly strong man there is a formidable woman.'

97

Justice versus Gold

On another quiet day at the durbar, Akbar turned to his trusted wazir and asked: 'Birbal, when passing judgements, do you think it is more important to be just or to be merciful?'

'That would depend on which side of the case one is on, Your Majesty,' Birbal replied. 'The victim of a crime will be hoping for justice. The perpetrator of the crime will be hoping for mercy. Justice and mercy are highly complex matters, wherein the expertise lies in tempering justice with mercy and mercy with justice.'

'That is true,' the emperor said, while the jealous courtiers grudgingly nodded in agreement. 'Now I have a tricky question for you, Birbal. If I gave you a choice between justice and a gold coin, which one would you choose?'

'O Most Righteous amongst Rulers, there is nothing tricky about the choice you have put before me. Without any hesitation, I would choose the gold coin.'

'You would prefer a gold coin to justice?' Akbar exclaimed in disbelief.

'Yes, Refuge of the World, I would pick the gold coin over justice,' said Birbal softly.

The other courtiers pretended to be shocked at Birbal's blunder but were secretly pleased that he had gone and damaged his reputation.

'Birbal, I don't know what to say. I would have been disheartened if any of my courtiers or subjects had said this, but I would certainly not have expected this of you,' Akbar spluttered. 'Coming from you, it is nothing short of scandalous. I was unaware that you were capable of stooping so low and being so avaricious.'

'Most Generous Majesty,' Birbal replied calmly, 'people usually ask for things that they do not have. Your wise and benevolent rule has ensured that every one of your citizens has access to justice. Because justice is readily available to me too, I opted for the gold coin, of which I am more in need.'

Placated and pleased by Birbal's reply, Akbar ordered his treasurer to give Birbal a purse containing one hundred gold coins. The disgruntled courtiers were disappointed that Birbal had not only triumphed again but had also been richly rewarded in the bargain.

98

Birbal Proves His Worth

His courtiers' jealousy of Birbal had become so routine that Akbar invariably chose to ignore their grumbling and complaints.

One day, when word reached him about a smarmy courtier's attempt to make a joke of the emperor's confidence in a country bumpkin who lived by his wits and was not half as clever as he made himself out to be, Akbar decided to put an end to the protests and backbiting once and for all.

'Since you are all against Birbal, I will leave it to you to sort out the next challenge that presents itself in my court,' the emperor told his courtiers. 'Birbal will stay out of it.'

The opportunity arose a few days later, when a stranger presented himself at Akbar's court one morning and introduced himself as a polyglot fluent in more than fifteen languages. 'Jahanpanah, I can speak many languages including Hindi, Urdu, Persian, Telugu, Tamil, Kannada, Marathi, Malayalam, Gujarati, Bengali, Odia, Punjabi, and others, each one as fluently as if it were my native tongue. I have travelled for many days to reach your durbar, and I'd like to put the wise men of your court to the test to see if they can identify where I am from, and which of the languages is my mother tongue.'

Impressed by the scholar's confidence, Akbar readily accepted the challenge. His courtiers hailed from all over Hindustan and its neighbouring countries, and one or other of them would definitely be able to figure out where the multilingual scholar was from. Birbal was to play no part in unravelling the mystery. For the entire day, one by one, each courtier spoke in his mother tongue with the stranger, who responded with the fluency of a native speaker. The scholar was so well acquainted with the poetry and prose of every one of the languages, that each of the courtiers was convinced that he hailed from his part of the country. They couldn't all be right, and not wanting to be proved wrong, the courtiers eventually admitted that they were unable to pinpoint the scholar's origins.

Akbar was about to give his courtiers a tongue-lashing, when Birbal came to their rescue. 'Jahanpanah,' he said, 'this has been a time-consuming exercise for the courtiers, and it is quite late. Let's offer our visitor hospitality for the night and resume the challenge tomorrow.' The stranger was taken to the royal guest house, where he enjoyed a lavish meal before going to bed.

In a deep sleep after his tiring day, the scholar woke with a start when he heard loud banging sounds behind his bed. In the pitch dark, in an unfamiliar room, unable to make out what was causing the noise, the bewildered scholar jumped out of bed and ran out of the room calling for help. Finding Birbal standing in the corridor, the stranger explained what had happened. Birbal calmed him down: 'There's nothing to worry about. Your window was left unlatched, and is banging against the frame because of the wind. You can safely go back to bed but make sure you latch the window first.'

The next morning, the scholar returned to court to thank the emperor for his hospitality before continuing on his journey. Before he could speak, Birbal stepped forward and declared: 'Your Majesty, we are honoured to have in our midst a man of great learning and erudition. It is not often that one comes across a person who can speak so many languages so fluently. I am certain that he comes from Gujarat and his native language is Gujarati.'

Birbal's announcement took everyone by surprise, not least the courtiers and especially the scholar. With folded hands, the scholar bowed to Akbar and then to Birbal. 'I am indeed a Gujarati,' he said. 'For the past thirty years I have travelled across the length and breadth of Hindustan and no one has been able to identify my mother tongue. Your educated and well-spoken courtiers tested me for the entire day yesterday but could not do so either. I'm amazed that Huzoor Birbal guessed correctly.'

'Tell us how you figured it out, Birbal,' Akbar commanded.

'I gave the matter some thought and came to the conclusion that when multilingual people feel fearful or panicky, they would instinctively speak in their first language...their mother tongue. Last night, when our guest was sleeping soundly, I repeatedly banged the window of his room rather loudly. Our guest woke up frightened and confused and rushed out of the room shouting in Gujarati, "What's going on? What's happening? God, please help me." And that's how I identified his native tongue.'

Akbar turned to face his courtiers. 'The charge of favouritism towards Birbal that you levy against me is blatantly false. I think you have seen for yourselves why I value Birbal so highly. He managed to figure out where our visitor was from without even conversing with him. He manages to solve mysteries that perplex all of you, even though he occasionally resorts to unconventional methods to do so. An adviser such as Birbal is worth his weight in gold to a king.'

Meanwhile, the scholar, adequately compensated for the inconvenience that had been imposed on him the night before, continued his travels around the country, singing the praises of the emperor and his wazir in a multiplicity of languages.

99

Question Time

Emperor Akbar's court was famous for its sharp and learned debates and discussions, where the cleverest ripostes usually came from Birbal. Soon, these regular question and answer sessions became a thinly veiled attempt by the emperor's courtiers—including the Navratnas—to get the better of Birbal, during which they would throw questions at him at lightning speed in an attempt to outfox him.

During one such gathering, Raja Todar Mal began the grilling: 'Name one trait that will stand a man in good stead throughout his life.'

'His own good sense,' Birbal replied.

Next, Faizi asked: 'Can you name an unconquerable enemy?'

'Death,' came the reply.

Abdul Rahim Khan-i-Khanan asked: 'Is there anything in the world that remains imperishable even after death?'

'One's fame.'

'Is there anything that cannot be regained once it is lost?' Mullah Do-Piyaza asked.

'Many things cannot be regained after they are lost,' Birbal replied. 'To name just three of them—life, a good reputation, and trust cannot be salvaged once they are lost.'

The court musician Mian Tansen asked: 'What is the most harmonious sound in the world?'

'A voice raised in prayer and praise of God.'

Fakir Aziao-Din asked: 'Can anything travel faster than the wind?'

'Yes, a man's thoughts.'

Finally, it was Emperor Akbar's turn. 'What are the qualities that make a king great?'

'Wisdom, humility, and compassion.'

'And what are the most undesirable qualities in a king?' Akbar asked.

'That's a good question, Jahanpanah. A king's virtues or vices always have direct consequences for his people, and history reminds us that a king who loves glory is far more dangerous than one who loves pleasure.... To my mind, injustice and lack of empathy can be the downfall of a king and his kingdom.'

Looking very pleased with these responses, the emperor said: 'You have taught us a lot today, Birbal. Do you have any questions for us?'

'Just one question, huzoor. When is this quizzing frenzy going to end?'

100

The Final Battle

Birbal was so trusted by Akbar, that he was often chosen to command the emperor's large army in combat. During a perilous battle in Afghanistan, Birbal was grievously injured and knew that the end was nigh. The men under his command wanted to send a messenger to Fatehpur Sikri to inform the emperor about Birbal's condition, but he prevented them from doing so.

In severe pain and drifting in and out of consciousness, Birbal dictated a letter to be handed to the emperor when the army headed back to Hindustan. The message read:

> My Lord and Master,
>
> It has been a privilege to have served in your court. Not a day has gone by over the last thirty years when I have not offered thanks to the hidden forces that led to a chance encounter with Your Majesty in a forest outside Agra. You were lost, but in that moment, I found a leader worthy of the name.
>
> From you I learned the power of humility, the importance of being open-minded, and the strength that comes from facing one's weaknesses.
>
> Your Majesty, do not grieve for me when I am gone. Think of it not as an ending but a new beginning for us both. Remember that everything happens for the best.
>
> Your humble servant,
>
> Birbal

History records that Akbar was devastated at the passing of his trusted adviser, who had served him faithfully for three decades, proclaiming it the greatest tragedy he had experienced since coming to the throne. So upset was the emperor that he did not eat for a few days and ordered two days of court mourning.

No one was appointed to Birbal's post for the rest of Akbar's reign. No one could ever take his place.

PART III

THE LORE OF COMMON SENSE

The stories in the last section of this volume are retellings of fables, folk tales, myths, and parables from around the world, centred on the disputes, dilemmas, misunderstandings, and predicaments that have overwhelmed humans since time immemorial and continue to do so. The cast of characters includes God, Love, the Devil, royalty, a cantankerous vampire, innocent children, wishful thinkers, daydreamers, foolish knaves, and wise animals; each in their own way becomes an object lesson in good sense and a reminder that disagreements only matter if we let them.

101

Time for Love

Legend has it that, a long time ago, all the emotions lived together on a large island in the middle of a vast ocean. Joy, Sadness, Unhappiness, Enthusiasm, Anxiety, Confusion, Concern, Curiosity, Fear, Panic, Pleasure, Confidence, Contentment, Friendship, Trust, Anger, Irritation, Optimism, Nostalgia, Misery, Love, Hate, Power, Pride, Kindness, Shyness, Sympathy—every feeling known to man—dwelt on the island, coexisting with each other regardless of their similarities or differences.

One day, the residents were informed that, because of warmer temperatures and rising sea levels, their island was in danger of sinking and they would all have to move. The news was received with mixed feelings: Enthusiasm cheerfully suggested that all the emotions immediately get busy and make boats to escape from the island; Irritation griped that the timing couldn't have been worse because he had just spent a fortune renovating his house; and Power was forced to admit that he was helpless when up against the vagaries of nature. Faced with looming disaster, many emotions got on board and began planning their getaway, everyone except Love. As the island slowly began to sink, and even Optimism began to face reality, Love was the only one who turned a blind eye to the fast-approaching calamity.

While most of her friends were packing their belongings and setting sail in search of a new home, Love—never one to give up easily on anyone or anything she cared about, especially in times of adversity—was still living in her dream world, reluctant to leave her beloved home on the sinking island, which was now inundated by seawater and lashed by heavy rain. Eventually, when the island was almost completely submerged and it was too late to build her own boat, Love decided to ask for help.

Seeing Contentment sailing by in a grand yacht, Love called out: 'Contentment, can you take me with you?'

'Sorry, I can't,' smiled Contentment. 'My boat is overflowing with many of the good things in life and I'm afraid there's no room for you.'

Pride was the next one to sail by, steering a stately vessel. 'Pride, can you please help me?' Love cried out.

'I can't help you, Love. You're wet and you'll only dirty my boat, of which I am very proud,' came the reply.

Love watched as Hate passed by in a black boat, followed closely by Sadness, so Love pleaded: 'My old friend Sadness, please let me go with you.'

'Oh, Love. I'm sorry but I'm feeling so miserable at having to abandon my home that I need to be by myself,' she moaned.

Next, Joy passed by, so cheerful and humming to herself that she didn't even hear Love calling out to her. Love watched helplessly as Anger rowed past furiously. Concern didn't seem to be bothered about anyone but herself. Shyness could barely be seen on her boat, which edged past very slowly, as if trying not to disturb the water's surface. Unhappiness was too busy trying to catch up with Contentment to stop to pick up passengers. Fear and Panic, who were sharing Anxiety's rickety and unsteady boat, were too scared to take Love on board, no matter how much she pleaded. Beginning to despair, Love called out to her ally, Friendship, who was clinging on to Nostalgia's creaky old dinghy and didn't hear her. Misery seemed desperate to get away from the island and couldn't see for crying, and Confusion was going backwards, so Love decided to steer clear of them.

Suddenly, a fierce storm broke out and Love was beginning to despair when a deep voice said: 'Come with me, Love.

I'll take you away from the island safely.' Love stepped into a boat that was being rowed by a tall and dignified man, with wavy white hair down to his shoulders and a long white beard. Her rescuer was struggling to keep them afloat in the lashing rain and surging waves. Love held on to the side of the violently rocking boat feeling too scared and nauseous to make conversation with him. Relieved to finally reach dry land, Love hastily got off the boat, but before she could thank the man or even ask him his name, he had rowed away.

Seeing Curiosity standing nearby, Love asked: 'Do you know the name of the man who helped me?'

'It was Time,' Curiosity replied. 'Didn't you recognize him?'

'Time?' asked Love. 'Why would Time come to my rescue?'

Curiosity smiled and said: 'Because only Time understands the value of Love, and how essential you are for the world. After all, it is only with Time's help that your true worth is revealed.'

The Richest Man in the Kingdom

Pandemonium broke out in the imperial palace following the royal soothsayer's alarming revelation to the privy council. 'I've had a strong premonition that the richest man in the kingdom will die before midnight tonight,' he declared worryingly. In two decades of service to the sovereign, the soothsayer's prophecies had always come to pass so there was no cause for doubt. Now, someone needed to inform the king.

The onerous task of passing on the bad news fell on the stooped shoulders of the chamberlain, who spent several minutes pondering how to break the news to the monarch. With only fourteen hours to go before midnight, there was not a moment to lose. Hastening into the hall where the king and queen were holding court, the chamberlain announced: 'I'm afraid I have bad news, Your Majesty.'

'Bad news?' the king exclaimed. 'Has the prince gone and done something foolish again?'

'No, Your Majesty. It's nothing like that.'

'What is it then? Are my enemies planning to wage war against me?'

'No, Your Majesty. It's much worse than that.'

'Are my own people and army planning a coup?'

'No, it's something of far greater importance,' the chamberlain replied. Taking a deep breath, he blurted out: 'The soothsayer has had a vision that the richest man in the kingdom will die at midnight tonight.'

It took a few seconds for the king to grasp the significance of the prophecy. 'Good gracious,' he exclaimed, 'the richest man in the kingdom would be me!'

Overcome by this proclamation, the queen swooned and nearly slid off her throne. While her ladies-in-waiting fussed around and tried to calm her down, the king instructed the chamberlain to summon his advisers.

Within minutes, they shuffled into the court and the chamberlain was ordered to give them the bad news. Clearing his throat, he announced: 'It has come to His Majesty's attention that the richest man in the kingdom will die at midnight tonight.'

The advisers turned to each other and expressed their shock and dismay at the news. As they gradually grasped the implications of the announcement, one of them exclaimed: 'But, Your Majesty, the richest man in the kingdom would be you! What shall we do?'

'That's for you to tell me, you fools!' the king roared. 'What do you think I'm paying you for? You are my advisers, so go ahead and advise me.'

The advisers went into a huddle to discuss the matter. One of them piped up: 'We think you should make a will.'

'I have already done that. You'll have to come up with a better plan.'

The advisers went into a huddle again and a frantic whispered discussion ensued for a few minutes. Finally, one of them said: 'We have a suggestion, Your Majesty. We are of the view that if you are not the richest man in the kingdom then you won't die at midnight tonight.'

'But I am the richest man!'

'You could save your life if you give your wealth away....'

'Give it away?' the king repeated slowly as if he could not believe his ears, while the queen fell into a faint and her ladies-in-waiting rushed to her side again, armed with smelling salts and lace handkerchiefs.

'The choice is yours, sire. Would you rather be poor or dead?'

'Neither!' the king yelled imperiously. 'I'd rather be alive and rich.'

'So you shall be, Your Majesty,' said the adviser. 'Here's the strategy. If you were to give away your riches to someone—only temporarily—then that person would be the richest man in the kingdom and would die at midnight tonight.'

'But that person will have all my money!' the king exclaimed, his voice rising several octaves. The queen, revived from her faint, turned ashen and looked as if she might collapse again.

'Your Majesty, whoever you give the money to cannot take it with him. You could collect it from the dead man's home tomorrow morning.'

'That's a brilliant idea,' the king beamed. 'I'd still be the richest man in the kingdom and I'd still be alive. We don't have much time, so don't just stand there, give my money away as fast as you can!' The queen passed out on hearing her husband's command.

The confused advisers asked nervously: 'But, sire, who should we give it to?'

'Give it to someone that nobody will miss.... Someone like Old George, the retired palace gardener.' The advisers, accompanied by the king's treasurer, made a hasty exit.

The day dragged on. Neither the king nor the queen, both feeling a bit queasy, had much appetite for dinner. They sat anxiously in court surrounded by their courtiers, advisers, doctors, and, of course, the soothsayer. The servants kept an anxious watch from a distance. Half an hour before midnight, the king instructed the doctor to check his temperature, pulse, and blood pressure at two-minute intervals. 'You are doing fine, Your Majesty,' the doctor reassured him. 'Everything is under control. Please don't worry.'

Unable to relax, the king summoned his treasurer and asked: 'You made absolutely certain that all my money was handed over to Old George?'

'Yes, Your Majesty, every last gold piece.'

'Do you think Old George suspected anything?'

'No, Your Majesty, not a thing. He's too simple-minded and trusting to suspect your motives.'

'That's good. So now I can be absolutely certain that he is the richest man in the kingdom?'

'Most definitely, Your Majesty. You don't have to worry on that score.'

As the clock began to strike twelve, the king visibly panicked. 'How am I?'

'You are absolutely fine,' the doctor reassured him.

The court froze in silence as everyone counted the sonorous bongs of the large palace clock. At the twelfth stroke, the queen fainted again, but the king, realizing that he was alive and well, resumed his air of bravado. The courtiers broke out into a loud cheer, and the king's advisers and soothsayer mopped their brows. The chamberlain suggested that their majesties and the court disperse to get a good night's rest.

Early the next morning the king and queen, accompanied by their retinue of courtiers and attendants, headed out to Old George's ramshackle cottage. The king peered anxiously from the window of his carriage as an attendant rapped on the door but got no response. After knocking several times, a courtier finally pushed open the door and entered the house followed by two other aides. Within a few moments, they emerged looking quite crestfallen.

'What's going on? Where's my money?' the king demanded haughtily.

'It's not there, Your Majesty,' the courtier replied nervously.

'What do you mean, it's not there? You did deliver the sacks, didn't you?'

'Yes, of course.'

By now, several curious villagers had gathered around the royal entourage. They bowed respectfully to the king as he descended angrily from the carriage and strode into Old George's humble hut.

'It's not there,' the king said, emerging from the cottage dazed and unbelieving. 'My treasure, my gold, my silver, my jewels, they've all disappeared. The only thing in the cottage is Old George's dead body.'

The queen swooned, predictably, on hearing this news. While her handmaidens rushed to attend to her, the king and his advisers were preoccupied with more pressing matters.

'What have you lost, sire?' a villager asked.

The king groaned: 'I've lost everything. My money, my treasure. It's gone. All gone!'

'Was it all in ten large sacks, tied up with red string?' a villager asked.

'Yes, yes,' the king replied eagerly. 'Do you know what happened to the sacks and their contents? Do you know where they are?'

'Yes, I do, as it happens. I've got a tiny bit of it, and so has the rest of the village.'

'Are you saying that you and the rest of the village have got parts of my fortune? Will someone tell me what's going on?'

The nervous villagers looked at one another and finally one of them spoke up. 'It's like this, Your Majesty. Last night, I was relaxing with my family after supper when Old George knocked on my door. I invited him in and he told me that he'd come into a bit of money rather suddenly and that he wanted to share his good fortune. He then asked if I would be so good as to accept a small portion of it. Of course, I readily agreed.'

A chorus of voices rose as one by one the rest of the villagers declared that Old George had also visited them to distribute his bounty.

'Oh no!' the king whimpered, his usually ruddy complexion now turned pale. 'The old fool has given it all away.'

This revelation proved too much for the queen, who collapsed again. Unconcerned at his wife's hysterics, the king began to weep uncontrollably. In between sobs, he suddenly had an epiphany.

'Wait a minute,' said the king, drying his eyes on a monogrammed silk kerchief. 'The prophecy said that the richest man in the kingdom would die at midnight. If Old George had given it all away, he couldn't possibly have been the richest man in my realm, could he?'

'With respect, Your Majesty, that's a debatable point,' a villager said hesitantly. 'For a few hours yesterday, Old George was the richest man in the kingdom in terms of monetary wealth. But even without your money and jewels, Old George always reckoned that he was the richest man in the world. "I haven't got a lot," he would say, "but I've got a roof over my head, food for my belly, and I'm at peace with the Lord." He didn't measure riches by money and possessions alone.'

As the villagers nodded in agreement, another spoke up: 'Yes, Old George always felt that he was blessed with wealth beyond measure. Therefore, he must undoubtedly have been the richest man in the kingdom.'

As the villagers' words sank in, and the king realized that he may not have been the richest man in the kingdom after all, and had mistakenly given his wealth away, his knees buckled and he fell into a faint on the ground.

103

Curious Creatures

They are an endangered breed, but we catch an occasional glimpse of one of them every now and again. Males and females of the species look like the rest of us, dress like the rest of us, earn a living like the rest of us, and may easily be mistaken for being one of us. We are talking, of course, about a community of curious creatures who live amongst us, and are often confused with regular human beings. These are the do-gooders.

What distinguishes them from us is their pathological compulsion to mind other people's business in addition to their own. Do-gooders will:

- Follow the golden rule by doing the right thing unto others.
- Support a friend in need.
- Always look on the bright side of life and be annoyingly optimistic.
- Help people even when they know people won't help them in return.
- Show sympathy for the less fortunate.
- Be punctual, respecting the value of other people's time.
- Render assistance to anyone who needs it even when not requested to do so.
- Drive cautiously, observe speed limits, and be courteous to other road users.
- Wait patiently at a pedestrian crossing for the WALK sign to light up, even when there are no cars in sight.

- Point out that your car has been parked incorrectly because the right rear tyre is on the white line instead of inside it.
- Queue patiently for a bus or train even when other commuters push past rudely.
- Give up their seat on a bus or train to anyone who needs it more.
- Hold open doors for ladies and elderly people, never minding that no one bothers to thank them for this courteous gesture.
- Bring ailing friends or family members tureens of chicken soup and other healthy foods for which said friend or family member will have no appetite.
- Return the airport or supermarket trolley to its designated area instead of abandoning it where it stands and thus blocking a parking space.
- Express genuine gratitude to cashiers, waiters, and all service providers.
- Be vigilant and keep a watchful eye on the neighbourhood.
- Keep the volume low when listening to the radio or watching television lest it disturb the neighbours.
- Be environmentally conscious, recycling paper, and avoiding plastic.
- Donate blood and contribute to charities.
- Be cheerful, courteous, and well-mannered.
- Volunteer at hospitals and homes for the elderly.
- Point out other people's indiscretions calmly and politely despite receiving rude gestures or abuse in response.

In short, do-gooders believe that you may not be perfect, but you must be good. They can and do get on other people's nerves. In our cynical modern world, where being good is considered foolish and somewhat pointless, do-gooders are laughed at for doing the right thing. Luckily, these paragons of virtue are oblivious to how 'normal' people view them. Though part of the human race, do-gooders are somehow cut off from it, always on the outside, looking in.

Social anthropologists have long deliberated whether it is heredity or environment that shapes these curious creatures. Do-gooders demonstrate their wholesomeness and righteousness from an early age—they are invariably teachers' pets, handpicked to be class monitors and prefects, and therefore doomed to be unpopular with their classmates for the rest of their schooldays. In the workplace, do-gooders will willingly volunteer to take on projects that their colleagues shun, earning the disdain of their bosses and the contempt of their co-workers.

Whether it's a defence mechanism or plain guilelessness, do-gooders themselves are blissfully unaware of their novelty value, oblivious to the fact that they don't fit in, mistakenly assuming that they are ordinary people, just like everyone else, and accepted as such. They go about their business cheerfully, unmindful of the eye-rolling, raised eyebrows, and widespread annoyance that their self-righteousness sparks in the general populace.

It is a sad reflection on our life and times that these maligned and misunderstood people are scoffed at and mocked for doing the right thing. Once in a while, non-do-gooders wonder whether the world would be a better place if there were more do-gooders around, but then quickly dismiss the weird thought. Do-gooders will always be a breed apart, unappreciated on earth but with their well-deserved reward surely awaiting them in heaven.

104

The Hare and the Tortoise Race Again

Speedy the hare had never lived down the ignominy of having lost a fabled race against Slomo the tortoise. The defeat had brought shame on the entire leporid family, and Speedy's life was never the same again. Overnight, he had changed from being frisky and confident to becoming depressed and withdrawn.

Not a day went by without him replaying the contest in his mind. He recalled sheepishly how he had taunted Slomo for being sluggish. 'Hey, slowpoke,' he used to call out to the tortoise, 'it's impossible for me to tell if you are coming or going or standing still. Why do you have to carry your house on your back? You should try to be more like me—fleet of foot and sharp of mind. We should have a race one of these days—the fastest animal in the forest outrunning the slowest.' Slomo, cool-headed and slow to anger, took Speedy's jibes in his stride, but eventually agreed to the contest, telling himself: Speedy may be fast, but I am tenacious.

On the day of the race, Speedy and Slomo lined up at the starting point. 'Ready, steady, GO!'

Speedy shot off like an arrow from a bow, while Slomo lumbered along, one slow step at a time. Speedy was sprinting along and was well in the lead when he spotted a field of cabbages alongside the path. I'm way ahead of the slowcoach so I can stop for an energy snack, he thought. After eating his fill, he looked back to check on Slomo's progress, but the tortoise was nowhere to be seen. I can have a short nap and run across the finish line before Slomo is even halfway down the track, decided Speedy as he lay down in a shady spot and fell into a deep sleep.

Waking up with a start, Speedy was surprised to see that dusk had fallen, and in the dim evening light he saw Slomo taking his last ponderous steps across the finishing line. 'What a disgrace this is for me,' he sobbed, deeply regretting his overconfidence. 'I'll never be able to live this down.'

When Speedy reached the finishing line, his face streaked with tears, Slomo said gently: 'Don't be so upset, my friend. It's not the end of the world. It just goes to show that a race is not only about speed but also about tenacity.'

Months went by and Speedy grew more and more depressed as word of his defeat spread and he became a laughing stock in the rabbit and hare communities. The only one who didn't taunt him or remind him of his setback was the gentle and compassionate tortoise. After a lot of soul-searching, Speedy realized that it was his cavalier attitude and brashness that made him lose the race, so he decided to challenge Slomo again. 'Listen Slomo, you won our first race fair and square. Would you be willing to race against me once more on the same track?' Knowing how important it was for Speedy to win, Slomo agreed to a second race.

This time, Speedy took no chances and sprinted to the finish line. The tortoise finally trundled up to it a couple of hours later and congratulated the hare on his impressive victory.

Trudging home wearily, Slomo realized that the odds were heavily against him in a race on land. With this in mind, he challenged Speedy to a third race, this time on land and water. Wanting to keep up his winning spree, Speedy took off from the starting point like a bullet and ran as fast as his legs could manage until he reached the river. The finishing point was on the other side of the water, so Speedy paced about restlessly on the riverbank, wondering how to get across.

A few hours went by until Slomo rolled up, his little legs working hard but steadily. With no break in his slow stride, Slomo walked into the water, swam at a gentle pace across the river, and crossed over the finish line on the other side.

The frustrated hare could not deny that Slomo had won the land-and-water race and congratulated him. 'Thanks, Speedy,' Slomo said breathlessly, 'it's easy if you can swim. But as I was walking along, trying to catch up with you and struggling not to think about the leaves I could be eating or how hungry I was, it occurred to me that we might actually achieve more if we work together, as a team.'

'What can you possibly mean?' asked the hare.

'Let's rerun the race tomorrow, and I will demonstrate,' said Slomo, 'but first I must eat some dinner, I've not stopped for a bite all day. I also need to rest my poor little legs. They're very tired from all that running.'

The next day, when they held the rerun, Speedy carried Slomo on his back until they reached the river, and then the tortoise took over, swimming across with the hare on his back. When they reached the opposite bank, Speedy again carried the tortoise until they reached the finishing line together, both cheering at their collaborative triumph.

Oddly, their joint accomplishment was much more satisfying than their individual victories: cooperating definitely felt better than competing. From that day on, their old rivalries forgotten, the hare and the tortoise became the best of friends and went everywhere together, crossing hilly valleys and rocky streams with ease.

105

God's Hat

On one of his occasional visits to earth, God decided to visit a small town in Africa. In his dazzling white robe and a large hat, he was a truly majestic sight as he strode along the main street that went through the centre of the town. Farmers working in their fields, townsfolk going about their daily business, and women doing their household chores, all greeted the elderly visitor respectfully as he walked past them.

It was a busy afternoon at the local store, but the garrulous grocer always found time to make small talk with shoppers. He asked a customer if she had noticed the distinguished-looking gentleman who had passed through their town.

'Yes,' said the woman. 'I found it strange that a man of his age was walking in the midday sun. I noticed that he was wearing a striking red hat.'

'First of all,' said the grocer, 'the man was not any ordinary elderly visitor but God himself. And second, I'm absolutely certain that his hat was blue.'

'I think you are mistaken,' the woman said firmly, unaccustomed to anyone disagreeing with her. 'It was definitely a red hat.' As the woman and the shopkeeper argued, others joined in the quarrel. In no time at all, the entire town was engaged in a heated debate, those on one side of the road certain that God's hat was red, those on the other side insisting the hat was blue.

As voices were raised and tempers flared, it became impossible to settle the argument amicably. After weeks and months of arguing, people were so enraged that they decided to build a wall through the centre of the town to separate the blue side from those who saw red. Once the dividing wall was put up, the people on one side became sworn enemies of those on the other side. Communications between the two sides ceased.

But life went on. On one side of the wall, people built a grand church with a tall steeple where they worshipped a god who wore a blue hat. On the other side of the wall, people erected an equally grand church where they worshipped a god who wore a red hat.

Years went by but the enmity persisted. Then, one day God visited the town again. This time, he was wearing no hat and was walking along the top of the wall. Recognizing the tall and majestic figure who had visited their town years earlier, people on both sides of the divide rushed up to the wall, pleading with him to settle their argument. Seeing the puzzled expression on God's face, a village elder explained: 'When you walked through our town many years ago, the people on the other side of the wall said you were wearing a blue hat. Those of us on this side all agreed that you were wearing a red hat. Please tell us, God, what colour was your hat?'

'I remember walking through this village years ago, but don't recall seeing this wall. On that day, I was wearing a hat that was blue on one side and red on the other.' With that, God walked along the length of the wall and off into the distance.

There was complete silence for a moment as the crowd on either side of the wall mulled over God's reply. Suddenly, the elderly villager who had asked the question picked up his walking stick and began hammering at the wall until a brick came loose. Through the hole in the wall, the villagers saw their estranged neighbours on the other side staring at them in confusion, until one of them widened the hole by breaking loose another brick with his hands. Soon, townsfolk from both sides joined in to tear down a wall that had divided them for many years because of their own folly.

The villagers worked together to build a new square in the centre of the town, where everyone could congregate at any time. In the centre of the square, the stones that had formed the wall were saved in high piles as a reminder of past differences. The one-time enemies also began to worship in each other's churches, determined never to let their beliefs tear them apart again. They had seen for themselves that there was one God, even though he wore a hat of many colours.

106

A King from Heaven

A long time ago, the kingdom of Prussia was ruled by a benevolent and popular king named Frederick William.

On a bright sunny day, the king decided to take a walk through the lush woods near his summer palace. He always looked forward to his summertime retreat, which provided a much-needed break from the bustle of the city and the burden of his royal duties.

Strolling slowly through the woods, the king marvelled at the beauty of nature, admiring the tall trees whose branches and leaves formed a canopy over the winding trail, through which rays of sunlight filtered down to make dappled designs on the pathway. Enjoying the solitude, the king reflected that the sound of chirping birds, the beauty of the wild flowers lining the path, and the splendour of nature brought him far more contentment than the palaces, wealth, gems, ermine, and silks that filled his privileged life.

His reverie was interrupted when he suddenly came to a clearing in the wood where a group of children were playing tag, laughing and squealing in delight as they chased each other with carefree and innocent abandon. King Frederick watched the lively little group with a smile on his lips. Calling out to the children, he asked them to sit with him in the shade for a few minutes.

The children immediately stopped their game and sat down in a circle around the tall, well-dressed, and distinguished-looking stranger, whose wavy blond hair seemed to form a halo around his head. 'Let's play a different kind of game, my happy little ones,' the king said, as the children looked up at him eagerly. 'I'll ask you a few questions, and the child who gives the best answer will receive a prize.'

The children clapped their hands in excitement and sat up straight, waiting for the first question. King Frederick held up a red apple and asked: 'We live in the kingdom of Prussia, but do you know which kingdom this apple belongs to?'

There was complete silence for a few seconds until a little boy raised his hand and said: 'I think it belongs to the vegetable kingdom, sir.'

'And what makes you think it is from the vegetable kingdom?' the king asked.

'Because apples come from a tree and all trees belong to that kingdom,' the boy answered.

The king smiled. 'You are right, and you shall have the apple as your prize,' he said, handing over the apple and a silver coin to the delighted little boy.

Next, the king took a gold coin from his pocket, and held it up for the children to see. 'And this coin, to what kingdom does it belong?'

Another clever little boy immediately shouted out: 'To the mineral kingdom, sir. All metals belong to that kingdom.'

'That's the right answer,' said the king, handing over the gold coin to the overjoyed boy.

Intrigued by the game and the tempting prizes, the children wriggled excitedly as they waited for the next question.

'My little friends, I will ask one more question,' King Frederick said, 'and you should be able to answer it easily.' He stood up and struck a majestic pose, back straight and head held high, and asked: 'To what kingdom do I belong?'

The children were confused. Some wanted to say 'to the kingdom of Prussia', others thought the correct answer would be 'to the animal kingdom', but not wanting to sound rude, they all kept quiet. The silence grew longer, and as the king looked around the group waiting for an answer, a little girl—the tiniest and youngest in the group—spoke up. Looking up at the king, she said shyly: 'I think you may be from the kingdom of heaven.'

The children were as surprised by their little friend's answer as by the stranger's reaction to it. They watched as King Frederick William knelt down beside the little girl and put his arms around her. With tears in his eyes, he planted a gentle kiss on the child's forehead and said: 'What a wonderful thought! I wish that it were so, my child, I wish that it were so!'

Then, pressing a few gold coins into the girl's hands, he bade goodbye to the children and swiftly walked away, deeply moved by the finest and most genuine compliment he had ever received, and firmly resolved to do everything in his power to live up to the innocent observation. King Frederick ruled wisely and well for many years, and his contented people often remarked that their king had been sent to them by angels.

107

No Place Like Home

Ever since he could remember, Bejan Behram Bamboat—Bambo to his friends—had planned on getting his post-graduation degree in England and eventually settling there. In the middle-class Parsi housing colony in suburban Bombay in which three generations of the Bamboat family lived in two small rooms, Bambo's parents and grandparents had pinned their hopes on him being their passport to paradise, their way out of India.

For many years, the Bamboats had looked on in envy as relatives, friends, and neighbours dispatched their sons or daughters overseas for further studies, most of whom did not return to India after completing their degrees. In the 1970s, members of the Parsi community were emigrating in droves to 'better their prospects' in Canada, the United States, or Australia. Bomanshaw Bamboat, the family patriarch, was determined that the only son of his only son should make England his destination, Canada being too cold, the United States too distant, and Australia not developed enough.

An Anglophile to the core, Bomanshaw, born in 1901, had lived through the twilight years of the Raj and prospered thanks to the British soft spot for and trust in members of the Parsi community. He had worked in a bank for forty-two years, starting off as a teller and ending up as the branch manager, known for his integrity and no-nonsense approach to customers and staff alike. Not averse to a little nepotism, Bomanshaw had inveigled a promising job at the bank for his son Behram, who had also worked his way up to the post of branch manager.

Behram's son Bambo had grown into a pale and skinny twenty-year-old, with a gaunt face, prominent hooked nose, sharply receding chin, and a nervous habit of rapidly blinking his close-set eyes while conversing with anyone. With a bachelor's degree in commerce, Bambo had studied hard to get good grades which won him a scholarship from a Parsi charitable trust that would partly pay for his master's degree in business administration. Thanks to the contacts of his grandfather and father, the necessary funds, bank loans, visas, tickets, foreign exchange, and accommodation were soon arranged, and Bambo was all set to leave for the promised land about which he had heard so much.

'This is a golden opportunity for you, my boy,' Bomanshaw proclaimed to his grandson. 'Britain is truly great! It is without a doubt the greatest country in the world. The British are brilliant administrators whose organizational skills enabled them to rule over three-quarters of the world. Learn from them. And if you get the chance to stay on and work there, grab it. Our country is going to the dogs thanks to overpopulation and rampant corruption. Things are going from bad to worse and the future here looks bleak.'

Despite the unearthly departure time of three o'clock in the morning, Bambo's grandfather, parents, relatives, neighbours, and friends were at the airport to see him off. With several garlands around his neck, Bambo posed stiffly for photographs in his new suit, which was tight-fitting and emphasized his scrawniness. He had a sinking feeling in his stomach as he turned to wave goodbye to his well-wishers before entering the immigration and customs hall.

Settling down in his window seat on the aircraft, Bambo felt light-headed and sick with excitement, nerves, and fear of the unknown. A plump woman seated in the middle seat next to him struck up a conversation, pulled out a packet of Glucose biscuits from her large handbag and offered him one. He nibbled at it, enjoying the sweetness, and felt much better.

The engines came on with a slow whine and the jet began its leisurely trundle to the runway. Silently muttering a prayer, Bambo experienced a rush of elation as the aircraft picked up speed and lifted off the tarmac with a slight wobble and a few thuds and thumps, taking with it the hopes and expectations of the entire Bamboat clan. Peering out of the window, he saw the shimmering lights of his home town disappear within seconds as the aircraft headed west over a sea of black and then rose above the clouds to cruise along on its long flight to London.

Bambo hardly slept a wink throughout the night, and was wide awake when the plane approached the verdant shores of England and the pilot announced that they would shortly begin their descent into Heathrow. It was a clear morning and he had a fabulous view of the enchanted land that he was to try and make his home. He caught his first glimpse of the fabled white cliffs of Dover and was mesmerized by the patchwork blanket of uneven squares of green and brown that stretched as far as he could see, with what appeared to be small towns and villages dotted here and there. He saw London basking in the morning sunshine and spotted the Thames snaking its way through the city. He was amazed at how much greenery there was, interspersed between row upon row of identical-looking houses. It really looks like the green and pleasant land Grandpa always talks about, he thought.

Disembarking at Heathrow with sore and bloodshot eyes, Bambo underwent a grilling by the unsmiling immigration officer, who repeatedly leafed through all the paperwork as if looking for a mistake and then grudgingly stamped his passport. Two of his father's friends had offered to meet Bambo at the airport and drive him to Birmingham, the location of his university. They had thoughtfully packed some food for him, but Bambo was so exhausted by the time they reached his student accommodation and he was shown up to his room that he went straight to bed despite it being only mid-afternoon local time.

Waking with a start, he saw it was pitch dark outside. He was cold and hungry. His watch showed it was 4 a.m. Indian time, 11.30 p.m. in Birmingham. He was grateful for the snacks his father's friends had thought to give him, for without them he would have gone back to sleep hungry.

His first few days at the university went by in a blur. Instead of blending in, Bambo became acutely aware of how much he stood out. His sing-song way of speaking, his accent, his clothes, all seemed completely out of place. In his first letter home, he forced himself to put a positive slant on his new surroundings. *I'm settling in well*, he wrote. *It is early autumn, and the whole place feels air-conditioned.*

My room is comfortable and the other students are very helpful. I've met people from many different countries and have never heard so many different accents. We think Bombay is cosmopolitan, but this country is something else! Will write again soon.

The weeks and months dragged on as Bambo struggled to cope with lectures, tutorials, and dissertations. At his college in Bombay, students had enjoyed enough free time to relax throughout the year, only having to buckle down a month before the final exams to cram from their prescribed textbooks. Here in Birmingham, there was no respite from continuous assignments and hard work. To add to the stress, he felt terribly homesick. He missed his family, his mother's cooking, his friends, and the comforts of his modest home in Bombay, where he had never had to cook or clean for himself.

Though his fellow students were polite, they were not exactly friendly and Bambo was never invited to join them at the cafeteria or on any of their outings. Being on a tight budget, trips to the cinema or dining out were unthinkable.

Without the company of friends, he became more and more isolated and depressed.

He found it surprising and somewhat annoying that many people couldn't pronounce his two-syllable name, acting as if 'Bejan' was an impossible tongue-twister. He struggled with the bitterly cold weather, and found it difficult to adjust to the fact that it was as dark as night by late afternoon during winter. In reality, England was a far cry from the utopia that Bambo's grandfather had described and that he had imagined, and was going through a period of discontent, strikes, and domestic turmoil.

Amidst all the political tumult, Bambo marvelled at the grit and determination of the Brits who seemed to take everything in their stride. Despite strikes by refuse collectors, the streets of Birmingham were still cleaner and litter-free compared to the dusty, crowded streets of Bombay. Traffic was disciplined and there was no honking or overtaking from the wrong side. Bambo was impressed by the courtesy of drivers who unfailingly stopped for pedestrians at zebra crossings. Best of all, there was no shoving and pushing to get on to buses and trains, because British people always queued in an orderly fashion no matter what the occasion, and he didn't see swarming, jostling crowds like he did everywhere in India.

To escape from the cold, Bambo would occasionally wander through the men's section of the overheated department stores on the high street. The snooty salesmen would pointedly ignore him and the attractive young ladies offering slips of paper doused with the latest aftershave somehow didn't seem to notice him. They appeared to have a sixth sense as to whether a shopper could afford to buy their overpriced products. He would walk up and down the aisles of shirts, trousers, jackets, overcoats, and underwear, recoiling at the exorbitant price tags. On his way back to his room, he would stop off at an Indian grocer's shop to buy bananas, a loaf of bread, and a packet of butter, which sometimes was all he could afford. One day, the grocer's wife brought out a tray of freshly made samosas from the kitchen, and the kind grocer added two piping hot samosas to Bambo's shopping bag but didn't charge him for them. Bambo thanked him and hastily left the shop with tears in his eyes, overwhelmed by this random act of kindness from a stranger.

One weekend, Bambo and two Indian friends on his course took a bus to the town centre, to an area they had heard was popular with students. All three of them gawped at the sight of young men staggering down the street in groups, clutching bottles of alcohol or cans of beer, many of them visibly drunk and shouting obscenities. The girls, sporting hot pants and miniskirts that displayed their pale legs turning pink from the cold, were equally inebriated and flirting brazenly with boys and older men. Bambo and his friends watched as three boys in their late teens staggered towards them, their arms around each other's shoulders, struggling to support the drunkest one in the middle who looked as if he was about to pass out. One of the teenagers called out to Bambo and his pals angrily: 'What the hell are you staring at? Go back to India, you filthy Pakis!'

By the end of his first year, Bambo concluded that he would never feel completely at home in England, because he would never really belong. At the same time, letters from his father and grandfather increased in frequency, urging him to try his utmost to find a job and stay on. Bambo mustered up his courage and wrote back:

> Dear Mama, Papa, and Grandpa,
>
> I hope this doesn't come as a disappointment to you, but I don't want to stay here once I finish my degree. England is a beautiful country and it has many plus points when compared to India, but I feel I will not have much of a future here. The political situation is quite bad and

> although I have been interviewed by several recruiters through the university, I only receive rejection letters from them citing the economic downturn and 'factors beyond our control'. As you know, I will not be allowed to stay on unless I have a job or a sponsor. The truth is that I don't fit in.
>
> You have made a lot of sacrifices to give me the opportunity to study here, for which I am deeply grateful. I have weighed the pros and cons of staying on or returning to India, and have made up my mind. I want to come home. I don't belong here.

On the plane back to Bombay, Bambo grew excited about his future in the country he had missed every day since being in Birmingham. Bombay will always be my home and there's nowhere like it, he thought, as he took his first breath of familiar muggy Indian air after they landed. His family and friends were there to greet him with garlands and bouquets and sweets and laughter, and he had never felt so happy or so loved.

Within weeks of his homecoming, Bambo got a mid-level administrative post in a reputed marketing and consultancy firm. Not being overly ambitious or pushy or charismatic, it was Bambo's diligence and dependability that enabled him to rise steadily through the ranks from section manager to senior manager, eventually ending up as a director of the company. He saved enough money to buy a small flat close to his parents' home, and a second-hand car. He had done well for himself, and his family was proud of his achievements.

Whenever he was in a pensive mood, Bambo often recounted stories about his student years in Birmingham to his daughter and son. He would remind them that everyone has a different idea of paradise, and that the grass is not always greener on the other side, no matter how pretty it may look from a distance. 'For me, paradise was feeling that I belonged somewhere, and knowing that I didn't want to be anywhere else,' he'd say, as his children listened wide-eyed. 'Each of you must make up your own mind about what you want to do when you grow up and where you want to settle. I'm convinced that I made the right decision to return to India. I'm happy with my lot, with my place in the world. For me, there was no place like home.'

108

A Lesson in Humility

A learned and revered yogi was in the habit of taking a dip in the holy Ganga every morning, and then sitting on the riverbank to chant and meditate for the rest of the day. On the opposite shore, he noticed a youth, dressed in white kurta and pyjamas, who also took a dip in the river before beginning his prayers and spending the day in meditation.

For several days, the yogi observed the young man, who spent hours in worship and spiritual contemplation. He seems like a devout and dedicated youth, and would make an ideal protégé, the yogi thought. I could teach him so much.... I've noticed that he chants Om only a few times before meditating. Perhaps he is unaware of the mystical and religious significance of chanting a mantra 108 times. I'd explain the importance of the number 108—that the twelve houses of the Zodiac multiplied by the nine planets is 108, that there are 108 Upanishads and that the number also signifies spiritual completion.... If he is taught about our beliefs and to do things in the stipulated manner, he could reach higher levels of enlightenment. He might even be able to levitate or walk on water! I shall offer to be his spiritual adviser.

He stood up, waved his arms, and called out to the young man to get his attention. On the opposite riverbank, the youth stopped his prayers and waved back. The yogi called out: 'Greetings, young man. I have noticed that you are very pious and God-fearing. So, as your elder, I am willing to guide you on the right spiritual path if you so desire.'

The youth cupped his ear with his hand and gestured to the yogi that he had not heard a word of what was said, the wind having carried the sound downriver. Signalling to the yogi to wait, the youth stepped off the grassy bank and walked deftly on the surface of the water until he reached the opposite shore. Bowing deeply, the young man asked: 'What were you trying to convey to me, yogiji?'

Humbled by the miracle he had witnessed, the yogi bent to touch the youth's feet and replied: 'I wanted to become your guru, but I see that you have already attained a far higher level of enlightenment than I have. I can learn far more from you than you ever will from me. I would consider it a privilege if you would accept me as your disciple.'

The young man smiled and said that the privilege would be his. 'But one act of humility alone will not enable you to walk on water, so you had better learn to swim if you want to spend time on my side of the river.'

109

Abu Kasem's Sandals

A long time ago, in the city of Baghdad, there lived a wealthy merchant called Abu Kasem, who was known far and wide for being tight-fisted not only with others but also with himself. 'What's the point of amassing all this wealth if he doesn't want to spend any of it?' people remarked. 'He doesn't even have anyone to leave it to.'

Impervious to the snide remarks being made about him, Abu Kasem continued with his miserly ways. All the shopkeepers and vendors in the bazaar dreaded dealing with him, because Abu Kasem would drive a hard bargain, offering them a quarter of the price they quoted and refusing to budge until they gave in just to be rid of him. He would buy expensive fabrics, exotic perfumes, incense, embroidered carpets, and rugs at low prices, and then cart them off to a distant town where he sold the goods at four times the price that he had paid. His customers had long since given up trying to bargain with him, knowing that he wouldn't lower his prices by even a dinar.

Aside from his miserliness, Abu Kasem was instantly recognizable wherever he went thanks to his scruffy, smelly, and threadbare sandals, which had seen better days at least a decade earlier. Whether at home or outdoors, Abu Kasem wore the same shabby footwear, blackened with age, worn out at the heels, with his bony toes and chipped toenails showing through holes in the front. Why he couldn't buy himself a new pair of shoes remained a mystery. Abu Kasem had become such an object of derision and ridicule, that the children in the town would follow him around the bazaar, singing:

Abu Kasem, Abu Kasem
We must ask him
Why he will not choose
To buy himself new shoes.

Abu Kasem, Abu Kasem,
Let's all ask him
Why his shoes have no soles
And are so full of holes.

In heaven there will be no reward
For wealth stored in his earthly hoard.
So, let's hope Abu Kasem becomes wiser
And stops being such a wretched miser.

'Mind your own business,' Abu Kasem would reply to his detractors, as he shuffled along in his worn-out sandals.

One day, after finishing his ablutions at the public bath, Abu Kasem found that his cherished sandals were missing. In their place was a brand-new pair of shoes, expensive and well made.

'Aha,' he cried. 'My friends are trying to trick me, but the joke is on them because I end up with a new pair of shoes.' Abu Kasem slipped his calloused feet with their yellowing toenails into the new shoes, marvelling at their softness and comfort and his good fortune, and headed home.

His friends had indeed played a trick on him, swapping Abu Kasem's tattered footwear with an expensive new pair that belonged to the local judge. When the judge emerged from the bath, he discovered that his new shoes were missing. In their place stood a ragged pair of sandals.

'My shoes have been stolen,' the judge exclaimed, as a small crowd gathered around him. Instantly recognizing the grubby sandals, one of the men in the crowd said: 'Abu Kasem must have stolen your shoes, Your Honour,' as the rest of the group nodded.

The judge immediately instructed one of his attendants to summon the thief to the court. As a confused Abu Kasem entered the courtroom, there was a roar of laughter from the crowd, because it was not often that a culprit wore the goods he had stolen when appearing in court. The judge was not amused. 'Abu Kasem, you are a wealthy man, and can afford to buy your own shoes instead of stealing from someone else....'

'But, Your Honour....' Abu Kasem interrupted, trying to explain.

'No buts,' the judge said sternly. 'I hereby order you to hand over the shoes you are wearing and to pay a fine of one hundred dinars. Then, take your disgusting old sandals and get out of my courtroom.'

Abu Kasem's delight at being reunited with his beloved sandals was outweighed by his dismay at having to pay the hefty fine. I have to face facts, he decided. These shoes have brought me bad luck. I cannot bear to lose more money. The time has come for me to part with my unlucky sandals.

On the way to his house, he spotted a man begging for alms on the side of the road. Abu Kasem went up to the beggar and said: 'You can have these,' as he bent down to remove his sandals.

Glancing at the stained and malodorous sandals, the beggar pleaded: 'I have no use for sandals, sir. I need a few coins to buy food.' Unwilling to part with any more money, Abu Kasem walked on until he came to a bridge that spanned the Tigris. Taking off his sandals, he threw them into the river and watched as they rapidly drifted downstream.

Abu Kasem had barely reached home, his feet sore from walking barefoot, bemoaning the fact that he would have to pay good money to buy a new pair of shoes, when there was a knock at the door. There stood a fisherman, holding Abu Kasem's soaked sandals. 'Look what I caught in my fishing net. Instead of fish, I found your sandals entangled in the netting and the buckles have made a hole in the net. I am a poor man and will have to pay a lot of money to repair my net so you must compensate me for the damage.'

A dejected Abu Kasem had no choice but to take back his soaked, tatty sandals and give a handful of coins to the irate fisherman. My sandals are causing me nothing but trouble, Abu Kasem thought. I'll put them out to dry on the parapet until I can figure out a way to get rid of them.

While he was thinking of ways to divest himself of the offending pair, he heard a ruckus on the street and opened the door to investigate. He found a crowd gathered outside his house, where a frail middle-aged woman was lying on the road, wailing in pain. A neighbour reported that he had seen a crow flying by with a sandal in its beak and that the bird had dropped the worn-out footwear on the woman's head. The woman was so startled by this unexpected projectile that she had fallen and broken her arm.

The woman's husband lodged a formal complaint with the authorities, claiming that his injured wife would not be able to work on their farm for several months. As everyone in town knew who the shoddy sandals belonged to, Abu Kasem was hauled into court and found himself facing the judge once more.

'You again!' the judge thundered. 'What is wrong with you? You and your sandals are causing harm to too many people. This farmer will now have to tend to his injured wife and will not be able to work on his farm. I therefore order you to take care of this peasant and his wife for the rest of your days. You can afford it and it's high time you put your amassed wealth to good use. What's the point of having all that money if you don't spend it?'

With the judge's words ringing in his ears, and aware that his painstakingly accumulated wealth was dissipating rapidly, Abu Kasem was nearly in tears. 'Your Honour, please help me to be rid of these cursed sandals. They've cost me a thousand times more than I paid for them.'

'Your sandals are your responsibility,' the judge said unsympathetically. 'Make sure that they cause no more trouble.'

Abu Kasem headed home, a broken man. Meeting a friend along the way, he begged him to help him get rid of the sandals. 'Throw them in the rubbish bin,' his friend advised. Abu Kasem followed his friend's advice and then waited in dread for the sandals to turn up again. Days passed, then weeks, months, and an entire year went by without a trace of the sandals.

In that one year, many things changed. People forgot about Abu Kasem's sandals and stopped laughing at him. The biggest transformation was in Abu Kasem himself. He stopped bargaining with the shopkeepers in the local bazaar, doled out money to the needy, and even bought himself several pairs of comfortable new shoes. He now found greater happiness in being generous and big-hearted than in hoarding his wealth. He had finally come to realize that it wasn't worth living poor to die rich.

110

The Promise

A once prosperous businessman had fallen on hard times and was struggling to make ends meet. The village priest advised him to offer prayers at the local temple, and to make a vow that if his problems were resolved and his business picked up, he would sell his valuable property and donate the proceeds to charity.

A few months later, when his business improved, the priest reminded the businessman of the vow he had made to the deity. Angry with himself at having made such a rash promise, the businessman announced that he would sell his house and land for one gold coin, on one condition: whoever bought the property would also have to buy his horse for a thousand gold coins.

As soon as the property and his horse were sold, the businessman kept the thousand gold coins for himself and donated one gold coin to charity. He had kept his promise.

111

The Kind Elephant

In the Indian village of Bhimapuram lived a wealthy merchant, who had an unusual pet—an elephant named Gajaraj.

Gajaraj's owner was rich but also tight-fisted, and made him work day and night to earn enough money for his upkeep. As everyone knows, elephants are high maintenance—an adult elephant can eat between 100 to 250 kilograms of food and drink up to 200 litres of water daily. Gajaraj was often sent to work in the jungle transporting heavy logs of wood. Occasionally, a howdah would be strapped to his back and he would carry people and their belongings from one place to another. On festive occasions, the docile and obedient Gajaraj led noisy processions to famous temples.

One day, the people of a nearby village began planning to celebrate their annual temple festival with the usual pomp and ceremony. However, the festival could not start until the temple's flag was hoisted. The temple had its own flag, but they needed a new flagpole. After some discussion, the villagers approached woodcutters in a nearby forest to chop down a large tree and make a sturdy flagpole from its trunk.

The towering flagpole was too heavy for the villagers to transport to the temple, so they hired Gajaraj for the job. The elephant would not only have to haul the heavy pole to the temple, but would also have to hoist it into the deep hole that had been dug to hold it in place.

The journey from the jungle to the village temple took two days. The villagers cheered when they saw Gajaraj lumbering towards the temple, pushing the large log along the ground in front of him with his trunk. The cheering got louder as Gajaraj rolled the log right up to the hole in which it was to be placed. Then suddenly the elephant stopped and pushed the log away from the hole.

The mahout, who was riding on Gajaraj's back, shouted orders for the elephant to lift the flagpole and place it in the hole, but the normally submissive elephant would not budge. He just stood there, flapping his enormous ears and swishing his trunk from side to side and to and fro. The mahout grew hoarse barking instructions at the elephant, but Gajaraj did not move. The impatient villagers added to the commotion by loudly berating the helpless mahout for the delay.

Upset by the hubbub, Gajaraj trumpeted angrily and lowered his head with a sudden jerk, causing the mahout to slip off and fall to the ground. Wiping the dust from his clothes, the mahout quickly moved away from the angry elephant as the crowd panicked and ran off in different directions.

Alone at last, Gajaraj slowly walked towards the hole, bent his forelegs and lowered himself to the ground. Placing his long trunk deep inside the pit, Gajaraj gently lifted out a tiny, terrified kitten. The little one had fallen into the deep hole and had been cowering there, unable to climb back out. The villagers and the mahout, who had been keeping an eye on Gajaraj from a distance, now realized why he had refused to obey the mahout's orders. The fragile kitten would have been crushed if he had put the flagpole in the hole.

After gently placing the kitten on firm ground a safe distance from the site, Gajaraj used his trunk to manoeuvre the flagpole into position in the hole that had been dug for it. The villagers rushed forward to bolster the pole and fill up the space around it with soil.

People visiting the temple offered sugar cane, coconuts, and fruits to the kind and clever elephant who had taught them an unforgettable lesson in compassion by showing that even the tiniest of lives is precious.

Elephants do not forget and nor did the kitten, who grew into a contented cat that lived at the temple and was looked after by the priests, who named her Kittu. Whenever Gajaraj came to the temple on festive occasions, Kittu would run up to greet her friend, stretching up on her hind legs to grab hold of Gajaraj's trunk, which he would playfully swish from side to side before scooping Kittu up and placing her on his head. Kittu would cling on for dear life as Gajaraj paraded around the temple grounds with her perched on his head, much to the delight of worshippers who saw this unlikely friendship as proof of the divinity and harmony of God's creatures great and small.

112

God Provides

Once upon a time there lived a king named Rajarao, who was much loved by his people for his kindness and generosity. Among the crowds that thronged to the palace every day were two hermits, who regularly sought alms from the monarch.

Whenever Raghav, the older of the two hermits, received food or alms from the king, he would bow and say: 'I'm thankful that God provides!' But when Balaraj, the younger of the two, received food or alms from the king, he would kneel in gratitude, saying: 'King Rajarao provides!'

Annoyed at the older man's response, Rajarao wondered why Raghav kept thanking God when it was he, the king, who gave him food and clothing! He needs to understand who is actually doing the providing, the king determined.

The next day, when Raghav and Balaraj arrived at the palace, the king instructed them to walk down a deserted tree-lined alley where he had placed a cloth bag containing ten gold coins. Rajarao gestured to Balaraj to walk down the pathway first. He was convinced that when the young man found the gold, the older man would surely realize where the bounty came from. Who but the king would place a bagful of gold coins in the middle of a pathway?

Wondering at the king's strange request, Balaraj walked briskly down the path, gazing up at the canopy of trees, not noticing the purse. When his turn came, Raghav walked down the pathway more cautiously, keeping his eye on the ground, and found the bag of gold.

When the two returned to the palace, Rajarao asked if they had found anything on the pathway. Balaraj replied: 'No, Your Majesty. I didn't find anything on the road but I admired the beautiful trees.'

Raghav said: 'I did find something! I found a purse full of gold coins. As always, I am thankful that God provides!'

Realizing that the hermit who did not find the purse of gold coins would be disappointed, the kind-hearted king had already devised a strategy to reward the loser. He'd instructed a courtier to put thirty silver coins in an earthen pot, and to cover the coins with grains of rice. The pot would be given to the hermit who had failed to find the gold coins. The king now reasoned that when Balaraj found the silver coins hidden in the pot, Raghav would surely realize that the king had put them there, and that it is not God but the king who provides!

Balaraj was handed the pot of rice but was unsure what to do with it—not having the facilities to cook it, and knowing it couldn't be eaten raw. Passing by a grocer's shop on his way home, he asked the owner if he would buy the pot of rice grains. Feeling sorry for the scrawny man, the shopkeeper took the pot and handed over a few coins in exchange. Balaraj headed home grateful to have at least earned a few coins for the pot. Our king is truly generous, he thought.

A short while later, Raghav walked by the grocer's shop. Despite having ten gold coins in his pocket, from force of habit he asked the shopkeeper: 'Can you spare a coin for a hungry old man?' Feeling sorry for the elderly man, the shopkeeper handed over the pot of rice grains, for which he had little need given that his shop was fully stocked. This man's need is greater so he is welcome to it, thought the grocer.

Raghav thanked the shopkeeper and headed back to his hut. As he poured the rice grains into a small pan to boil the rice, he was delighted to find the silver coins at the bottom of the pot. 'God provides! God is great!' he exclaimed.

In his durbar the next morning, King Rajarao eagerly waited for the hermits to arrive. 'Did anything out of the ordinary happen to you yesterday?' he asked Balaraj.

'No, Your Majesty, but I did manage to earn a few coins by selling the pot of rice you gave me!' came the reply.

The king was dismayed. 'What about you?' he asked Raghav.

'I was truly blessed. Not only did I find those gold coins on the roadside but on my way home, a shopkeeper gave me a pot of rice in which I found thirty silver coins! I'm so thankful that God provides.'

The king sighed, somewhat defeated. 'You are right. It is said that man proposes, but God disposes. Ultimately, God does provide, because it is he who determines where to bestow his bounty.'

113

The Wise Men of Gotham

A long time ago, England was ruled by King John, a cruel despot who showed no consideration towards his people, and was feared and despised by them. As a result, when residents of the small Nottinghamshire village of Gotham heard that the king and his royal party planned to travel through their village, they were greatly concerned and agitated. The king's impending visit would spell doom for their peaceful hamlet, because in those days, any road that the king travelled on had to be converted into a public highway.

The good people of Gotham did not want a public road disrupting the calm of their sleepy community and immediately called a meeting of the village council to figure out a way of preventing the king from passing through their neighbourhood.

After considerable discussion, the villagers devised a cunning plan—they chopped down a number of tall trees and blocked the roads leading into Gotham with their large trunks and heavy, leafy branches. When King John and his men rode up on their horses to the outskirts of the village, they were unable to enter. The infuriated king had to turn back but instructed a few of his soldiers to clear the obstruction and punish the villagers by chopping off the noses of all the men in the village.

The villagers took great fright on hearing of the king's decree, and hastily called another village council meeting. They had very little time to think of a strategy because the soldiers were strong and able. They would easily clear the path within a matter of hours.

A villager said: 'We've kept the king out of our village by using our wits, so now our wits will have to help save our noses. But how?'

A village elder responded: 'In my three score and ten years, I've seen many a man being punished for being wise, but I've never heard of anyone being harmed for being foolish. When the king's officers enter our village, let's all act like fools. The soldiers are bound to feel sorry for us and will leave us alone.'

'That's an excellent idea,' the villagers proclaimed. Every resident was advised to behave as foolishly as possible to keep the soldiers at bay.

Dusk had fallen by the time the king's officers and their horses finally manoeuvred past the felled tree trunks and broken branches. As they were cautiously making their way along the narrow streets, the soldiers came across a man riding a donkey. The man looked exhausted, bent forward under the weight of a large sack of grain that was slung across his shoulders. As they rode past the man and his donkey, one of the king's men asked: 'Why are you carrying that heavy sack on your shoulders, my good man? Why don't you put it on your donkey's back?'

The man replied: 'My donkey has been unwell for the past few days. As he was already carrying my weight, I thought I would ease his burden by carrying the sack on my back.'

'But don't you see that if you're carrying the sack and riding on top of the donkey, he is still carrying your weight and also that of the sack?'

'What nonsense!' the man muttered, giving the king's entourage a disdainful look as he went on his way. The king's officers shook their heads in disbelief at the arrogance and stupidity of the villager. Deeming it pointless to argue with fools, the soldiers rode on.

As the evening shadows lengthened, the soldiers came across a man banging his head repeatedly against a brick wall. Stunned by the man's actions, the officers stopped and asked him: 'Why are you banging your head against the wall?'

'Because it feels so good when I stop,' the man replied.

Shaking their heads even more vigorously, the king's men went on their way until they came to an inn where they decided to stop for the night. The innkeeper welcomed the officials warmly. 'I usually charge two silver coins per person for a night's stay but seeing that you are men of means and can afford it, I will charge you only one silver coin each.' Smiling at the innkeeper's lack of logic, the officers settled down for the night.

Shortly before dawn, the soldiers were awakened by a hubbub from the street. A small crowd had gathered by a cheese vendor, who was taking large rounds of freshly made cheese from a sack, wrapping them in cloth and then rolling them down the hill with all the strength he could muster, as the crowd cheered.

'What's going on here?' the king's men asked imperiously.

The cheese vendor replied: 'To save myself the trouble of carrying my homemade cheese all the way to the market, I'm rolling them down the hill and across the bridge. I've instructed the cheese to stop at the market entrance and wait for me there.'

At a complete loss for words, the king's men decided to head back to London as soon as possible to inform King John of the strange goings-on in Gotham.

While discussing the bizarre events they had witnessed, the soldiers rode past a large field where a handful of men were diligently labouring. Reining in their horses to observe the work in progress, the soldiers saw the men working in pairs. One man would dig a deep hole, and another would immediately fill it up with soil. Unable to make sense of the men's actions, one of the soldiers called out to them: 'Good day to you all. What is this strange task you are engaged in where one man digs a hole and another instantly fills it up?'

'Good day to you too, sire. The man who is supposed to plant saplings in the holes is off sick today. But even though he's absent, we're continuing to do our jobs.'

The soldiers sighed and continued on their way. They had not gone far when they came to a pond where several villagers were shouting advice to two men who were struggling to hold on to a large, slippery eel that was slithering and writhing in their hands.

'What's going on here?' one of the king's men asked. 'Why all the noise?'

'It's like this,' one of the villagers explained. 'Last year, we placed all the surplus fish that we'd caught into this pond, hoping they would multiply and spare us from having to go out to sea to fish. But when we came back a few days ago, all we found in the pond was this fat eel. It's obvious that it has eaten all our fish. We spent two days thinking how to punish the eel and we have finally agreed that the best penalty is to drown it, so we're trying to throw it back into the pond.'

The king's men were now convinced that there was an epidemic of insanity spreading through Gotham. These imbeciles actually thought they could drown an eel in water! 'It appears to me that the people of this town are all fools,' one of the soldiers said.

'That's true,' said another. 'It would be wrong to punish such simpletons. The king has ordered that we cut off the noses of all the men in the village, but by doing so we would be spiting *our* faces if we harm such harmless folk.'

The officers returned to the palace and informed the king that the people of Gotham were too simple-minded to pose a threat to anyone but themselves. In those days, there was a widespread belief that madness was contagious, so the king and his officers decided to keep as far away from Gotham as possible.

From that day forward, the residents of Gotham gained a reputation for being foolish. But the villagers were unperturbed. 'We know that more fools pass through Gotham than remain in it,' they declared confidently, looking out onto the lush green fields surrounding their village—fields that would have been replaced with a noisy public highway, had the villagers not shown that they were stupid enough to have driven away a powerful army.

114

A Vampire Tests a King

The adventures of King Vikramaditya and Vetal are based on Baital Pachisi, *a collection of twenty-five stories believed to have been written in the eleventh century by poet Somadeva Bhatt, based on tales that had been passed down for centuries. These enduringly popular tales centre on the king's promise to a mystic that he will capture Vetal, a vampire-like spirit who lives in a corpse and hangs from a tree, and the many difficulties the king faces in fulfilling his pledge.*

The selected anecdotes below illustrate that since time immemorial, storytellers' vivid imaginations have known no boundaries.

Wise and adventurous King Vikramaditya ruled over a prosperous kingdom from his capital at Ujjain in central India. One day, a yogi came to the durbar and presented the king with a raw pomegranate, which the king handed over to an aide to store until it ripened.

The yogi repeated this ritual for several days, but one day the pomegranate accidentally fell from the king's hands and split open, revealing a large blood-red ruby instead of edible seeds. The surprised king ordered an aide to check all the fruit that the yogi had brought to the palace, and found a priceless ruby concealed in each one.

Delighted but puzzled by such strange bounty, the king summoned the yogi. With much daring, the yogi refused to go to the palace, insisting that the monarch should meet with him after sunset, on the night before the new moon, under a banyan tree which stood in the middle of a cremation ground outside the city.

Not too happy about the yogi's choice of venue, the king headed for the designated meeting point on a cloudy, dark, and humid night. He found the yogi sitting cross-legged on the ground, a short distance from a smouldering pyre. Gesturing to the king to sit beside him, the yogi said: 'Pardon me, sire, for insisting that you meet me here, even though I am the one who needs your help. There is a task that only someone as brave and noble as Your Majesty can perform for me. It will enable me to gain occult powers and mastery over the forces of nature, after which I shall serve you faithfully for the rest of my days.'

The king urged the yogi to continue, curious to hear what his task could be.

'About four miles south of here, there is a burial ground near the forest at the centre of which stands an ancient siris tree which has a corpse hanging from one of its branches. I need you to bring the corpse to me but be mindful not to utter a word on your return journey. That is very important. Once the corpse is in my possession, it will give me extraordinary powers that will benefit us both and make you the most powerful man in the world.'

Despite an unseasonal downpour, accompanied by drumrolls of thunder and flashes of lightning, the brave king set off to retrieve the corpse. After several hours, soaked to the skin, he reached the siris tree from a branch of which hung a body, head downwards, swaying to and fro in the gusty storm. The corpse's greenish-brown eyes were wide open, its mouth appeared frozen in a grimace, the frizzy hair and wizened skin were as brown as a coconut, and the skeletal body was hanging from a branch by the tips of its toes like a bat. Drawing his sword, the king slashed at the branch to which the creature was clinging, causing it to drop heavily to the ground. Landing with a thud, the corpse began groaning as if in intense pain. Surprised at this sudden return to life, the brave king asked: 'Who are you?'

The creature responded with a piercing cackle, gleefully leapt into the air, and suspended itself upside down on a higher branch of the tree. Only Vetal, a vampire possessed by an evil spirit, would do such a thing, deduced the king.

Six attempts to subdue the vampire failed, and the king was beginning to lose patience when he recalled the hermit's warning and realized that the capricious creature escaped every time he spoke. He eventually subdued Vetal at the seventh attempt, silently tied him securely in his large shawl, hoisted him over his shoulder, and prepared to carry him back to the yogi.

Impressed, or possibly cowed, by the king's perseverance, the vampire finally spoke: 'I, the unconquerable Vetal, have surrendered to the indignity of being trussed up and carried like a helpless infant. But listen to me carefully, mighty Vikram. I must warn you that I am talkative by nature and have many intriguing stories that I wish to share with you. It is nearly an hour's walk to the place where your friend awaits you. But before we set off, we have to make a deal. At the end of each story, I shall ask you a question. If you choose to answer me, I shall immediately fly back to my favourite resting place on the branch of the siris tree, forcing you to start your journey all over again; and if you keep silent, whether from ignorance or confusion, I shall smash your head into a thousand pieces.'

Not accustomed to being spoken to so rudely, the wise king kept quiet, and with the vampire wrapped tightly in the shawl and slung over his shoulder, he began the long walk back to the cremation ground where the yogi awaited him.

~

It had stopped raining but the forest had come alive with bats circling between the trees, owls hooting persistently, and jackals howling hungrily. Popping his head out of the king's makeshift sack, the vampire said in his grating nasal voice: 'Listen carefully to my story and answer my questions judiciously, Vikram. Otherwise, the consequences for you will be dire....'

> A long time ago, a trader named Surya and his friend, Chandra, visited a famous temple dedicated to Durga, goddess of war, in the city of Pataliputra. While they were chanting their prayers, Surya spotted a beautiful young woman seated on the opposite side of the prayer hall making an offering to the deity. Although the girl's head was covered by the pallu of her sari, he could see that she was petite, with delicate features that were bestowed a captivating luminosity by the light of the flickering oil lamps. Surya had never thought it possible, but he had truly fallen in love at first sight.
>
> As they left the temple, Surya told Chandra that he was determined to marry the young woman, so the friends set off to meet the girl's parents to ask for her hand in marriage. Sundari, the aptly named beautiful maiden, had noticed Surya staring at her in the temple, and had been similarly enchanted with him. Given the mutual attraction, Sundari's father gave the young couple his blessings and the wedding ceremony was arranged within a few days.
>
> The day after the wedding, the young bride took tearful leave of her parents and set off for her marital home in a large horse-drawn carriage accompanied by her husband and his friend. In the fading evening light, while they were crossing through a forest, their carriage was attacked by a gang of bandits. While Sundari called out desperately for help, Surya and Chandra put up a valiant battle against the thieves but their lathis were no match for the bandits' swords and daggers. Sundari handed over

all her jewellery and money, but the bloodthirsty bandits chopped off the heads of the two men before riding off into the forest with their loot, including the horses and carriage.

Sundari was beside herself with grief, hoarse from crying and helplessness. She had been married for only a day and was already widowed! Unable to bear her anguish, Sundari decided she would end her life by hanging herself from the branch of a tree with her bridal sari. She was on the verge of taking this drastic step when Goddess Durga appeared. 'You have been a steadfast and loyal devotee for years,' the goddess said, 'so I will repay your faith in me by bringing these two men back to life if you put the head and body of each of them together.'

Still in deep shock and panic-stricken, Sundari picked up the severed heads with trembling hands, but mistakenly placed them on the wrong bodies. Within moments, the goddess brought both men back to life through her divine powers.

'Now tell me, O Wise King, whose bride is this young woman and who is her rightful husband?' Vetal asked mockingly. 'Is it the man with her husband's head or the one with his body? If you don't give me an answer, I shall have to make your head explode. Trust me, it is never a pretty sight.'

Drawn in by the story and the young bride's dilemma, King Vikram replied: 'The parts of a human body are unique in their abilities; each possesses a characteristic or function that is vital to life. But the master of all these is always the head. It is the command from the brain that makes a person's body function. Therefore, Sundari's rightful husband is the one to whom his head has been attached.'

'That's a highly perceptive answer, Vikram,' Vetal said scornfully. 'But you're not as smart as you think you are. You seem to have forgotten that the moment you speak I shall be released from your clutches.' With that the vampire leapt into the air gleefully and flew off in the direction of the siris tree. Wielding his sword, King Vikramaditya had no option but to give chase to his perverse and wily tormentor.

~

When King Vikramaditya reached the siris tree he found Vetal had suspended himself on a high branch. I wonder how long I will have to put up with his wiles, he thought. Climbing up to reach him, Vikram once again forced the vampire to the ground with a sharp blow from his sword, wrapped him tightly in his large shawl and set off to meet the yogi, careful not to utter a word. The brazen Vetal laughed out loud and launched into another tale.

> A long time ago, a king named Roopsen ruled over the kingdom of Vardhaman. One day, a tall and robust man named Veerdev arrived at the palace seeking a job.
>
> The kind king smiled and said: 'If I do find a job for you, what wage would you expect?'
>
> 'One hundred gold coins a day,' came the reply.
>
> 'That is a very large amount,' the surprised monarch said. 'Do you need the money because you have a large family to support?'
>
> 'No, sire. There are only four of us, my wife and I, and our son and daughter,' Veerdev replied.
>
> Something in the man's demeanour impressed the king, who hired Veerdev as his personal bodyguard on night duty. Veerdev began work the following evening, and returned home every morning with a bag containing a hundred gold coins. Wondering what Veerdev did with his earnings, the king instructed his spies to find out how the money was spent. After a week, the spies reported that Veerdev distributed most of his earnings amongst the poor and needy, and made donations to various temples and

their priests, keeping only five mohurs for his family and himself. The king was pleased to hear this and felt he had made the right decision to employ such a generous man.

One night, loud screams pierced the silence of the sleeping palace. Woken from his slumber by the hubbub, King Roopsen ordered Veerdev to investigate. Outside the palace gate, the bodyguard saw a middle-aged woman weeping and in great anguish. The woman explained that she was a psychic and had dreamt that the king's life was in grave danger. She added that the only way the king's life could be saved was if someone sacrificed his son at the local temple before dawn to appease the gods.

The king, who had watched the entire scene, wondered what action Veerdev would take and decided to follow him.

Veerdev rushed home, woke his wife and children, and told them what the psychic had said, adding that it was his responsibility to safeguard the king's life at any cost. His son readily agreed to be sacrificed, and all four of them headed towards the temple. The boy lay down on the altar and was beheaded by Veerdev. His distraught daughter, unable to bear the loss of her brother, grabbed the sword from her father's hands and slit her throat. Veerdev's wife, aghast that both her children were dead, picked up the sword and killed herself. Seeing his entire family lying dead in front of him, Veerdev used the bloodstained sword to end his own life.

The king, who had watched the horrific killings from behind a temple pillar, was overcome by grief and guilt at not intervening to protect his bodyguard or his wife and children. He blamed himself for destroying an entire family and decided to end his life. King Roopsen unsheathed his sword and was about to kill himself when the goddess of destruction appeared and said she would grant him any boon he desired. The monarch fell to his knees before the

> goddess and implored her to bring his faithful servant and his family back to life. The goddess granted the king's wish, and raised Veerdev and his family from the dead. The very next day, King Roopsen divided half of his kingdom with the loyal bodyguard.

'It's your turn to speak now, Vikram,' Vetal continued. 'Tell me, between Veerdev, his family, and the king, who was the greatest fool?'

'If by the greatest fool you mean the noblest mind, then without hesitation that honour would go to King Roopsen,' the wise king replied.

'Why?'

'Because Veerdev was duty-bound to give up his life for a master who treated him so generously; the son could not disobey his father; and the women instinctively killed themselves because the example was set to them. But Roopsen was willing to give up his life and ended up giving up half his kingdom in gratitude. For this reason, I consider him the most meritorious.'

The vampire laughed out loud. 'Vikram, why are you wasting your time running back and forth in this jungle when you could be sleeping comfortably in your bed in your majestic palace? Aren't you tired of chasing after me? You may be a wise king but as you have not kept silent despite my many warnings, I have to take your leave and head back to my home on the siris tree.' And off he flew, with the valiant king chasing after him.

∽

It was now nearing three o'clock in the morning, and King Vikramaditya used his sword for the fifteenth time to dislodge his tormentor from his perch on the tree, bundled him up in the shawl, and began to trudge back to the cremation ground. Although he was tiring of Vetal's capriciousness, his stories did relieve the monotony of the long walk and helped to keep his mind off the eerie night-time sounds of the jungle.

'I hope you are ready for my next story, O Wise King,' Vetal chortled. 'I'm sure you will ultimately succeed in your mission to reach the cremation ground, but before that I must keep you entertained....'

There once lived a king who had three beautiful daughters who were extremely delicate. His eldest daughter was so sensitive that her skin would break out in blisters even in moonlight. His second daughter was unable to tolerate loud sounds and would lose consciousness if anybody spoke loudly. The youngest daughter was so fragile that even if a rose petal touched her skin, she would bruise.

News of the princesses' strange afflictions had spread far and wide and no cure had been found. The eldest princess was never exposed to sunlight or moonlight but stayed in the shade at all times; everyone spoke in whispers when the second princess was present; and the youngest princess made sure that nothing and nobody touched her. The king was deeply concerned about his daughters and wondered if they would ever be able to marry or lead a normal life.

To keep them as safe as possible, he had hired a maid to take care of them personally. One day, the king gifted the maid an elegant filigreed necklace made of gold in appreciation of her devotion to the princesses. As the maid was heading home, a beggar asking for alms at the palace gate implored her to give him the necklace, saying that he would give it to his daughter who was getting married soon. The kind-hearted maid handed over the necklace but the king and the princesses were very upset that she had given away his gift.

A renowned vaidya who had been invited to the palace by the king with the hope that he could cure the princesses, had witnessed the episode involving the maid. When the king asked the doctor which of his daughters was the most sensitive, the doctor burst out laughing. He refused to treat any of the girls and left the palace.

'Tell me, Vikram, was the vaidya right or wrong? Who was the most sensitive princess amongst the three?'

'The princesses were delicate, but certainly not sensitive,' Vikram replied. 'In my opinion, tenderness of heart is more important than tenderness of the body. In your story, the most sensitive person was the maid who gave the necklace to the beggar. If someone's heart is not tender, then tenderness of the body is useless. That is why the vaidya refused to treat the princesses.'

'You are right as usual, Vikram,' Vetal said as he wriggled out of the sack and flew off to his resting place on the siris tree.

Captured for the twentieth time and unceremoniously bundled up in the king's shawl, Vetal was unabashed. 'My next story is about a love triangle.'

Many years ago, the kingdom of Kanakpur was ruled by a young king named Yashodhan, whose kindness and impartiality earned him the respect of his people, his army, and his courtiers. Some distance from the palace, there lived a wealthy businessman with his wife and daughter, Roopali, a slim, beautiful, and gentle young girl who was now of marriageable age.

The businessman's friends often commented on Roopali's elegance and good looks, adding that only Yashodhan could be a suitable match for her. Encouraged by his friends, the businessman sent a letter to the king, extolling his daughter's virtues, and inviting him to visit them. The judicious young monarch, used to receiving similar propositions and proposals, sent three of his courtiers to visit the businessman and his family to assess whether Roopali would make a suitable queen.

The courtiers spent a few days as the businessman's guests and were impressed not only by Roopali's beauty but also her calm and gracious temperament. Word soon spread in the town about the purpose of the courtiers' visit, and a jealous neighbour, who had years earlier been punished by the king for breaking the law, decided to get his revenge.

He waited until the courtiers were strolling alone in the town one morning. As they passed the local flower stall, he introduced himself and started a conversation about roses, saying there was nothing more beautiful in nature than the petals of a fresh bloom. When the courtiers predictably extolled Roopali's natural beauty in comparison, the neighbour slyly pointed out that Yashodhan, being young and vulnerable, would become so enamoured of her looks that he would neglect his royal duties and bring havoc to the realm. He repeatedly sowed seeds of doubt amongst the courtiers until they began to believe him.

Returning to the palace soon after, the courtiers reported that the girl would not be a suitable match and, indeed, could be a curse. Therefore, the king did not make a formal proposal.

A few months later, the businessman and his wife arranged their daughter's engagement to a handsome young commander from the king's army. The young couple were deeply in love and looked forward to their wedding.

One day, the king happened to see Roopali in a passing carriage, and was immediately captivated by her beauty. He asked his courtiers, including the commander, to track down the girl immediately and ask for her hand in marriage.

> The young commander put his loyalty to the king above all love for his fiancée and broke off the engagement, thus clearing the way for his master to marry Roopali. A few days before the wedding, a courtier revealed the truth about the commander's sacrifice to the monarch. Being a fair and decent man, Yashodhan arranged for Roopali to marry the commander instead, the man she loved.

'The question for you, Vikram, is straightforward. Whose sacrifice is greater—the king's or the commander's?'

Vikram replied: 'The commander was merely doing his duty by giving up his fiancée out of loyalty to his king. To my mind, the king's sacrifice was greater because he could easily have used his power and authority to marry the girl. But being a highly principled man, he did not do so because he did not want to get in the way of true love.'

Vetal made no comment but immediately slipped out of the sack and flew off to his perch on the siris tree, with King Vikramaditya in hot pursuit.

∽

The cycle of capture and escape had been repeated so many times that both Vikram and Vetal were tiring of the game.

'Why do you trouble me so much?' the exasperated king asked.

'Whatever I've done is for your good. A time will come when you will be obliged to me,' Vetal said. 'It's nearly daybreak, O Powerful King, but you still persist in trying to subdue me. I like to rest during the day, so I'll keep my next tale short....'

> My story is set in a time when the world was going through the Kaliyug with widespread pestilence and war, and there was death and destruction everywhere.
>
> In the midst of this mayhem, a father and his young son who had survived a brutal battle were heading to their

> home town. On the way, they came across a queen and her daughter who were also fleeing from soldiers who had taken over their kingdom. The four of them decided to travel together, hoping for safety in numbers. Soon after reaching their destination safely, the princess married the father and the queen married the son. A year later, the father and the princess had a daughter, and the son and the queen had a son.

'My question for you, Vikram, is simple. What is the relationship between the two new-born children?'

For the first time since his quest began, Vikram was silent, his head spinning from lack of sleep and physical exhaustion. He trudged on in silence and had nearly reached the cremation ground where the hermit awaited him, when Vetal made a shocking revelation. 'Vikram, this yogi is untrustworthy and is planning to kill you. He will ask you to kneel before him and when you do so he will behead you with a sword.'

The king didn't respond or react but kept walking towards the cremation ground. When the yogi saw King Vikramaditya approaching with Vetal slung over his shoulder he greeted him warmly. 'Well done Vikram, you are truly courageous. You will now rule the realm without any obstacles.' The hermit drew his sword and killed Vetal, then tossed the body into one of the pyres. Turning to the king, the yogi said: 'King Vikramaditya, you can now attain your ultimate blessing by prostrating in front of me.'

'I am a king, I do not prostrate in front of anybody,' King Vikramaditya replied.

'In that case, I shall prostrate myself before you.' As the yogi bent down before the king, the king cut off his neck with his sword. Suddenly, the king heard loud laughter reverberating through the forest and was astonished to see that it was Vetal, laughing with his head thrown back.

'Is it really you, Vetal?' Vikram asked. 'I thought you were dead.'

'Yes, it is me,' came the reply. 'If you hadn't killed the yogi, I could not have been born again.' The king noticed that Vetal's appearance had completely changed—he had transformed into a handsome young man. Vikram asked him: 'What are your plans?'

'To follow your orders,' Vetal replied. Vikram offered the young man the post of a minister in his court, which was gratefully accepted. King Vikramaditya and his newly appointed minister set off for the palace as the sun began its steady rise on the horizon, bringing with it the promise of a new day.

115

Straightening a Dog's Tail

Tenali Ramakrishna, also known as Tenali Raman, was one of eight Telugu poets known as Ashtadiggajas in the palace of King Krishnadeva Raya, who reigned over the Vijayanagar empire from 1509–29 and was one of the most powerful Hindu rulers in India. A scholar and royal adviser known for his quick wit, Tenali Raman soon became as indispensable to King Krishnadeva as Birbal would to Emperor Akbar half a century later.

During his reign, King Krishnadeva Raya had earned the reputation of being equally adept at war as at peace, and took pride in encouraging intellectual and philosophical discussions in his court. One day, the topic under discussion was whether it was possible to change the basic nature of any living thing, be it a man or an animal. Opinion on the matter was divided, with some of the king's courtiers convinced that it was possible, while others were of the view that just as a dog's tail cannot be straightened, similarly, a man's nature cannot be changed. One of the courtiers countered: 'I believe that if one tries hard enough, even a dog's tail can be straightened.'

The king laughed on hearing this, and threw open a challenge. He ordered six puppies to be brought to the durbar, and offered a reward of one hundred gold coins to anyone who could straighten a puppy's tail within the next three months. Six of the courtiers, including Tenali Raman, accepted the challenge and carried a puppy home, confident that they could straighten the tiny creature's tail in the allotted time.

Ingenious strategies were devised to try to straighten the puppies' tails. One man tied a heavy stone to the tiny creature's curved tail, hoping the weight would straighten it out. A second bound his puppy's tail in a splint made out of two pieces of wood. A third person massaged an expensive potion prescribed by a doctor on the dog's tail three times a day. A fourth person hired a godman, who conjured up a magic spell that had to be chanted a hundred times daily to straighten the tail. The fifth person approached a doctor to break the bones in the animal's tail in a futile attempt to straighten it, but the doctor refused to do so.

Raman shook his head in disbelief when he heard about his competitors' efforts. He had decided not to spend any money on straightening his own puppy's tail. All he did was keep the little pup indoors, giving it just enough food to ensure its survival. The tiny pooch began to get weaker by the day, and its tiny tail began to droop, looking limp and inert, but straight.

Three months later, the six owners turned up at King Krishnadeva's palace along with their charges. The tails of five of the puppies were still curved, despite their owners' desperate attempts to straighten them. When Raman presented his pup for inspection, the malnourished animal was unable to stand or wag its tail, which hung straight and limp between its hind legs.

'Look, Your Majesty,' Raman said proudly, 'I have straightened the puppy's tail.'

'You scoundrel,' the king shouted. 'You have starved the helpless little creature and nearly killed it. He doesn't even have the strength to wag his tail!'

Raman replied: 'I was merely following your orders, Your Majesty. Your command was to straighten the puppy's tail, which is not normal and against the laws of nature. The only way I could do this was by keeping the little one hungry. I wanted to make the point that no living being's nature can be changed forcibly. Trying to do so does more harm than good.

In fact, it can be very dangerous to meddle with nature, very dangerous indeed.'

Tenali Raman had answered the question about whether a living being's nature could be changed or not. He headed home carrying his reward in one hand and the puppy in the other. From that day onwards, the dog was well fed and looked after. He grew big and strong, and frequently wagged his curled and bushy tail.

The Right Man for the Job

A generous patron of the arts, King Krishnadeva Raya decided to have his portrait painted by the famous artist Tyagarajan. The king was so pleased with the flattering painting that he appointed the artist to the important post of minister of administration. Undoubtedly a gifted artist, Tyagarajan tried his best to make a good impression running the affairs of state but was completely out of his depth. Public services were affected, supplies were not ordered on time, salaries were delayed, and people began to suffer. The king's other ministers frequently dropped hints about the alarming state of affairs, but their warnings were ignored. Eventually, the ministers turned to Tenali Raman to help. 'Leave it with me,' the adviser promised. 'I'll think of a way to show the king his error.'

A few days later, Raman invited the king to his house for dinner, saying he would be honoured if the monarch attended a special family celebration. The king arrived punctually and was warmly welcomed by the host and his family. Raman had taken great pains to make it a memorable evening for the king. He had borrowed gold plates and chalices in which to serve the food and drink and had rented a thick carpet and plush silk cushions to seat the esteemed guest.

Krishnadeva Raya was pleased with the lavish arrangements and looked forward to the meal. He was a connoisseur of good food and liked to try a variety of dishes. Observing the elegance of the other arrangements, he was sure that the dinner would be a culinary feast. However, when Raman's wife served the food, the king was very disappointed to see that there were only a couple of dishes: a large portion of lumpy pilaf, two watery vegetable offerings, and a pile of thick chapattis.

Despite the unappetizing appearance, the king took large servings of every dish, broke off a piece of chapatti, scooped up some of the curried vegetable in it and popped it into his mouth. The vegetables were tasteless and the chapatti was thick and chewy. Too polite to show his displeasure, the king battled with the unpleasant mouthful for a full minute until he finally managed to swallow it with a large gulp of nimbu pani from his golden chalice.

'Raman,' the king said, pushing his plate away. 'Who has done the cooking?'

'A friend of mine,' Raman replied. 'He's a cobbler.'

'What?' the king laughed. 'No wonder the food tastes like leather. You can't expect a cobbler to cook good food.'

'Why not, Maharaj?' Raman asked innocently.

'Because a cobbler is trained in shoemaking, not in cuisine.'

'But Maharaj, if a painter can run an administration, why can't a shoemaker cook a royal feast?'

Realization dawned on the king. 'I've made a big mistake, haven't I?' he said. 'I appointed Tyagarajan to the ministerial post as a means of honouring him. How can I take back the honour without upsetting him?'

'Your Majesty, Tyagarajan is indeed a good man and an excellent artist. But he is hopeless at administration, and he knows it. That's why I'm certain that he'll help you resolve this situation without any dishonour to you.'

The following day, Raman made sure that Tyagarajan heard about the inedible food that the cobbler had cooked for the king. Soon after, the artist resigned from his post as minister of administration, no longer fearing that this would offend the monarch, because he had a more important job to do. He focused on being the talented painter that he was meant to be by completing portraits of the royal family. The king was amazed by such brilliance and ordered the paintings to be hung in the royal dining room, where he held sumptuous banquets prepared by the finest chefs in the land.

117

Thieves to the Rescue

The citizens of Vijayanagar were greatly perturbed. A gang of thieves had been robbing homes across the kingdom, ransacking one town after another and successfully evading the police. When the chief of police approached Tenali Raman for his help to catch the thieves, he readily agreed. 'There's no point going after the crooks,' he said. 'We'll make them come to us and that's when you must nab them.'

The next day, under Tenali Raman's instructions, his wife began to spread a rumour that the king had gifted her husband a bag of gold coins. The news spread like wildfire and soon reached the thieves.

Heading home later that evening to his large house surrounded by acres of fields in which he grew vegetables and rice, Tenali Raman spotted two men lurking behind the trees outside his gate and knew his plan had worked. Ignoring his wife's greeting as he entered the house, he instead loudly declared: 'The king has received word that thieves are on the prowl in the area and all citizens have been urged to lock up their valuables.'

'Oh dear, what should we do?' his wife asked.

'Put the bag of gold coins along with all our silver, jewellery, and money into a trunk and I'll throw it into the well for safekeeping. No thief will ever think of looking for it there.'

His wife put a heavy grinding stone into the trunk and Tenali Raman made a great show of dragging the heavy chest to the well. He lifted it up with a grunt and a groan, and pushed it into the well, where it made a mighty splash. He then had his dinner, made sure that the doors and windows were latched and bolted, and prepared for a good night's sleep.

When the house was dark and still, the thieves got to work. They began to drain the well, drawing up bucket after bucket of water and pouring it into the fields. Working silently and swiftly through the night, the thieves were exhausted by the time they finally got hold of the trunk. Before they could recover from the shock of finding that the crate contained nothing but a grinding stone, Tenali Raman crept up behind the thieves and said: 'Thank you, my good men. You've done an excellent job of watering my crops.'

The startled thieves turned to make their escape but were caught by the police who were lying in wait in the street outside Tenali Raman's house. King Krishnadeva Raya decided to reward Tenali Raman with a purse of gold coins for his assistance in catching the crooks.

118

Gold for the Afterlife

Once, when King Krishnadeva Raya's vast orchards yielded a bountiful crop of mangoes, his elderly mother had expressed her desire to distribute the luscious fruit to the kingdom's poor, but died shortly after the fruit was harvested. While the court was plunged into mourning and funeral arrangements were made, the fruit had rotted and was good for nothing. Nevertheless, the noble king was determined to fulfil his mother's last wish.

He summoned one hundred Brahmins from around the kingdom and told them that he feared his mother's unfulfilled desire would prevent her from finding peace in the afterlife. The Brahmins shook their heads from side to side and looked perturbed. 'Do not despair, Your Majesty,' the head Brahmin said after giving the matter some thought. 'The only way of providing peace to your mother's soul is by giving a hundred Brahmins mangoes made out of gold equal in weight to the mangoes your late mother had wanted to give away in charity.'

'Will my mother's soul definitely reap the benefit if I follow your advice?'

'Indeed it will, Your Majesty,' the Brahmins assured him. 'It has been a long-standing and proven tradition.'

Never one to question tradition, the trusting king ordered his goldsmith to make a hundred mangoes of pure gold, each one weighing as much as a real mango. It was an expensive undertaking but the king deemed it worth the expense to safeguard his mother's soul. When the hundred gold mangoes had been crafted, the Brahmins were summoned and the gleaming fruits were distributed among them.

As the Brahmins were leaving the palace with their bounty, Tenali Raman sent a messenger to summon them to his house, saying that he too wanted to attain peace for his mother's soul. The Brahmins eagerly headed to Raman's house and were shown into a large room that had a blazing brick oven at one end. When the Brahmins were seated, Raman signalled to his servant, who stuck two iron rods into the fire.

'My late mother suffered from severe rheumatism and was often in pain,' Tenali Raman explained to the Brahmins. 'One day she told me that if I applied a hot iron to her skin, it would alleviate her pain. Sadly, she died before I could fulfil her desire so I want to make sure that she's not in pain in her afterlife and that her soul gets peace.' Tenali Raman then gestured to his servant, who pulled the red-hot iron rods from the oven and approached the priests.

'What are you doing?' the Brahmins shrieked, backing away in alarm.

'Since I couldn't do this for my mother in her lifetime, I must do it to you, because you're obviously able to fulfil desires on behalf of the departed and transfer the benefits to them.' He then nodded to the servant again, who advanced towards the Brahmins with the hot irons.

'Are you out of your mind?' the priests shouted. 'Tell your man to stop at once!'

'But what about my mother's soul? She needs to be at peace, and you are the only ones who can provide it.'

'No, no, we can't,' they screamed. 'How can we possibly do that? Your mother is dead. Her body has been cremated, and her ashes are in the river. Who knows where her soul is! How can we bring her peace? We have no way of reaching her.'

'But you promised the king that his mother would find peace through you.'

'That was just a ruse. We admit that we misled the king. Please tell your man to stop,' they begged.

At Tenali Raman's nod, the servant halted, but he still stood pointing the rods at the Brahmins.

'What about the gold mangoes?' Tenali Raman persisted.

'That was sheer greed. You are welcome to them,' the Brahmins said, and emptying their bags, they ran out of Tenali Raman's house.

The next day Tenali Raman returned all the expensive fruits to King Krishnadeva Raya, saying: 'The queen mother was a pious and charitable lady who performed good deeds all her life. Have faith that she will find peace in heaven based on her own actions. She does not need the help of greedy priests or gold mangoes.'

119

Brain versus Brawn

Following his retirement, Tenali Raman and his wife were passing through a small town on their way to visit relatives when they noticed a large crowd gathered outside a temple. At the centre of the throng, towering above everyone else, stood a bodybuilder. The man, who was more than six feet tall, had a bulging gunny bag slung over his left shoulder and was nonchalantly waving to the crowd with his right hand.

Awed by this display of superhuman strength, a man standing next to Tenali Raman said: 'It's unbelievable. The rice in that sack weighs five maunds*! But he's carrying it on one shoulder as if it were as light as a feather!'

'That's nothing,' Tenali Raman retorted, loud enough for everyone around him to hear. 'I can carry a hundred times more weight than that.'

Everyone looked at Tenali Raman in amazement, including his wife, who had not known her husband to carry so much as a bucket of water from the well to their house. Before she could say anything, her husband added: 'I can easily carry that hill on one shoulder,' pointing to a nearby peak.

The excited crowd cheered loudly. 'That would be amazing! We'd love to witness such a show of strength!' they exclaimed.

'Be patient, my friends,' Tenali Raman urged the crowd. 'I can carry the mountain, but not right away. Carrying such a heavy weight will take months of preparation.' Then turning

---

*About 185 kilograms.

to the bodybuilder, he asked: 'How long did you have to train to lift this bag of rice?'

'Nearly three months,' came the reply.

The village chief came forward. 'How long will you require to prepare for your show of strength?' he asked.

'Mine is a much more difficult and challenging task,' Tenali Raman replied. 'It will take at least six months of rigorous training, at least three wholesome meals a day to build up my muscles, plus a massage twice daily.'

Cottoning on to her husband's plan, his wife added: 'As you know, we are not from this town so we'll also need a place to live.'

'I'll personally see to it that all arrangements are made for you,' the village chief promised. 'Good luck with your training. We shall assemble here exactly six months from today to witness this marvel.'

For the next six months, Tenali Raman and his wife did not have to worry about their stomachs. The villagers brought them delicious home-cooked meals, plied them with sweets made with pure ghee, and made sure that they never went hungry. Both Tenali Raman and his wife enjoyed the villagers' hospitality with gusto. Everyone noticed that the husband and wife were steadily gaining weight, but no one ever saw Tenali Raman doing any strength-building exercises.

Six months went by, and the day of reckoning finally dawned. The entire town gathered outside the temple to witness Tenali Raman's show of strength. The village chief and the bodybuilder had positioned themselves to get the best view. All eyes were transfixed on Tenali Raman as he slowly took a few steps forward and sat down in the centre of the temple's courtyard.

'I'm ready,' he announced loudly.

The crowd looked puzzled. The village chief stepped forward and said: 'We're ready too. What are you waiting for?'

'I'm waiting for the men from your village to place the hill on my shoulder,' Tenali Raman replied coolly.

'But who is going to lift the hill and carry it here?'

'That's your problem, not mine! I had only promised to carry the hill on one shoulder, not to lift it up and place it there.'

Realizing that they had been duped, the crowd dispersed, laughing. The bodybuilder stood there shaking his head, admitting that strength is no match for shrewdness.

The Bell of Atri

A long time ago, in the Italian town of Atri there lived a wise king who took great care of his subjects. One day, the king ordered a large brass bell to be erected on top of a tall tower that stood in the middle of the town square. The townsfolk wondered about the bell's purpose, but were confident that it was being built for their benefit. When the construction was completed and the finishing touch—a long plaited rope made of hemp and reaching to the ground—was attached to the bell's clapper, the town crier announced:

Hear ye! Hear ye! Good people of Atri,
This bell is a gift for you from His Majesty,
Who has decreed that this will henceforth be
A call for speedy justice for all the citizenry.
Whenever justice is delayed or denied
People inevitably feel dissatisfied.
Therefore, His Majesty has let it be told
That all justice seekers, be they young or old,
At any time of day or night may this bell ring
To summon three judges, who'll swiftly bring
Their complaint or grievance to a conclusion
By providing an appropriate and fair solution.

Over the years, through sunshine and storms, heat and cold, the bell of Atri was rung many times. Though the bell was kept gleaming and polished, the rope began to fray and became shorter when bits of it began to fall off, making it difficult for a child to reach.

A new custom-made rope was ordered from a neighbouring town but it would take several weeks to reach Atri. What was to be done while they were waiting for the rope to be replaced? A local grape farmer came up with a solution. 'I have a strong vine of the right width and length that will serve our purpose until the new rope is ready,' he said. The farmer tied the vine to the shortened rope ensuring that the bell of justice remained within easy reach of adults and children.

Now, in the hills near Atri, there lived a retired soldier who had amassed great wealth over the years. He and his trusted horse had survived many a battle but both now lived a quiet life. One morning, the soldier looked out of the window of his villa and saw the old horse grazing in the yard. 'There is no point in keeping that old mare any longer,' he muttered. 'She's of no use to me now and is an unnecessary expense. The time has come to get rid of her.'

The next day the soldier set off with his horse. He walked beside her for several miles and eventually abandoned her in a secluded spot a long way from his home.

It was a hot summer that year, and the land was parched and dry. No one knows for how long the old and starving animal wandered across hill and dale in search of food and water. But one stiflingly hot afternoon, when all the residents of Atri were enjoying their siesta, the weary horse, its head drooping, plodded slowly into the town square. Spotting the vine tied to the rope of the justice bell, the starving horse pulled at the vine to bite off a leaf. 'Dingggg dongggg,' went the bell, its rich tones vibrating through the silence in the slumbering town, startling both the horse and the residents of Atri. As the old mare reached for more leaves from the vine, the bell tolled again and again.

The judges hastily got out of bed, wiped the beads of perspiration from their faces, put on their robes and headed for the town square in response to the urgent summons.

A few curious people also gathered at the spot and stared at the frail and fatigued four-legged supplicant. One of the townsfolk recognized the starving animal and cried out: 'This horse belongs to the soldier who lives in the big house on the hill.'

'Summon the soldier immediately,' the judges ordered, hoping that they wouldn't have to stand around in the heat for too long. When the soldier arrived, he hung his head in shame and had nothing to say in his defence.

The judges reprimanded him sternly. 'Abandoning an animal because it has grown old and is of no more use is as great an offence as deserting your elderly parents or family members. We could impose a hefty fine on you for abandoning your horse, but instead we order you to care for it as long as it lives. You owe a lot to this faithful animal.' The soldier apologized for his mistake and promised to obey the judges' order.

The people of Atri were delighted that the bell in their town would henceforth be remembered for bringing justice to all—even to an old horse, who now lived in equine luxury in a large warm stable that the soldier built with his own hands, in time for winter, from the finest oak in the realm.

121

Let's Team Up

Legend has it that a long time ago, the gods became deeply concerned about the rise of misconduct and wrongdoing in the world. Theft, bribery, fraud, and murder were on the rise and even swift justice and harsh punishments did not bring down the crime rate. The gods therefore decided to send a representative to earth to spread the message of ethics and principles.

A beautiful and gentle young woman named Neeti (meaning integrity) was appointed the emissary of morality and was dispatched to spread her message amongst human beings. Dedicated to her mission, Neeti did her best to get people to change their ways, to no avail. Her homilies about the need to be truthful, to not cheat others or destroy their property, and to treat others as they themselves would want to be treated were ignored and even laughed at.

After months of being mocked and made to feel unwelcome wherever she went, Neeti had become unrecognizable. Blaming herself for being an utter failure, she had lost weight, and her hair had turned white. She looked old and haggard. Still, she persisted in her quest. One evening, after a frustrating day when she had knocked on several doors only to have them slammed in her face, she was tearfully walking along a deserted road heading to a new town, when a handsome young man riding a magnificent black horse, stopped and asked her where she was headed.

Neeti was so taken aback by someone actually stopping to talk to her that she burst into tears and told the handsome youth about her unsuccessful assignment.

'What an amazing coincidence,' the young man said. 'I'm a writer and my name is Dastan, which means story. I think you and I could work well together, and I can help you to spread your message. Let's team up.'

That was the start of a fruitful collaboration between the emissary of ethics and the storyteller, who between them wrote hundreds of stories that each ended with a valuable moral, setting a trend that outlived them both and inspired generations of writers and readers.

Neeti and Dastan both learned a valuable lesson from their partnership: if you can't manage something alone, you may be more successful if you work as a team, where everyone brings something different to the table, but all have a common goal.

A Helping Hand

A farmer was making his way home along a country road on his two-horse wagon loaded with hay, when it began to rain heavily. Within minutes, the farmer, his horses, and the hay were soaking wet, and the muddy road had turned into a squishy pool of sludge. The horses slowed down and strained to proceed along the path as their hooves sank into the mud, then suddenly came to a standstill with a jerk as one of the rear wheels sank halfway into a rut, causing the wagon to tilt precariously.

The farmer dismounted to survey the damage, cursed his bad luck but made no attempt to try and lift the wheel out of the pothole. Instead, he closed his eyes, turned his wet face towards the weeping skies, and appealed loudly to Heracles to come to his rescue. 'O Mighty Heracles, God of Strength, I beseech you to come to the aid of a humble and hapless devotee. My wagon is stuck, my horses and I are fatigued. If we do not get back to the farm before nightfall, we may not survive the storm.'

Hearing his loud and impassioned plea, Heracles appeared, accompanied by a bolt of lightning and a resounding clap of thunder, and was surprised to see the farmer standing helplessly beside his wagon feeling sorry for himself. 'Don't just stand there, my good man,' Heracles roared. 'You need to put your shoulder to the wheel and spur on your horses. The wagon is not going to get out of its rut simply by your looking at it and moaning about it. I cannot help you unless you make some effort to help yourself.'

The farmer put his shoulder to the wheel and made loud clicking sounds to goad his horses. The wagon rocked slightly, slipped back a bit and then with a mighty heave from the farmer, the rear wheel slid out of the pothole and the trio were able to make their slow and cautious way home.

From that day onwards, the farmer remembered that the best place to find a helping hand was at the end of his own arm.

123

The Value of Things

A wealthy but miserly merchant converted his life's earnings into gold coins, and stored his stash in a metal box that he buried under an apple tree in his garden. Every evening, before nightfall, the miser would dig up the treasure and count the coins one at a time to make sure they were all there. A thief, who had watched the merchant painstakingly dig up the box, count its contents, and then bury it under the tree again, crept into the garden in the middle of the night and made off with the treasure.

When the miser discovered that his life savings had been stolen, he was distraught, and began beating his chest and loudly lamenting his loss. Hearing the uproar, a passer-by stopped to find out what had happened.

'My gold! My life savings! Disappeared! Stolen!' the miser cried hysterically, pointing to the hole in the ground under the apple tree. 'My life is ruined. I have been robbed and left with nothing.'

'You put your gold in that hole?' the bewildered passer-by asked. 'Why on earth would you do something so foolish? Why would you bury your gold under a tree instead of keeping it safe in the house, where it would be within easy reach when you needed to buy things?'

'Buy things? What things?' the miser yelled angrily. 'I did not spend any of my gold. I wouldn't dream of using any of it, not even a single coin.'

On hearing this, the stranger picked up a large stone and handed it to the miser. 'Take this stone instead, bury it under your tree, and pretend that you have gold there. If your heart and soul are obsessed with collecting things instead of using them, then this stone should serve the same purpose as the treasure you lost! Because even when you had the gold you might as well not have had it—wealth not used is wealth that doesn't exist.'

The miser could not argue with the stranger's logic, and saw his own folly. He picked a few ripe apples from his tree and handed them to the stranger. 'Thank you for showing me the real value of things. I realize now that I have not lost much at all, because what I had, I never used, so should not miss it.'

124

The Farmer's Secret

An elderly farmer worked hard throughout his life to provide for his three sons. As the boys grew up, they occasionally helped till the land, sow the seeds, and reap the harvest, but most of the hard work was left to their father.

After years of back-breaking toil, the patriarch was now old and ailing. Recognizing that he was dying, the farmer summoned his sons to his bedside. 'My boys,' he began, 'I may not have long to live but need to share an important secret with you. I'm aware that you're not keen to follow in my footsteps and take up farming, but I urge you not to sell the lands and property that have been in our family for generations, and which I shall bequeath to you. The reason I want you to hold on to your inheritance is because somewhere on the estate there is buried treasure. I cannot remember the exact spot where the wealth is hidden, but I know it is there. I want the three of you to work together and put all your efforts into finding your fortune.'

A few weeks later, the farmer passed away and soon after the funeral his sons began the laborious task of digging up the vast estate in search of the treasure. The three boys worked from dawn to dusk, repeatedly turning up every foot of ground with their spades.

Months went by. The boys did not unearth any buried treasure, but at harvest time they were overjoyed with their bounteous crop and found that they had made a far greater profit from their land than any of the neighbouring farmers. Their diligence and unity had paid off—they had earned the fortune that their father had promised.

The brothers went on to care for the farm, as did their wives, children, and grandchildren, who were often told the story of the buried treasure hidden somewhere on their land, which they might find some day if they kept digging.

125

Teaching a Donkey to Read

Till Eulenspiegel is a popular character from sixteenth-century German folklore, known for his chicanery. 'Eulenspiegel' literally translates as 'owl mirror' (hence his moniker Owlglass), and has been interpreted to mean 'wise reflection'. While playing the part of a fool, Owlglass holds up a mirror for society to look in and judge itself. As in many folk tales, social criticism is cloaked in humour.

Footloose and fancy-free, Owlglass had come up with a new scam, going from one university to another in his native Germany, posing as a learned scholar and engaging in debate with academics. Being something of a smart aleck, with a superficial knowledge of many subjects and mastery of none, Owlglass came up with such baffling and ambiguous answers to the questions posed to him that even the most erudite cross-examiner would lapse into bemused silence. Buoyed by his success, Owlglass began to boast that he could teach any animal to read.

When word got around in the university town of Erfurt, in central Germany, that Owlglass was gracing them with a visit, the dean and the professors were determined to call his bluff. 'We must take him at his word and put him to the test,' said the dean.

They bought a donkey, dragged the bewildered animal to the inn where Owlglass was staying and asked him if he was a good enough teacher to be able to teach the donkey to read.

'Yes, of course,' Owlglass replied. 'It will be as easy as ABC.

But a donkey being an especially dull and stubborn animal, it will also take a long time.'

'How long?' asked the dean.

Owlglass considered the question for a few minutes. I think I should give myself enough time...say, twenty years, he thought. A lot can happen in two decades—the dean might die, the donkey might succumb from the pressures of learning to read, and in the worst-case scenario, I might die and that would be the end of the problem.

'My guess is that it could take me at least twenty years,' he told the dean, who mulled over the matter for a few seconds before agreeing that it seemed a reasonable estimate, given the complexity of the task. 'And I will charge a fee of five hundred guilders for my services,' Owlglass added, 'one-fifth of it to be paid in advance to cover my expenses.'

'If you do not succeed in teaching the donkey to read, you will not get a single guilder from us and you will also have to return this advance payment,' the dean warned as he handed over one hundred guilders to Owlglass and left him to deal with his four-legged pupil.

Owlglass housed his student in a stall behind the inn. The unlucky animal's training began that evening, when his tutor stuffed bits of hay and oats between the pages of a large tome, which he placed in the food trough, forcing the hungry donkey to leaf through the book with his tongue to get to the food. When he'd gobbled up the last of the hay and oats, the donkey raised his head and brayed loudly: 'Eee-aw, eee-aw.' This process continued for a whole week, at the end of which Owlglass visited the dean and invited him to see the donkey's progress.

The dean, somewhat sceptical, asked: 'Has your student managed to learn anything so soon?'

'Oh yes,' Owlglass replied. 'He has already mastered two letters of the alphabet, as you will see for yourself.'

Later that day, the dean and a few of his associates came to the inn and Owlglass led them to the donkey's stall. He placed the tome in the trough, but this time without any hay or oats scattered between its pages. The donkey, who had not been fed all day, eagerly turned the pages of the book with his tongue, and not finding any feed, let out a loud 'Eee-aw, eee-aw' in protest.

'As you can see,' said Owlglass proudly, 'he has already learned the letters E and O. Tomorrow I will start teaching him the remaining vowels before moving on to the rest of the alphabet.' The dean and his party looked at each other in surprise, at a loss for words as realization dawned that Owlglass was making a fool of them.

Later that evening, Owlglass put up a notice on the college door declaring that his student, the donkey, was now fully competent not only to instruct the other donkeys of Erfurt but also to be the head of the university. The dean and his colleagues, outraged at Owlglass' impudence, tore up the notice and headed straight for the inn to confront the upstart. But Owlglass had already left town, taking with him the advance that he felt he had deservedly earned.

'The knave has made a fool of us,' the dean sighed. 'We may be a hundred guilders poorer, but it's good riddance to bad rubbish. We must ensure that the scoundrel never sets foot in our town again.'

The good people of Erfurt were astounded that a nonentity like Owlglass had outsmarted the town's leading academics. 'It goes to show that even wise men cannot anticipate the extent of a knave's folly,' they said. The only good thing that came out of the embarrassing episode was that there was an outpouring of public sympathy for the donkey, who lived out the rest of his days in a barn near the university campus, became a mascot for the college, and never had to read a book ever again.

126

The Crumbling House of Starving John

Starving John earned his nickname because everyone in his home town knew that he had no regular source of income and that his family—a wife and four children—lived from hand to mouth.

One day, John's pet cat, who was also famished, managed to hunt down a rabbit. Before the cat could enjoy his kill, John's wife, Maria, snatched the rabbit from the cat's jaw, skinned it, and cooked up a flavoursome stew. Handing a steaming bowl of stew to her hungry husband, Maria said: 'Quick, take this stew and go and eat it as far away from here as possible before the children and the cat finish it off.'

Making sure not to spill the stew, John walked quickly into the forest some distance from his hut. Reaching a shady spot, he sat down on a fallen tree trunk to enjoy his meal. Before he could have even a spoonful, he saw a scary-looking old woman standing in front of him. Dressed in black, the woman was thin and hunchbacked, with wrinkled, yellowish skin, a sharply hooked nose, and thin lips. Staring at John with dark, piercing eyes, the woman made him feel so uncomfortable that he asked if she would share his meal. The woman took the dish from John's hands, sat down on the log next to him and finished the entire bowl.

Licking her lips, the old woman exclaimed: 'That was delicious, John, thank you.'

John's stomach let out a growl. 'How do you know my name?'

'I know everyone's name,' replied the hag. 'Let me introduce myself. I am Death and I've been around for hundreds of thousands of years.' Seeing John's startled expression, she continued: 'Please don't be scared. I'm not going to hurt you. You were good enough to share your meal with me, so I will repay the favour. But first, let me give you some advice.'

John ignored his pangs of hunger and concentrated on what Death had to say. Any advice from Death herself had to be worth paying attention to. 'Do go on....'

'I advise you to become a doctor because it will make you very rich.'

'Thank you, dear lady,' John replied respectfully. 'But I've no idea how I could possibly become a doctor because I can't even read or write.'

'Don't be silly, my good man,' Death replied. 'Do you really think that reading and writing are essential to become a doctor? When I decide that the time has come for someone, I drag him or her off without consulting their doctor.' John thought about this and realized Death was right—a doctor wasn't always around for her to consult with, to fight for life; sometimes she acted alone, taking people by surprise. He had seen it happen many times.

'Just do as I tell you to,' continued Death. 'Whenever you are called to attend to a patient, all you need to do is to keep a lookout for me. If you see me standing at the head of the bed, you'll know that the patient's time is up. All you have to do is say so, and people will find that you are right. If you don't see me there, you can prescribe a dose of clean water with something harmless added to it, and the sick person will recover.'

Death stood up to leave. 'Don't forget my advice,' she said.

'I won't,' said John. 'But before you go, and as repayment of the favour, could I ask that you stay away from me for a good number of years?'

'Don't worry about me, John. I won't come for you until your house begins to fall to pieces.'

John headed home and told Maria about his strange encounter with Death. In no time at all, Maria let the entire town know that her husband had the medical know-how to tell whether a patient would live or die merely by looking at them. The townsfolk laughed at the very idea of Starving John giving an accurate medical prognosis just by looking at someone, and mockingly started to call him the Shock Doc.

A few weeks later, the townsfolk decided to play a practical joke to show how little the Shock Doc knew about doctoring. They arranged for a group of young girls to go on a picnic to pick wild berries in the forest. The plan was that Lucy, the smallest of the girls, would pretend to be in pain after eating the wild berries and while a few of her friends carried her home to her bed, the rest of the girls would run to fetch the Shock Doc.

When John was summoned, he had misgivings about relying on Lady Death's advice, but Maria pushed him out of the house and told him to attend to the ailing girl. As soon as he entered the house and went into Lucy's room, he saw Death standing at the head of the bed.

'This child is gravely ill,' John said solemnly. 'There is nothing I can do for her. She will likely pass away before the night is through.' As he left the house, the family called out: 'Charlatan! Fake!' and started laughing at him.

Unfortunately, in the excitement of having a picnic, Lucy had eaten too many wild berries and had genuinely fallen ill. To everyone's horror, she was dead before morning.

From that moment on, Starving John's luck changed. He was called upon to visit patients near and far, and the money came pouring in. The transformation in John had to be seen to be believed: his gaunt face filled out, his skin became smoother, he put on weight—even developed a paunch—and was now dubbed Spot-on John because of his accurate diagnoses.

Making the most of his good fortune, John built a large and strong house, hired two maids to assist Maria with the housekeeping, and made sure that his four children were well educated and then gainfully employed. Above all, he spared no expense in keeping his house in good repair. The roof was inspected regularly, the walls were painted, and the tiled floor was maintained in pristine condition, for John remembered Death's promise that she would not visit him until his house crumbled to pieces.

As the years passed, John's fortune grew, but age began to catch up with him. He lost his hair, then his teeth, his spine became bent with age, and he developed severe arthritis and found it difficult to walk. Death sent several emissaries to warn John that she would visit him soon, but he paid no attention to them and shooed them off one after another. Eventually, he had a stroke, which left him paralysed and bedridden. After several months in this pitiable state, Death knocked at John's door, but he was adamant that she should not enter the house. Creeping in through a window in the dead of night, Death stood in front of his bed. Her chilly presence soon woke John up.

'Dear lady,' said John, suddenly very cold, 'need I remind you that you said you wouldn't come for me as long as my house was not crumbling to pieces? Please look around and you'll see that my house is in perfect condition.'

'It's not the brick house you live in that matters to me, John,' Death replied. 'Your body—the house that is equipped with everything you require to keep you alive and determines the quality of your life—has fallen to bits. Your strength has gone, you've lost your hair and your teeth, and you can't even get out of bed! So I'd say that your house has been crumbling away.'

'When you said "house", I thought you meant the place where I live. I have kept my house in good shape but have let myself go in the process. Your visit has come as a shock to me,' John mumbled, his teeth chattering now.

Death answered, somewhat icily: 'If people kept their houses in order, they could delay my arrival and I should take fewer by surprise. But come along now John, say your goodbyes. You're coming with me tonight.'

127

From Little Acorns....

On his way home from work, a man noticed that a new shop had opened on his town's high street. Not a particularly keen shopper, the man felt strangely drawn to the shop, which looked different from those around it, and had a welcoming and inviting air.

Entering the store to pick up a few provisions, the man was surprised to find the interior filled with a luminous and welcoming ambience. He was even more surprised to see God standing behind the sales counter. Walking over to it, the man asked: 'What are you selling, sir?'

'What does your heart desire, my son?'

The man thought for a few seconds and replied: 'For myself and my family, I would like good health, happiness, and peace of mind. For the rest of the world, I would also request well-being, prosperity, freedom, justice, and peace.'

God smiled, shook his head slowly, and said: 'I don't sell fruit here, I'm afraid. Only seeds.'

128

The Hospital Window

Andrew and Michael, both seriously ill and bedridden, shared a room in an overcrowded hospital. Their room had a small window, a door leading out to the general ward, and a plastic screen positioned between their beds to give each of them privacy.

Andrew's bed was next to the window and he was allowed to sit up in his bed for an hour or so twice a day to do breathing exercises that helped drain the fluid from his lungs. Following a serious car accident, Michael had one arm and both legs in plaster. He was not allowed to sit up, and had to lie flat on his back all day long.

With nothing else to do in their pitiable state, the two patients talked to each other for hours on end, the plastic partition proving no barrier to their growing camaraderie. They reminisced about their families, their homes, their favourite vacation spots, their careers.

Every morning and afternoon, when Andrew had finished his exercises and physiotherapy, he would describe to Michael all the things he saw outside the window. He told his bedridden room-mate how the window overlooked a park full of flowers and trees and paths on which couples walked hand in hand and mothers pushed their babies in strollers. He described how young and old sat on prettily painted benches and tossed breadcrumbs to the ducks and swans in the pond, while bright-eyed children sailed their paper boats and ran about happily.

Day after day, the only thing that Michael had to look forward to were those short interludes when Andrew would give him a glimpse of the exciting and vibrant world that lay right outside their hospital room. As Andrew vividly described the world outside the window, Michael would close his eyes tight and begin to picture the enjoyable scene—the colourful daisies and dahlias, carefree and playful children, people enjoying a leisurely stroll, the city skyline in the distance....

Many months went by. One morning when the nurse entered the room to check on the two patients, she found that Andrew had died peacefully in his sleep some time during the night. The hospital attendants were called to take the body away.

Although saddened by his room-mate's death, Michael was eager to move into Andrew's now vacant bed and see for himself the sights he'd heard so much about. As soon as it seemed appropriate, he asked if he could be shifted to the bed next to the window. The nurse agreed and arranged for him to be moved. After making sure the patient was comfortable, she left him alone.

Slowly, painfully, Michael propped himself up on one elbow, excited to take his first look in months at the real world outside. Turning his head slowly, he looked out of the window beside his bed. All he could see was a brick wall.

Puzzled, Michael rang the bell to summon the nurse. 'There is nothing to be seen from this window except a brick wall,' he complained. 'Where are the flowers, the park, the lake, all the people that my room-mate Andrew saw? Why would he tell me about things that don't exist?'

The nurse shrugged. 'I think he probably just wanted to cheer you up and give you something to look forward to,' she said. 'You see, your room-mate, Andrew, had age-related macular degeneration and was blind.'

Michael lay in his bed, fighting back tears of disappointment and confusion, wondering why Andrew had made up stories for him day after day. He had yearned to be able to look out of the window and enjoy the view, and now he was faced with no view at all.

A few days later, he began to see things differently. Perhaps the nurse is right and Andrew was only trying to give me hope, he thought. I must admit that his stories did make me feel better. Instead of letting me wallow in misery, he gave me a reason to smile.

A few weeks later, when Michael was able to move about in a wheelchair, he asked the nurse if he might visit other bedridden patients in the hospital. She thought it was a fine idea, and as it happened, his fellow patients looked forward to Michael's visits as much as he enjoyed chatting with them. He realized that even a few minutes of conversing with the elderly or the ailing cheered them up considerably. Michael was determined to keep Andrew's legacy alive by opening a window of hope for the sick and lonely, because he knew how important hope could be, and how everyone needs something to look forward to.

129

The Man and the Lion

A lion and a man were travelling together through a forest. The journey was long and tiring and to while away the time, the two travel companions discussed a number of topics amicably, but when they began talking about themselves, pride and prejudice got in the way and they began to quarrel.

The lion boasted: 'I am hailed throughout the world as king of the jungle, renowned for my hunting prowess and bravery.'

The man scoffed and replied: 'The jungle occupies a very small space in the larger world. Nothing and no one can compare with mankind for our physical and mental superiority.'

After a few hours of walking in sullen silence, the pair reached a clearing in the forest in which stood a large statue depicting Heracles tearing open the jaws of the Nemean lion. Turning to the lion, the man said: 'Now, you can see for yourself how strong men are. This statue is proof that men are stronger than lions. Even the Nemean lion, a vicious monster whose claws were sharper than mortals' swords and whose fur was impervious to attack, was slain by a man. It's obvious that the king of the jungle is like wax in our hands!'

'That's just a myth!' the lion exclaimed. 'If men fought us fairly instead of with spears and guns, they would be no match for us. This statue was made by a man, so one cannot take it too seriously. If lions could carve sculptures, they would have presented quite a different picture of a man subjugated by the king of the jungle. As you know, the story changes depending on who is telling it, and I've come to realize that depictions of men who don't survive battles with a lion are not very popular subjects in art.'

130

Judgement

A story is told about an incident that happened during the 1930s in New York, on one of the coldest days of the year. The world was in the grip of the Great Depression, and all over the city, the poor were close to starvation.

It so happened that the judge sitting on the bench that day was hearing a complaint against a woman who was charged with stealing a loaf of bread. She pleaded that her daughter was sick, and her grandchildren were starving because their father had abandoned the family. But the shopkeeper whose loaf had been stolen refused to drop the charge. He insisted that an example be made of the poor old woman as a deterrent to others.

The judge sighed. He was most reluctant to pass judgement on the woman, yet he had no alternative. 'I'm sorry,' he turned to her and said, 'but I can't make any exceptions. The law is the law. I sentence you to a fine of ten dollars, and if you can't pay I must send you to jail for ten days.'

The woman was heartbroken, but even as he was passing sentence, the judge was reaching into his pocket for the money to pay off the ten-dollar fine. He took off his hat, tossed the ten-dollar bill into it, and then addressed the crowd. 'I am also going to impose a fine of fifty cents on every person here present in this courtroom for living in a town where a person has to steal bread to save her grandchildren from starvation. Please collect the fines, Mr Bailiff, in this hat and pass them across to the defendant.'

And so the accused went home that day from the courtroom with forty-seven dollars and fifty cents—fifty cents of which had been paid by the shame-faced owner of the grocery store who had brought the charge against her. As she left the courtroom, the gathering of petty criminals and New York policemen gave the judge a standing ovation.

131

Men at Work

A townsman was walking back from the market one afternoon, lamenting how bored he was at work, how tough it was becoming to cope with rising costs and keep his family happy, when he came across a sprawling building site near the town square, which had been cordoned off and piled high with huge granite boulders, timber, and other construction material. Walking past the area, the townsman observed three masons at work, using strong hammers and chisels to chip chunks of granite from large blocks.

The first mason appeared to be doing his job mechanically, showing no enthusiasm and repeatedly looking at his watch as if anxious to get away. When the townsman asked him what he was doing, the mason replied: 'I think it should be perfectly obvious that I'm hammering away at this blasted rock. I can't wait until it is five o'clock so I can skedaddle home.'

I hope his workmanship is better than his attitude, the townsman thought as he walked away. The second mason he approached seemed more engaged in his work and was hammering away diligently at another boulder.

'May I ask,' said the townsman, 'what you are doing?'

'My task is to shape and smoothen this rock so that it can be used with others to construct a wall,' said the man. 'It's back-breaking work, and quite honestly, I'm only in it for the money. I'll be glad when the last stone's laid.'

A short distance away, a third mason was hammering away at his block with the greatest concentration, his lips pursed tightly. Every now and again, he would stop hammering and step back to survey his handiwork, his head tilted to one side.

When the townsman asked the mason what he was doing, the man stopped for a moment and proudly declared: 'I'm building a cathedral! I have the best job in the world.' The townsman shook the grinning mason's hand, wished him luck and went on his way.

That evening, as was customary, the townsman sat by the fire with his children to tell them a story before bedtime. He told them about the three men he'd met in the square, with their heavy tools and their vastly different attitudes.

'And they were all doing the same job, Papa?' asked his son.

'Indeed, they were, my boy. They were all chipping away at a rock.'

'Isn't it hard work, whoever's doing it?' asked his daughter.

'Absolutely, my dear. It can be soul-destroying work—if you let it. You can be negative and miserable...or you can be positive, and imagine you're a part of something special and new and exciting, which fills you with pride and makes you enjoy your work. What I observed was that the first two masons were in it only for the money. The third man had a special calling and was passionate about his work. What a commendable attitude!'

The next morning, the townsman set off to his job with a veritable spring in his step and a vastly altered outlook. Noticing fresh blossoms on the trees in the park and a piercing-blue cloudless sky, he smiled and decided: Today is going to be a good day. I am certain.

132

The Rumour

A long time ago, there were two villages that stood side by side, separated only by a small stream spanned by a bridge. In fact, if it hadn't been for the stream, it would have been impossible to tell where one village ended and the other began.

One day, when the children from one of the villages were playing in the street, they saw a nomad walking past. The man's eyes were watering because specks of dust had got into them and he was wiping away tears that clouded his vision. The children watched curiously as the man repeatedly wiped his eyes with the end of a turban that was wrapped around his head to protect him from the harsh sun. Assuming that they were tears of sadness, the children began to speculate why the stranger was crying. Their imaginations running wild, somehow a rumour started that the man was weeping because a close relative of his in the neighbouring village had died from a highly contagious illness.

The rumour also spread to the second village, where the residents claimed that the first village was the source of the dreaded disease.

As the story spread, children in both villages were prohibited from playing outdoors and forbidden from crossing the bridge to visit their neighbours. The residents of both villages began to avoid each other, and all communication between the villagers ceased completely. Eventually, as the animosity between the former neighbours grew, both villages decided that living conditions had become too dangerous, and the residents moved out, lock, stock, and barrel to set up home elsewhere.

For centuries thereafter, descendants of the original villagers told the same tale of how their ancestors had been forced to leave their homes and resettle elsewhere because of the terrible and deadly disease that had plagued their neighbours.

Who would believe that residents of two entire villages could be blinded by a few particles of dust in a stranger's eyes?

133

The Ties That Bind

A father and son were out having a stroll one afternoon when they came to a vast field in which a visiting circus had pitched its colourful tents alongside several cages for animals. The young boy was fascinated by the jugglers rehearsing their routines, the clowns doing cartwheels, monkeys leaping about in their enclosure, and the fierce-looking lion pacing up and down in its cage.

What caught the father's attention was the sight of an elephant standing calmly at one end of the field, shovelling leaves and branches into its mouth with its trunk. There was no chain or cage or barbed wire enclosure for the huge creature. It was being held only by a small rope tied to its front leg, the other end of which was tethered to a peg sunk into the ground. The elephant could have broken free from the rope at any time, but stood there placidly, enjoying its lunch.

'Do you see that, Aaron?' he said to his son. 'That ginormous animal is being kept in its place by a thin rope that it could easily break free from, but for some reason it doesn't.'

'Why doesn't it want to escape, Daddy?' asked the lad.

'Let's find out,' his father replied. Spotting a trainer inspecting some cages, the man asked him why the majestic elephant just stood there and made no attempt to get away.

'Well, you see,' the trainer began, 'when the elephants are very young and much smaller, we use the thin rope to keep them in place and prevent them from running away. At that age, the rope is strong enough to hold them and even if they try, they can't escape it. Elephants are famous for having excellent memories, so even when they're fully grown, they remember that they cannot break the rope. They're so conditioned into believing that it can still hold them, that they never even try to break free.'

'Isn't that amazing, Aaron?' the man asked, looking at his son. 'The elephant could easily break free from its bonds, but because it believes that it can't, it remains stuck where it is. Many people are also like that. They convince themselves that some task is impossible, simply because they failed at it once before....'

'Daddy, can we not show the elephant how easy it is to escape?' Aaron asked.

'It may be too late for the elephant to be taught new tricks,' the father advised, 'but it's not too late for you.' Bending down to be at his precious son's height, he told Aaron: 'Don't let failures prevent you from aiming for success, and never allow someone else's limiting beliefs to prevent you from fulfilling your dream. Remember, my son, you can do anything you set your heart on, no matter who tries to hold you back.'

134

Fatherly Advice

A farmer had worked hard for many years to support his wife and only son, but had become so old and feeble that he could no longer tend to his land. His wife had passed away years earlier but their son was still working on the farm. Day after day, the son would go out into the fields and whenever he looked up from his tilling or sowing or ploughing, he would see his father sitting on the porch.

He doesn't do a thing except sit there staring vacantly into the distance, the son thought. He's absolutely useless.

Eventually, the son became so frustrated by his father's helplessness that he built a wooden coffin, dragged it over to the porch and told his father to get into it. Without a word, the father followed his son's instructions and climbed into the casket. Closing the lid, the son dragged the coffin to the edge of a high cliff near the farm.

As he was preparing to tip the coffin over the cliff, he heard a light tapping on the lid from inside the box. Opening it, the man saw his father lying in the coffin peacefully, his hands folded over his chest.

'Son,' said the father, looking up at his son, 'I know you are going to throw me over the cliff, but before you do, may I make a suggestion?'

'What is it?' the son asked tersely.

'You may throw me over the cliff if you like,' said the father, 'but don't waste this sturdy, well-built coffin. Your children might find good use for it one day.'

135

The Politician's Shadow

It was a bright, sunny day, and a politician was walking briskly from the parking lot to his office, hurrying to seal a deal with a business tycoon that would generate a hefty kickback for him. As he strode along, smirking while he contemplated ways to spend his ill-gotten gains, the politician was surprised to see his shadow slinking away from him.

'Come back,' he called out to his shadow. 'Where do you think you're going, you scoundrel?'

'If I were a scoundrel,' his shadow replied, picking up speed, 'I would not be leaving you.'

136

Finding Fault

Commanded by the king of the gods to mould mankind out of clay, Prometheus, the god of fire, came up with a novel design for his creations—deciding to hang two sacks from the necks of every man, woman, and child. The bag hanging in front of them was filled with other people's flaws and defects, while the one hanging behind their backs contained their own failings.

This unique feature caused unforeseen problems and almost led to Prometheus's downfall. He had failed to anticipate humans' propensity to effortlessly spot the faults and failings of their fellow beings, and their great difficulty in noticing or acknowledging the imperfections that they were carrying on their own backs. The design flaw led to endless bickering and finger-pointing, often ending in violent conflict and war.

With the situation getting out of control, the sacks were removed, but the habit of people finding fault with others whilst turning a blind eye to their own has persisted. To this day, the gods are debating whether the world might have been a better place if the original positioning of the sacks had been reversed.

137

The Ant and the Grasshopper

The autumn air was blustery and chilling to the bone
But the busy ant diligently trudged uphill to his home,
Carrying food, grain, and anything edible upon his back,
Ensuring that the harsh winter brought his colony no lack.

A happy-go-lucky, cheerful grasshopper who lived nearby
Watched the ant's frenzied activity from the corner of his eye.
Life can be so joyful if you sing and dance, he thought,
But an ant's life with so much needless pain is fraught....

He toils so hard, so purposefully, from morning until night,
That watching him tires me out and gives me quite a fright.
I wish that he could be more relaxed, happy, and carefree;
This busy ant could surely learn a thing or two from me.

But soon the bitter winter winds began to swirl and blow
Carpeting the countryside under a blanket of thick snow.
With no food to be found and on the brink of starvation
The cold, hungry grasshopper grew desperate with frustration.

Recalling that the ant would have plenty of food in store
The famished grasshopper knocked at the muddy anthill's door.
'Good neighbour,' said he, 'the winter's been terribly cruel.
Would you be so kind as to spare me a plateful of gruel?'

'I'm sorry,' said the haughty ant, 'but I have no food to spare
For someone as irresponsible as you, who didn't bother to prepare.
In fact, all autumn you sang and danced throughout the day,
Not concerned that in winter, hunger would be a high price to pay.'

The dejected grasshopper took his leave, determined to mend his ways.
Thenceforth, he gathered enough food to sustain him through wintry days.
As for the illustrious ant, years of ceaseless toil eventually took their toll
When he succumbed to a sudden heart attack while out for an evening stroll.

138

Hardware Store Heroics

A piece of iron, an axe, a saw, a hammer, and a tall candle stood side by side on a shelf in a hardware store. Proud of his perfect symmetry and gleaming surface, the iron ingot often boasted that he was the strongest of them all.

'I'll prove you wrong,' said the axe, and immediately began striking heavy blows on the iron slab. After nearly a dozen attempts, the axe gave up because each blow had only blunted its edge, forcing it to stop.

'Don't worry, I'll take care of it,' said the saw, before the iron slab had a chance to object. It began working backwards and forwards on the iron slab's surface with such force that its jagged teeth were soon worn and broken. The saw also had to admit defeat and retire hurt.

'Oh dear!' said the hammer, ignoring the iron ingot's sniggers. 'I knew it would be tough for you, so let me show you how it's done.' But at the first fierce blow, off flew the hammer's head and the piece of iron remained as unharmed as before, quite smug in the belief it was the strongest.

'Shall I give it a try?' the candle asked softly.

The blunted axe, the toothless saw, and the headless hammer laughed and shook their heads, or what was left of them. 'What can you do that we couldn't?' asked the saw, whose teeth were very sore.

'At least let me try,' said the candle. Determined to prove itself the strongest, the candle wrapped its small but steady flame around the iron slab. While the others watched in amazement, the iron bar soon began to melt under the scorching flame, which despite being the size of a thimble, was more effective than all the boastful tools.

'Do you see,' said the candle, 'all your pounding, sawing, and hammering had no effect on the iron slab, but my warm embrace makes it melt. It just goes to show that you can be gentle *and* strong.'

The axe, the saw, and the hammer could not argue with that, but they did notice that although the boastful iron slab had now melted down to a misshapen molten lump, in the process the elegant candle too had burnt down to a stubby stump of wax, no bigger than a walnut.

'Both the victor and the vanquished have become a shadow of their former selves,' observed the axe.

'The candle, in its effort to be the best, ended up cutting off its nose to spite its face,' remarked the hammer, noting the irony, given that he lost his own head while trying to show his might.

'Indeed, I'm seeing that strength does not always need to be demonstrated, proven, or witnessed,' said the sore saw. 'It can be hidden, used only when it benefits all parties. It is especially not advisable to use your strength to your own detriment. I should know. If I had stayed on the shelf, I wouldn't have the worst toothache ever, and I hate going to the dentist!'

139

The Messenger of Love

Deep within a dense forest in northern Germany stands a tall oak, which has the distinction of being the only tree in the world with its own postal address. Doubling as a mailbox, the 500-year-old tree, known as Bridegroom's Oak, has dozens of letters deposited into a knothole in its massive trunk almost daily. At around midday, every day of the week—barring Sundays and holidays—lonely hearts looking for a soulmate trudge to the forest to see if the mail has brought them a letter that carries within it a promise of true love.

The Bridegroom's Oak is believed to possess magical matchmaking powers, being at the root of more than a hundred marriages. Anyone seeking proof of the tree's supernatural powers need look no further than the story of Karl-Heinz Martens, a mailman with Germany's postal service, Deutsche Bundespost, who delivered mail to the tree for more than three decades, and ended up finding love himself.

Martens, known as the messenger of love, was not what you would call a romantic. A cynical, middle-aged divorcé, who was fed up with women, and had given up dating, Martens never really enjoyed having to deliver love letters to a tree and was openly sceptical about stories of the many romances that the letters triggered. But the magical oak tree would soon make him change his mind....

German folk tales are replete with stories of lonely princesses, handsome princes, enchanted forests, magic spells, and true love. With several of these elements present in anecdotes about the matchmaking powers of the Bridegroom's Oak, tourists began to flock to the forest, usually coinciding their arrival at the tree with Martens' postal delivery. To make the most of the tourist attraction, Deutsche Bundespost instructed Martens to tell visitors about the tree's history. Martens would relate the story of the son of a prince who was abandoned in the forest with no one to care for him. 'One day, the youth was rescued by a beautiful girl. To thank her for rescuing him, he planted a tree. That seedling eventually grew into this mighty oak,' he would tell visitors with a dramatic flourish.

In reality, the tree became known for matchmaking in the 1890s. A youth from a nearby town fell in love with the forester's daughter, but her father disapproved of the relationship. The despairing lovers took to leaving each other notes in the knothole of the oak tree. Eventually, the girl's father had a change of heart and hosted a wedding ceremony at the spot where his daughter's love had bloomed. There, in the shadow of the branches, the bride and groom exchanged their vows, and the tree found its name. Soon after, other love letters started to arrive.

By 1927, there was so much mail addressed to the Bridegroom's Oak that the post office decided to give the tree its own mailing address. Deutsche Bundespost even erected a 10-foot-tall ladder up to the mailbox, to help people reach in to open, read, and respond to love letters at the senders' return addresses. There was only one strict rule: if someone opened a letter and didn't want to respond, they had to place the letter back in the tree for someone else to find.

Martens was in his late thirties when he started delivering mail to the Bridegroom's Oak in 1984. The delivery route was tough. It involved a mile-long detour, and the mailmen weren't exactly thrilled at having to go out of their way to deposit what they thought were sentimental, soppy letters in the trunk of a tree. But when Martens heard story after story of couples who had found 'love at first sight' after sending a letter to the tree, he began to think that there might be some truth to the tales.

One day, as Martens climbed the wooden steps to the Bridegroom's Oak, he reached into his mailbag and noticed a letter that was addressed to him. The letter was from Renate Heinz, a divorcée in her late fifties, who had watched a television programme about the Bridegroom's Oak in which Karl-Heinz Martens had been interviewed. 'I want to get to know you,' her message read, with the directness typical of a strong woman who knows what she wants.

Renate lived in a town some distance away, near the French border. Too lazy to write, Martens preferred to call Renate and soon he was running up huge telephone bills because they would talk for hours. When they eventually met, they took an instant liking to each other. So much so, that their first date lasted two days. They moved in together in early 1990, and four years later, they got married in the town hall, and were then treated to a surprise buffet in the shade of the Bridegroom's Oak, hosted by their friends. They had been married for twenty-four years when Renate passed away from lung cancer.

His own fairy-tale romance and happy marriage convinced Martens that there was more to the Bridegroom's Oak than merely lucky coincidences. 'I do believe there's something magical about the tree,' he admitted.

Several months after his wife's death, Martens went to the Bridegroom's Oak and pulled out a letter from a woman. '*Hello dear stranger,*' he read. '*If you like to laugh, enjoy the quiet moments of life...then you should definitely contact me.*' There was a pause as Martens read and reread the last sentence: '*When you're alone, everything is half as much fun.*'

The woman's letter struck a chord: his life had indeed been far more enjoyable with Renate in it. Thanks to the Bridegroom's Oak, he had found his soulmate. But now, it was time for him to give someone else a chance at happiness.

Martens replaced the letter in its envelope and put it back in the tree, hoping it would enable some other lonely heart to live life to the fullest with someone at their side to love.

140

The Black Dot

Chatting happily, the students returned to their classroom,
Glad that school had reopened after many months of gloom
In which a deadly virus launched its indiscriminate assault
On young and old alike, bringing the whole world to a halt.

'Welcome!' the teacher said as they all took their places.
'It's been a long while since I saw your smiling faces.
I'd like to start today's lesson with an easy writing test
And I hope each of you will give it your absolute best.'

Caught unawares, the students had no room for doubt
As the test papers, face down, were swiftly handed out.
Turning the page over, they found the white sheet was blank,
Except for a black dot right in the centre—was this a prank?

The teacher, noticing his students' clear bewilderment
Hastened to put an end to their collective predicament.
'Your assignment is to write about exactly what you see,'
He said firmly, giving them no chance to question or disagree.

Assignment over, students read out their essays to the class,
Which is something their teacher had never before asked.
'No grades will be assigned for this test,' he averred,
'But I want all of you to reflect on what you've just heard....

'Every essay honed in on the dot—its colour, size, position,
Whereas the white part of the paper didn't even get a mention.
It's the same with life: we tend to overlook all that goes well,
Focusing only on its rocky patches, complaining and raising hell.

'The lesson I want you to take away today is that in every life
There's no escaping ups and downs, some happiness, some strife,
But always be grateful for the blessings, of which you have lots,
And spend less of your time fixating on life's pesky little dots.'

141

Wisdom, Wealth, and Nourishment

Tired of always being on the move, going from one place to another and being frequently separated, the three friends Wisdom, Wealth, and Nourishment decided to find a place where they could live together comfortably. Setting off on foot, they began the search for their dream home.

Passing through the outskirts of a small village, the trio saw a shepherd sitting in the shade of a gao tree, chewing on a blade of grass and keeping a half-hearted eye on his flock of sheep.

'Where are you headed?' the shepherd asked, recognizing all three of them instantly.

'We're looking for a suitable place to live,' they replied.

The shepherd mulled over this for a minute and then turned to one of the friends. 'Nourishment, you are more than welcome to come and live with me and my six children,' he said. 'With you in the house, my family will never go hungry and I can send these sheep to slaughter and get rich.'

'Thanks, but no thanks,' Nourishment replied. 'If you had made a smarter choice, all three of us could have lived with you. I prefer to provide for everyone, not just your loved ones, so we'll have to keep looking.' And off they went.

At the edge of a thick forest, the trio came across a woodcutter, hard at work chopping a massive tree trunk into smaller bits of firewood. The man was scrawny and simply dressed. He lay down his axe, wiped the sweat off his brow, and raised his kufi cap in greeting to the three men. 'What brings you to these parts?' the woodcutter asked. 'Where are you headed?'

'We are looking for a place to live,' they replied.

'I'd be very happy to invite Wealth to live with me in my humble home,' the woodcutter said, without hesitation. 'With a limitless pot of money and my wood-chopping skills, I could travel the world to chop down whole forests! I would be rich beyond my wildest dreams.'

'Money won't buy you happiness though,' Wealth replied. 'If you had been more wise, then all three of us could have lived with you. Without my companions Wisdom and Nourishment, I could not have stayed with you long, I assure you.'

The weary threesome continued on their way. After a while, they reached a village. As they wandered down a steep, cobblestoned hill, they saw a bookshop tucked away in a small side street. Going in to investigate, they found a shop so full of books that there was hardly any place to stand. The walls were lined from floor to ceiling with books of all shapes and sizes, and Wisdom noted titles of various genres from all around the world, on all sorts of topics, for all types of interests.

Quietly impressed with such a vast amount of knowledge in one room, they introduced themselves to the bookseller, a serious, busy-looking man with a pile of books under his arm and a pair of glasses on the end of his nose, that seemed about to fall off.

'How can I help you, my good men?' asked the bookseller, keen to get on with his filing.

'We are looking for a place to live,' they said in unison. 'Can you help us?'

The bookseller rubbed his chin with his free hand, eyeing all three as if choosing a cream cake in a bakery. Decision made, he replied: 'Wisdom, you are most welcome to come and live with me, because this is a house of knowledge, and you will agree that no one can have too much of that.'

Wisdom was nodding and grinning from ear to ear, but before he could answer, Nourishment addressed the bookseller:

'Since you have chosen Wisdom to live with you, I will live with you too and make sure you never go hungry. I know that we'll be comfortable here.'

Wealth added: 'You've made a wise choice, sir. I'll be happy to stay here along with Wisdom and Nourishment. We work well together, the three of us, you'll see. We won't give you any trouble, and you will want for nothing.'

The bookseller was delighted to welcome all three into his modest home at the back of the store, also lined with rows of dusty books but very cosy and inviting. The trio took off their shoes and put their feet up.

It was the bookseller's thirst for knowledge, not riches, which enabled them all to live harmoniously together for many years. And with the three friends' help, the bookseller was able to provide hot soup, a good book, and a small bag of coins to anyone who came to his door in need.

142

It Only Matters If We Let It

On a wildlife reserve, an unlikely friendship developed between a lion and a chital. Orphaned shortly after they were born, the lion and the chital had grown up together in a fenced-off enclosure, and became inseparable over the years.

One swelteringly hot summer's day, the two friends were lounging by the lake when they got into an absurd argument.

'We'll have to put up with this heat for a few more days,' the lion roared. 'As everyone knows, it gets cold only when the moon decreases in size, going from full moon to new moon. We're still two days away from a full moon.'

'Wherever did you get that idea?' the chital asked. 'Everyone knows that it's exactly the opposite: when the new moon becomes a full moon, it brings cool weather in its wake.'

The two friends continued arguing, voices raised and tempers flaring, aggravated by the heat. Each insisted that he was right and his friend was wrong. Matters became so unpleasant that they began trading insults and calling each other names. Eventually, they decided to ask one of the gamekeepers to resolve the argument.

After patiently hearing both sides of the disagreement, the gamekeeper spoke: 'In my humble opinion, I think it can be cold in any phase of the moon, be it from new to full and back again. It's the wind that brings cold weather with it from the west or north or east, not the moon; the moon's job is to bring us tides to keep our oceans moving, not weather. So in a way, both of you are right and neither of you is wrong.'

As the lion and the chital thanked him and turned to leave, the gamekeeper stopped them. 'You've been such good friends since childhood that it upsets me to see the two of you get into arguments about inconsequential matters. The bond you share is unique and special. You mustn't let anything come between you, no matter how right you think you are. Sometimes you have to know when to back down, let it go, swallow your pride. Always remember that alone you can do very little but together you can do a lot.'

The lion and the chital nodded and resolved to not let petty differences get in the way of their friendship again. That evening, they decided to take a dip in the lake to beat the heat. An almost-full moon shone brightly in the sky and many of the animals were hovering around the lake where it was coolest.

'It's easier to find food at night when there's a full moon,' commented the chital, gazing at the lush riverbank as he floated in the shallow water. The bank was teeming with shrubs and reeds and grasses that were vibrant green in the moonlight.

'I disagree,' countered the lion. 'I have much more success when the moon is barely there and everything is very dark.' He had already noticed a family of mongooses approaching the lake, unaware of his presence, but it was such a nice evening and so menacingly hot that the lion decided he couldn't be bothered to chase after baby mongooses, so stayed where he was, enjoying the tranquillity.

He didn't want to argue with his friend, the chital, either. They'd done enough of that earlier. 'What is sauce for the goose may not be sauce for the gander,' said the lion, putting a friendly paw on the chital's speckled back. 'I think we should agree to disagree. That way we will remain strong—a unit—and not fight against each other like two enemies.'

'I agree with you there,' smiled the chital, nudging the lion's mane with his muzzle. 'Sometimes neither of us is right or wrong, and sometimes both of us are. At the end of the day, it only matters if we let it.'

143

The Daydreaming Milkmaid

It was a sunny autumn day, and a pretty milkmaid named Heidi was walking to the market with a bucket of milk balanced on her head, humming merrily. In a cheerful mood and enjoying the warm weather, Heidi began to daydream about the money she could earn from selling the milk.

Thinking out loud, Heidi said: 'Let's see. I have ten litres of milk in the bucket, and if I sell it all, I will have enough money to buy four dozen eggs. After I take the eggs back to the farm, I'm sure that at least forty chicks will hatch. A week before Christmas, the chickens will be big enough for me to sell at the market and they'll fetch a good price. I will use the money to buy myself a new dress, maybe a sky-blue one to match my eyes. Yes, that's what I'll do, because I deserve to spoil myself after working so hard all through the year.

'I'll wear my pretty new dress to church on Christmas Day and curl my hair into loose ringlets. I'm sure that all my ardent admirers will vie with each other to walk me home. But I won't encourage any of them. In fact, I won't even look at them,' said Heidi, tossing her head haughtily, causing the bucket to tip over. In a trice, the milk spilled into a puddle on the ground, some of it splashing on the hem of her skirt and on her shoes, forcing Heidi to face the reality of her shattered daydream. She wept at the thought of having no milk to sell, and definitely no pretty dress to wear.

Upset at her foolishness, disappointed to return with nothing, Heidi picked up the empty bucket and turned to go home, sobbing and sniffling. Just then, a carriage drawn by two large horses appeared on the path. It slowed as it drove past her, and Heidi heard a man's strong voice instruct the coachman to stop. A handsome young gentleman descended from the coach, doffed his hat and asked: 'Is everything okay, miss? I'm Henry. I live in the neighbouring village, just over that hill....'

Heidi felt she looked a dreadful sight in her old market dress now stained with mud and milk, her eyes red from crying, and her cheeks streaked with tears, but she thanked the young man for his concern and explained what had happened.

'Did no one ever tell you not to cry over spilled milk?' laughed Henry, leading Heidi to his carriage. 'Come on, I insist on taking you home.'

Heidi and Henry's chance meeting turned into a friendship that developed into a romance and ended in a long and happy marriage. For sixty years, on every wedding anniversary, the couple raised an unusual toast—to the bucket of spilled milk that had brought them so much happiness.

144

Wishful Thinking

Once upon a time, in a small village in Japan, there lived a stonecutter named Ishizu. He had a tiring job, hewing boulders from the mountainside, then hacking them into the shapes needed by his customers. Ishizu worked so hard all day long that the skin on his hands was rough and calloused, his back ached, and his clothes were always filthy, sweat-stained, and tatty.

Never having known anything different, Ishizu was quite content with his lot, until one day things changed. He was hard at work, sweating in the hot sun as he cut and shaped a large boulder. Suddenly, he spotted a long procession passing by the spot where he was working. As the procession neared, Ishizu saw several soldiers walking alongside a norimono in which sat the king, being fanned by attendants on either side.

'How wonderful it must be to be the king!' Ishizu said out loud. 'What an easy life he must lead, being pampered day and night. I'd be very happy if I were the king instead of a lowly stonecutter.' As soon as he said the words, a miraculous thing happened: Ishizu's ragged clothes disappeared and were replaced by an expensive shirt and trousers enveloped in a kimono of the finest silk. His hands were soft, the nails unbroken, and he was being carried in a comfortably cushioned and gently swaying norimono.

As the procession moved on, the sun rose higher in the sky and Ishizu the king began to feel uncomfortably hot in his silk kimono. The attendants fanning him on either side were merely blowing hot air in his direction. Perspiring heavily in his finery, Ishizu began to wonder if being a king was all it was cut out to be. I'm surrounded by great fanfare, he thought, but I am powerless when compared to the sun. I'd be better off being the sun than a king.

In a trice, Ishizu became the sun, beaming down on the earth from high up in the sky. Delighted at having so much power at his fingertips, Ishizu the sun shone so brightly that he scorched the forests and fields, and turned the oceans into vapour that formed vast clouds over the land. Soon, the haze completely blocked his view of the ground, and though Ishizu shone even brighter, he could not penetrate the thick blanket of clouds.

Ishizu hadn't realized that clouds could be more powerful than the sun. I'd much rather be a cloud, he thought, and quick as a flash, he was transformed into a billowing dark cloud. Trying out his new power, he poured rain down on the land, causing rivers to swell, triggering floods, and creating havoc. From high up in the sky, Ishizu the cloud watched as trees came crashing down in the forest and houses were swept away in the torrential downpour, but then suddenly, he noticed that the rock which he had been cutting in his earlier avatar as a stonecutter stood unaffected and unmoved. Even when he poured down relentlessly on the boulder, it stood firm and unchanged.

Perhaps clouds are not so powerful after all, mused Ishizu the cloud. That rock appears to be far more powerful than I am. Only a stonecutter could alter the rock with his skill. How I wish I were a stonecutter!

As soon as he expressed the wish, he found himself sitting atop a huge boulder. The skin on his hands was rough and calloused, his back ached and his clothes were tatty, but Ishizu the stonecutter was back where he belonged. He picked up his tools and happily set about tearing down the boulder to then shape it into something new—something that made him proud, something only he could do.

145

The Shrinking Forest

Some of the oldest trees in the forest had stood there for hundreds of years and could remember a time in their youth when the woods had stretched for miles around them. In fact, it was not until they had reached middle age, and had grown tall and strong, that the aged trees had finally been able to look into the distance and see where the vast forest began and where it ended.

From their vantage point, the mighty trees now observed that their forest was shrinking rapidly, that fires burned at its edges and roads were being built in place of trees. They needed to do something to safeguard their future, to secure their centuries-old home.

By curious coincidence, an axe showed up and appealed to the trees to elect him their representative and spokesman. 'I am sharp and strong and can safeguard your interests in the outside world,' the smooth-talking axe promised.

The trees mulled over the matter for a few days. 'The axe is indeed sharp and strong,' said an elderly tree, who was bent with age and had lost many of his leaves and branches, 'but I'm not sure if we should trust him completely. I don't like the look of his shiny blade.'

'The blade is only a small part of the axe,' a younger tree, standing straight and tall, scoffed. 'It is so tiny, I don't think it can do much harm to us strong and sturdy trees. Besides, more than four-fifths of an axe is made of wood, which means he is one of us. He will be on our side and will protect us.'

And so, the trusting, rustling trees cast their vote in favour of the axe, convinced that he was one of them and would have their interests at heart because his handle was made of wood.

Indeed, an axe is strong, and one alone can only do so much damage. An army of axes, however, can wipe out a whole forest. Had the gullible trees thought about things further, their forest may have survived. Instead, the older trees watched as the tallest and straightest trees were felled, one by one, and fashioned into smooth, sturdy handles for more busy axes.

146

A Question of Attitude

A shoe manufacturing company sent two salesmen to Africa to gauge whether it could be a possible market for their products. The first man was sent to the east coast, while the second was sent to the west coast. Both salesmen surveyed the target market and reported back to the office.

The salesman who went east informed the company's headquarters: 'No one wears shoes in these parts. There is no market for footwear here.'

The salesman who travelled west reported: 'No one here wears shoes, so there is tremendous scope for us to introduce and establish our brand in this region! We could capture the market if we act swiftly.'

The first salesman was assigned a back-office job and never sent out on a business trip again. The second salesman landed a lucrative post as manager for the new Africa office, and generated huge profits for the company from the hitherto unexplored market.

147

Knowing When to Stop

The ancient Greek philosopher Socrates, believed to be the wisest man in the world, was standing in the marketplace deep in thought when a young man approached him and asked to become his student. 'You are renowned as a philosopher, teacher, and debater,' the youth said. 'Can you please teach me how to become an orator?' The youth then launched into a lengthy discourse to impress Socrates with his vocabulary and eloquence.

After listening to the youth's flowery speech for a few minutes, Socrates signalled for him to stop talking. 'I will have to charge you twice my usual fee,' he told the young man.

'Why is that?'

'Because my work will be doubled. I will have to teach you two vital sciences. The first of these is to learn how to hold your tongue, and the other, how to speak. The first science is not only more difficult but also more important, and you must aim for proficiency in it or you will suffer greatly and create no end of trouble. People will listen more if you talk less. That is how you learn to speak.'

148

Room at the Inn

This is the story of how a young boy added a new—and unforgettable—touch to his school's Christmas pageant in a small town in the American Midwest.

Nine-year-old Wallace Purling was a little slow in the learning department and still in the second grade. Gentle and kind by nature, he was popular with his classmates, even though he was older, taller, and stronger than them.

Wallace had not taken part in his school's Nativity pageant before. He really wanted to play the role of a shepherd, but the director thought he was better suited to play the innkeeper. After all, he wouldn't have to memorize too many lines and, because of his size, he would be able to present a more forceful refusal to the much smaller Joseph.

Students, parents, and townsfolk crammed into the school hall on the big night and waited for the curtain to go up. Backstage, Wallace was so excited that the director had to hold on to his sleeve to stop him from wandering onstage before his cue.

Then it was time for Wallace's big scene.

Exhausted from their long journey, Joseph and Mary entered the stage and slowly approached the entrance to the inn. Joseph knocked on the door, which opened immediately. There stood Wallace, who asked in his gruffest voice: 'Can I help you?'

'We are looking for a place to spend the night,' Joseph replied.

'You will have to look elsewhere,' Wallace said curtly. 'There is no room at this inn.'

'Sir, we have stopped at many inns and lodges along the way but have been turned away from them all. We have travelled many miles, and my wife and I are exhausted.'

'There is no room at the inn,' Wallace repeated sternly. The director, watching anxiously from the wings, breathed a sigh of relief that Wallace had not forgotten his lines.

'Please, good innkeeper, I implore you to help us,' Joseph pleaded. 'My wife, Mary, is expecting our first child and needs a place to rest. Surely you can find a small corner for her? She is so tired.'

It was then that the audience noticed that the innkeeper, swayed by Joseph's heartfelt plea, let down his guard a little. There was a long pause...and an even longer silence.

'No! Goodbye!' said Wallace eventually, his voice shaking.

Joseph looked at Mary, put his arm around her, and with heads bowed, they slowly walked away. But the innkeeper didn't close the door and go inside. He stood there with his mouth open watching the forlorn couple leaving his establishment. He was genuinely upset. His eyes filled with tears.

Then, quite unexpectedly, with a broad grin lighting up his face, Wallace said loudly and clearly: 'Wait, Joseph. Don't go. You can have my room.'

Joseph and Mary looked stunned at this unscripted turn of events but pretended they hadn't heard and exited stage left as they were meant to do. The director put her head in her hands and burst into tears, but the show went on, the shepherds and wise men turned up on cue, and baby Jesus was born in a manger.

A few in the audience felt Wallace had ruined the pageant. The majority, however, thought it was the best Nativity play they had ever seen. When it was his turn to take a bow, the nine-year-old who had demonstrated the true spirit of Christmas received a standing ovation and rapturous applause.

149

Clearance Sale

It had been many years since the Devil had done any spring cleaning and his vast storehouse had become cluttered with the tools of his trade, tightly stacked from floor to ceiling. Pride, Arrogance, and Vanity had an entire section of the storehouse to themselves, while Dishonesty, Discouragement, Cowardice, Anger, Hatred, Greed, Injustice, Insecurity, and other deadly sins were also stacked in large heaps. The place was in such a mess that the Devil decided to have a sale, which he falsely advertised as a 'going out of business' clearance at 'throwaway prices'.

As expected, customers turned up in large numbers and were awed by the astonishing range of sinful merchandise on sale. Rummaging through heaps of products, the customers were surprised to see that Jealousy not only had the largest section in the store but also the highest price tag amongst the Devil's tools.

'Why is that one so expensive?' a customer asked.

'Oh, it's quite simple,' the Devil replied. 'Jealousy is pricey because it is my most effective and therefore favourite implement. It covers a multitude of sins from greed to wrath, from lust to loathing, and everything in between. It has always been my best-selling item.'

The customer gasped in amazement. He had never seen Jealousy for sale before and had no idea that it would be so much in demand. He watched as politicians, statesmen, businessmen, executives, officials, husbands, wives, single people, professionals, white-collar workers, labourers, students, siblings, and even friends waited patiently in line to take their pick from the vast selection in front of them. The Devil was right: he would make a killing from the sale of Jealousy.

'Thanks to Jealousy,' continued the Devil, as he watched items flying off the shelves, 'I can intrude in almost everyone's life and cause all kinds of mayhem. It can make mountains out of molehills and destroy the perpetrator along with his victim. Individually and collectively, it can drive mankind to do terrible things. I think of Jealousy as my weapon of mass destruction.'

The customer didn't much like the sound of that, and thought Jealousy was perhaps too dangerous an item to purchase, no matter how popular. 'Thanks for your help,' the customer said, 'but I'll give Jealousy a miss because it's way beyond my budget.'

Reluctant to let a customer leave empty-handed, the Devil persisted. 'In that case, let me recommend a starter kit of Insecurity, which is available in the neighbouring section in the stall between Suspicion and Vengeance. Insecurity belongs to the same family as Jealousy but is a mildly watered-down version and therefore cheaper. I highly recommend it as a good investment. Based on my long years of experience, I can assure you that every human being experiences insecurity at some point in their life. You never know when you'll need it.'

The customer moved along to explore the adjoining section. He knew that people rarely admit to being insecure but felt it would be a safer and less destructive transgression to acquire than the omnipotent green-eyed monster, who was cackling with glee at maintaining his Number One position in the Devil's clearance sale.

150

Giving the Devil His Due

Buoyed by the success of his clearance sale and confident that he would never go out of business, the Devil decided to get away from the heat, take a few days off, and catch up on his reading, especially books that centred on him.

'I don't know why I'm always being depicted in a negative light,' he said to his assistants. 'If I really were dastardly and evil, I wouldn't have such a prosperous business and a worldwide following. I don't personally know this American chap Ambrose Bierce, who claims to have compiled my dictionary, but I hope he has taken a balanced view of my areas of expertise.'

As he browsed through the book, the Devil couldn't help smiling, grinning, and even laughing out loud at some of the definitions. 'I couldn't have put it better myself,' he smirked. 'I'm so glad that I'm finally being understood.' Unused to seeing their boss in such good spirits, his assistants urged him to share the jokes.

'This guy really knows how I think,' the Devil began. 'Listen to this: he classifies love as *a temporary insanity curable by marriage*, a bride as *a woman with a fine prospect of happiness behind her,* and patience as *a minor form of despair, disguised as a virtue*. He sees a political boundary as *an imaginary line between two nations, separating the imaginary rights of one from the imaginary rights of the other* and a capital city as *the seat of misgovernment*, which it so often is.'

As his assistants nodded in agreement, their boss continued browsing through *The Devil's Dictionary.* 'This guy Bierce is really perceptive. He is aware that what humans call knowledge is merely *the small part of ignorance that we arrange and classify*. Diplomacy, for him, is *the patriotic art of lying for one's country*, a year is *a period of three hundred and sixty-five disappointments*, and friendship is *a ship big enough to carry two in fair weather, but only one in foul*. He even seems to share my views on immigration, describing an immigrant as *an unenlightened person who thinks one country better than another*.

'There is, however, one definition that I have a quibble with,' the Devil declared. 'According to him, war is *God's way of teaching Americans geography*. That is a brilliant observation, but why does only God get the credit, when I play a major role in all conflict and oftentimes, even bring about these tragedies single-handedly? I think people are jealous and reluctant to give me my due, even though my popularity is growing and my followers are multiplying by leaps and bounds.'

Acknowledgements

Writing a book is a task undertaken by one person that can only be accomplished with the support of many—and I am deeply grateful to all those who made it possible for the book to exist.

First and foremost, I am thankful to David Davidar, Publisher, Aleph Book Company, and an accomplished writer himself, and Aienla Ozukum, Aleph's Publishing Director, for getting me started on this journey. As part of Aleph's freelance copy-editing team, I have worked closely with Aienla on more than six manuscripts on a range of topics. In my new avatar as a writer, it has been a pleasure working with Aienla, and I greatly benefited from her advice and support throughout the writing and editing of this compilation.

There was no lack of suggestions for stories to include in the collection from friends whose varied backgrounds and diverse interests resulted in a wide range of recommendations. I am deeply grateful to Armene Modi, founder of Ashta No Kai, a non-profit organization that educates and empowers women and girls in villages in Pune District, for her help in tracking down stories from local sources; to Rustom 'Rooky' Dadachanji, actor, teacher, and storyteller, for his suggestions; and to my well-read friends Ebrahim Chaney, Soumitra Gokhale, and Sumedha Varma for sharing stories from their vast repertoires.

Picking and choosing the stories took as much time as reworking and retelling them. I am thankful to my sister, Rutton, and my brother-in-law, Zulfikar Bharmal, for hosting my extended stay in the United Kingdom, where the first draft of this book was pulled together.

Many of the stories and folk tales in this compilation have long been in the public domain and have been retold by multiple sources. For the anecdotes featuring Mullah Nasruddin, I am deeply grateful to the Idries Shah Foundation for permitting me to use stories from *The Pleasantries of the Incredible Mulla Nasrudin*; to Ron J. Suresha for allowing me to adapt stories from *The Uncommon Sense of the Immortal Mullah Nasruddin* (2017, 3rd edition); and to Rodney Ohebsion for letting me recreate several amusing tales about the mullah's escapades from the collection published on his website.

I am thankful to the following writers for granting me permission to include versions of their work in the third section of the book: to John Fewings for readily giving me consent to adapt his play *The Richest Man in the Kingdom*; to Jeff Maysh for permission to adapt his story, 'The Tree With Matchmaking Powers', which first appeared in *The Atlantic*; to Meena Arora Nayak for letting me retell stories based on Tenali Raman from her book *The Blue Lotus: Myths and Folktales of India*; and to Margaret Silf for allowing me to reproduce the story titled 'Judgement' from her book *One Hundred Wisdom Stories from Around the World*.

I must also acknowledge Google, Wikipedia, and hundreds of Internet resources and websites that yielded a treasure house of information. I couldn't help wondering how writers of the pre-Google era managed to find answers to such imponderables as when mirrors were invented, when people began using tiles, and whether crows had tongues. For the wealth of information now available at the click of a button, I am much obliged to the scores of anonymous and unsung storytellers and raconteurs whose folklore and fables have added immense value to the growing store of worldly wit and wisdom.

My sincere thanks to Bena Sareen for the cover and book design and Priya Kuriyan for bringing my word portraits to life with her vivid illustrations.

Above all, my deepest gratitude to friend and former colleague Rachelle Claret, for her patient review of and comprehensive comments on my manuscript through its various iterations. I am greatly indebted to Rachelle, an experienced editor, who is currently completing her own first book, not just for her honest assessment of my work but also for bringing her impressive writing skills and quirky sense of humour to bear on many of the stories. By adding a twist to the tales wherever she deemed fit, she added much wit to their wisdom.

Select Bibliography

BOOKS & ARTICLES

Baldwin, James, *Fifty Famous Stories Retold*, Createspace, 2014.

Bierce, Ambrose, *Fantastic Fables*, London and New York: G. P. Putnam's Sons, 1899.

———, *The Devil's Dictionary*, New York and Washington, D. C.: Neale Publishing, 1912.

Friedman, Amy, *Tell Me a Story: Timeless Folktales from Around the Word,* Friedman & Danziger, 2010.

Lal, Anupa, *Birbal the Clever Courtier*, New Delhi: Scholastic India, 2007.

Maysh, Jeff, 'The Tree With Matchmaking Powers', *The Atlantic*, 19 June 2019.

Mudholkar, Ramesh, *175 Stories of Akbar and Birbal*, Pune: Anmol Prakashan, 2007.

Naim, C. M., 'Popular Jokes and Political History: The Case of Akbar and Birbal and Mulla Do-Piyaza', *Economic and Political Weekly*, Vol. 30, No. 24, 17 June 1995.

Nayak, Meena Arora, *The Blue Lotus: Myths and Folktales of India*, New Delhi: Aleph Book Company, 2018.

Parker, Dorothy, 'Good Souls', *Vanity Fair*, June 1919.

Shah, Idries, *The Pleasantries of the Incredible Mulla Nasrudin*, London: ISF Publishing, The Idries Shah Foundation, 2015.

Siegel, Lee, *Laughing Matters: Comic Tradition in India*, Chicago: University of Chicago Press, 1987.

Silf, Margaret, *One Hundred Wisdom Stories from Around the World*, London: Lion Books, 2011.

Suresha, Ron J., *The Uncommon Sense of the Immortal Mullah Nasruddin*, New Milford: Bear Bones Books (3rd edition), 2017.

Vas, S. R. Luis and Vas, S. R. Anita, *Solve Your Problems the Birbal Way*, New Delhi: Pustak Mahal, 2010.

BLOGS & WEBSITES

Afghan Network <www.afghan-network.net>
All Time Short Stories <alltimeshortstories.com>
Amar Chitra Katha <www.amarchitrakatha.com>
Bed Time Short Stories <www.bedtimeshortstories.com>
Blue Planet Journal <http://www.blueplanetjournal.com/index.html>
English for students <English-for-students.com>
Guideposts <https://www.guideposts.org/>
Indira Gandhi National Centre for the Arts <http://ignca.gov.in/>
Kids Gen <https://www.kidsgen.com/>
LokHindi <https://www.lokhindi.com>
Moral Stories <www.moralstories.org>
OSHO <www.otoons.com>
Reader's Digest <https://www.rd.com/>
Rodney Ohebsion <http://www.rodneyohebsion.com/folktales.htm>
Speaking Tree <https://www.speakingtree.in/>
Story World <http://worldwithstory.blogspot.com/>
The Unbounded Spirit <https://theunboundedspirit.com/>
ThinkRight.me <https://www.thinkright.me/en/>
Unitarian Universalist Association <www.uua.org>